POTIONS & PERILS

An Evermoss Cozy Fantasy

RECK WELL

Additional DTP Titles

Augmented by MJ Douglas

Echo by MJ Douglas

Thank you for buying this Dragon Tomes Publishing book.

To receive special offers, bonus content, and info on new

releases and other great reads, sign up for our newsletter on our

website at www.dragontomespublishing.com

Potions and Perils An Evermoss Cozy Fantasy
Copyright © 2024 Reck Well
All Rights Reserved.
Publishing by Dragon Tomes Publishing, LLC
Topeka, KS

Dragon Tomes Publishing
www.dragontomespublishing.com

Name: Well, Reck, author
Title: Potions and Perils An Evermoss Cozy Fantasy / Reck Well
Description: First edition/ Kansas: Dragon Tomes Publishing, 2024
Subject: Cozy Fantasy
Cover Design: Sienna Arts
Chapter Illustrations: Amy Cerasi
Book ISBN: 978-1-963198-04-1

Chapter illustrations created by Amy Cerasi! Check out her books and website at
www.coloringbookofshadows.com!

Dedication

To Jen – No love potion required.

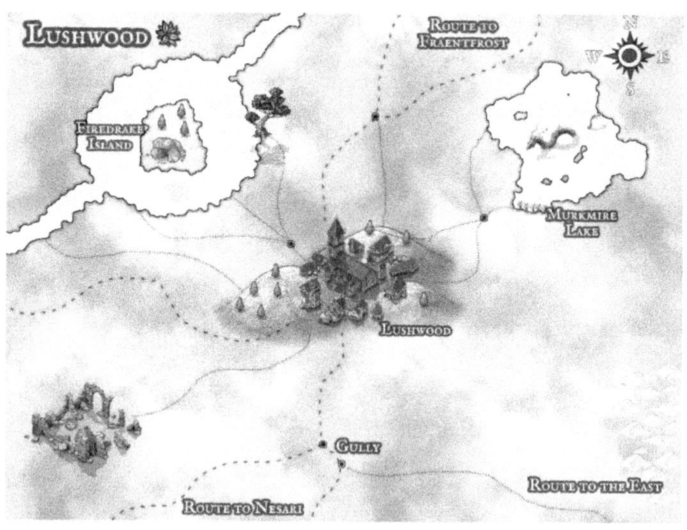

Lushwood
Firedrake Island
Route to Fraentfrost
Murkmire Lake
Lushwood
Gully
Route to Nesari
Route to the East
N
W
E
S

Chapter 1

"I'm going to tell Evelyn about this," Chester growled as he slammed the door to her shop, stomping away. A gust of frigid winter air swirled around like one last act of the man's defiance.

Eshail schooled her face for one last moment before breaking into a grin.

"What do you think, Druff?" Eshail's black cat looked up with wise eyes, face almost set in a matching grin. "I do hope Evelyn takes his complaint seriously and stops by." Eshail sighed wistfully as she set a kettle to boil, deciding a black tea with a touch of lavender would be an excellent way to banish Chester's negative energy and the cold. If her crush, Evelyn, the town herald, happened to stop by, it'd also be a good excuse for the woman to linger a bit longer.

She walked over to the front of the store, flipping her sign from open to closed. With one last glance about the desolate street, Eshail pulled the curtains tight, shutting out the view of the frozen cobblestones and sealing in the warmth of her sanctuary.

"It's been a long winter, hasn't it?" The spring equinox had come and gone, and yet snow still fell on the countryside. Eshail ran her hand along Druff's long, silky fur. Witches had a reputation for talking to their familiars. For her, it'd been a habit built on long periods spent alone. Druff hadn't answered—not yet—but there were legends.

The honey oak shelves of her store stood bare in testament to the long, frigid season. Eshail walked over to the chalkboard on which she kept her list of chores and added, "Stopping by Chester's." Tania, his second daughter and more favored, had gotten sick with a fever. Chester's description had indicated to Eshail that she'd likely pull through fine; the girl was usually quite healthy, and he kept his family well-fed. He was just nervous. The long winter was making them all nervous.

Denying him a curative had been based on her dwindling supplies and his overreaction to his daughter's illness. She had no witchy premonitions one way or another. She'd check in person on the morrow. The flu roaming the village shouldn't be fatal, as long as the girl didn't catch a secondary infection.

Even if Chester had brought her the necessary nutmeg, mustard seed, mace, and brendlewood thorns to infuse a tincture, she'd have insisted on waiting. The unnaturally long winter should have broken weeks ago.

Eshail itched for a simple problem to solve. The tingling in her hands had gotten worse lately. She needed to brew, harvest, or walk among the Evermoss.

Druff brought her back to the present by pressing his lean body against her leg. The kettle began whistling, and his eyes slaked back in annoyance.

Removing the kettle from the stove, Eshail poured hot water into her favorite flowered porcelain cup. The sunflower patterns always cheered her up in the dreariness of the winter. Within moments, she stood cradling the hot cup as a small linen bag of tea leaves steeped and the wholesome smell of cinnamon and orange filled her nose.

"Come, Druff. It's time for dinner." Eshail and the cat walked to the upstairs workroom, which contained what was left of the season. A small collection of dried herbs hung from the ceiling, the remnants of her warding spells for the year. They wouldn't ward off much these days, covered more in dust than the protection spell's power.

Her primary worktable sat in the middle of the room, blanketed by the expected recipe books and plant identification charts. The aged wooden shelves surrounding the room held dusty, empty bottles and a few more books. Eshail examined them briefly, pondering whether she should reread one of the romances to pass the time.

Rrrowl! Druff pulled her back to her task. He knew it was dinner time.

"Give me a minute," she told the small impudent beast as she sat down her tea. She took one more look through to the adjoining room at the door, willing the knock of the Herald. Evelyn had been avoiding her most of the winter—she had made it apparent she wasn't interested.

Eshail went to the corner of the room and flipped over the rug that disguised the trapdoor to her cellar. She poked at a knot in the floor, revealing a handle. With an expert tug of long experience, a steep, rickety staircase leading to darkness was revealed.

The witch worried the stairs would be her death one day. All witches kept their true workrooms secret when possible. Some rumors of witches *were* true, and keeping those works out of the public eye was best. Her anxiety, though, forced her to imagine falling down the stairs, dying, and no one finding her for days.

Concentrating, the witch cast a simple cantrip. A small glowing ball came into existence, no more prominent than the flame of a candle. The bit of magic brought a smile to her lips, even though she could feel its drain adding to the load of magic she already sustained.

Eshail removed her eyes from the flame and looked into the pitch-black cellar. With an annoyed wave, she mentally directed the glow to hover just behind her head so the glare of it wouldn't continue to ruin her night vision. She carefully made her way down the stairs, Druff on her heels.

The cellar wasn't in any better shape than her workroom upstairs. The shelves, ordinarily full of glass canned goods, root vegetables, and ingredients, were instead full of cobwebs. She kept her emergency stockpile of food and a few essential potions every witch held in reserve. Other than that, however, she had nothing.

Eshail added spring cleaning to her list of chores. However, if spring came the next day, she'd be woefully unprepared to process anything in a sanitary way. She noted the purple glow behind the panel of shelves concealing her stash—her special potions she couldn't use or destroy. She added renewing the charm of hiding to her list.

A shank of meat hung in the corner. Druff stood with two feet on the wall, stretched out for his meal, willing it to fall from its hook. As a familiar, his intelligence surpassed a normal housecat, but she still couldn't trust him to not try to eat the entire shank in one sitting.

She'd paid the wandering folk a handsome sum last summer to enchant the corner of her cellar. They made a living with such enchantments, as well as the gossip and finding out things they shouldn't. She didn't worry about them knowing of her hideout; they understood needing to take precautions, being who they were. The enchantment enabled the already cool underground temperature to drop even further, allowing her to keep some rarer potions, ingredients, and meats fresh longer.

Ottow, the tanner, had paid with the meat shank. He'd begged her to give him the last antiseptic ointment she'd had in stock—something she'd been saving for emergencies. To Druff's delight, he'd grudgingly paid a steep price. Eshail wasn't one to argue with her cat. She drew her athame from its sheath. The bone handle was cold and smooth in her hand. She effortlessly sliced off a few pieces of lamb for the hungry cat. The slices fell neatly into her outstretched hand, ignoring his open mouth.

He squeaked. She didn't have to cast a cantrip to translate what he was trying to communicate.

"Not down here. Last time I let you eat down here, I couldn't get you up the stairs!"

He gave her a baneful glare and neatly trotted up the steps, tail straight up in judgment. Eshail looked around one last time, grabbing one of her remaining precious jars of soup. If things didn't change soon, the entire village would go hungry, her included.

A starving village wasn't suitable for anyone, especially the local witch. People would grow desperate, angry, and look for someone to blame. Witches were easy targets, no matter if they'd saved your kid, calf, or entire farm the previous season. They were outsiders, frequently misunderstood, and when their pantry was empty, there wasn't much they could do to help.

Chester's daughter would survive, but what about the next villager who knocked on her door? If the winter lasted too much longer, she'd be turning people away even though they really did need her help.

Eshail was shuffling up the stairs when the front door jingled—another customer.

"I'm sorry, we're closed for the night!" she called, annoyed. Everyone knew better than to bug her when she closed for the night. What if she'd been mid-brew? A gust of air, light, or general concentration disturbance could throw off a working.

A woman's gruff voice answered with an odd accent, "Nevertheless, I am here."

Eshail blinked. She knew all three hundred villagers' voices and names. She could even identify the babies by a cry or gurgle. She didn't recognize the woman. The accent was as misplaced as the arrogance.

"One moment." She tried to convey confidence as she picked her footholds on the stairs carefully. She felt vulnerable in a way she hadn't in a long time. The town of Lushwood was small. Everyone knew their neighbors, the drunks, and what the troublemakers could do. Everyone was a known quantity.

Strangers were treated with hospitality but with a touch of suspicion. Everyone, even the visitors, respected a witch's work enough not to come barging into their shop once the door had been closed. Eshail cursed herself for being complacent. She'd gotten out of the habit of bolting her front door.

Her head broke into the stillroom, and she looked toward the front. Stupidly, she was so curious to see who this stranger was that she lost control of her cantrip. The glowing ball embarrassingly sped straight for the intruder, whose face flashed with fear before relaxing as the bright ball simply hovered over her head. The loose spell had the unfortunate effect of drawing the stranger's eyes straight to Eshail's hidden stairwell.

Eshail blushed crimson as she emerged. The stranger was tall and firmly built. She had darker skin, which was uncommon in the northern swamp. Her hair was unusual. Those of the Evermoss tended toward blond, brown, and reddish hues. Her hair was dark, almost black, with ringlets of curls encircling her face.

Eshail frowned, thinking it had to be dyed but unable to recall a single dye that would have that effect. The only people who had hair like that were from the Eastern Empire. Seeing one of them here was as likely as Druff doing a jig. The few Easterners allowed into the West stuck to the major cities and the trade routes leading to the sea. She'd never seen one in all of the Evermoss, let alone in a small village like Lushwood.

The woman stood bemused, looking up at the glowing light. Eshail was beyond irritated. She snapped her fingers harshly, snuffing the spell.

"Greetings, stranger. Most don't venture into a witch's shop uninvited." Eshail's voice was cold. She felt off-balance by this intrusion and wasn't good at hiding it.

"Good evening, witch." The appellation was said with disdain.

Eshail was on guard immediately. Druff, dinner forgotten, had jumped onto the worktable, arched his back, puffed his fur out, ready to attack. This person was not a friend or a desperate villager looking for a cure-all. Whatever they were here for, they hated the necessity, and they hated witches. It was further evidence the person was an Easterner. In the East, they hunted her kind down, hanging, burning, or quartering anyone discovered or suspected of witchcraft.

She held the meat scraps for Druff in one hand and calmly slid her other hand within her robes, putting her fingers on the smooth corners of her knife. The handle's coolness was reassuring.

"Apologies, good mother, I mean you no harm." The woman had noticed Druff and remembered her manners. She stepped back, toward the door, and held her empty hands out. It was meant to show she meant no harm, but the woman's hands were big like the rest of her. This woman didn't need a weapon to do harm.

"What brings you into my shop?" Curt, her question brokered no room for jest.

"I'm a traveler"—Eshail snorted at the obviousness of the woman's statement—"looking for trade. Talin sent me here and told me you'd be the person who possibly had what I seek."

"And what be that?" Eshail winced. She'd slipped into a bit of her country talk. It crept into her language when she was happy or stressed—such a witch's sense of balance.

"A potion, a brew. I'm a trader of sorts, and I've got

a client looking for something specific. I had to travel west. It's not something"—she coughed, self-conscious of what she was going to say—"it's not something you can find in the Empire."

Eshail breathed a sigh of relief. If this woman was looking for a bit of magic—a magic potion—then she probably wouldn't drag her off and accuse her of heresy. Feeling more comfortable, she walked into her showroom, stepping behind the sales counter. Eshail found comfort in the act of negotiation and bargaining. This was a space where she could operate confidently.

"And what are you looking for? I'm running particularly low on ingredients and ready-made brews these days. The winter, you see, has been long." She kept her eyes on the stranger as she dropped Druff's meal into his bowl. The cat, still on edge at the intruder, ignored the gift. He jumped on the counter, green eyes glued to the woman.

Even if she had what the Easterner was looking for, it served her to play up the long winter and her prices. She wouldn't fleece the local villagers. For a moment, she thought of the lamb shank in the cellar. She wouldn't fleece the local villagers *too much*. But she had no qualms about taking from a traveling merchant looking for a hard-to-find bit of magic. Even if she was handsome, she was an Easterner, and they deserved a stupidity tax.

Sensing the change in mood, the woman smiled like a seasoned barterer. "I came prepared. I've brought enough herbs and other ingredients that even if you don't have something ready, I'm sure we can find what you need in my stock."

Eshail lifted an eyebrow. That was quite the statement. The woman must have driven in with a wagon or small caravan to make that claim. Talin was likely drooling at the prospect of getting restocked. He owned the inn/tavern/town reserve in the city. He also served as mayor. He'd been anxious the last month as winter still held firm.

"Well, I'm sure we could work something out. This must be a highly sought-after bit of magic." Easterners didn't believe in magic, not really. They hunted witches and hedge wizards and burned them at the stake. What could an Easterner possibly want from her?

"It's simple. I need a simple brew, and I'm prepared to pay for it." It was an unusual tact for a traveling merchant to take. To give ground on the price before they even started bickering. Eshail's curiosity was piqued. And then, "I need a love potion."

Eshail's curiosity was instantly extinguished. A rage boiled in her veins, and she answered with it: "Absolutely not. Get out. Now."

The traveler was shocked. She didn't expect this reaction. Well, the feeling was mutual. No one asked Eshail for a love potion. They all knew better.

"Out." The witch pointed at the door as though ordering vermin out of her store.

As the shocked traveler turned to leave, Eshail pushed with a bit of magic to make her feet move quicker. The door slammed closed as soon as her boots crossed the threshold. And for the first time in years, Eshail slid the bolt into place.

Eshail stood staring at the bolt.

The nerve of Easterners.

The witch stomped around the shop with a broom. She was a tornado of action, removing dust and dirt, heating her soup only to have it sit and cool on the counter while she reorganized her spice cabinet. Two fingers of a candle later, she sat with a self-aggravated thump, holding a cold bowl of soup and her strong, icy cup of tea.

Eshail brought warmth to the congealed black bean spice soup, prioritizing food over tea with her last cantrip of the day. This wasn't the first time someone had asked her for a love potion, and the woman *was* a stranger, so she didn't know her general stance on such things. She allowed a niggle of guilt at how she'd treated the woman. Easterners put her on edge. They didn't deserve kindness from witches, but she'd have done it if asked for a healing potion, an antidote, or any of the fifty enhancements Eshail could make. She'd have done it for the right price.

Love potions. The witch shook her head. There was no price high enough to make her sell a love potion. She'd left matchmaking and love brewing behind a long time ago.

Chapter 2

Eshail woke up grumpy. The woman was stuck in her head. The itch to brew had become a cramp, aching every time she moved. Druff didn't notice. He was curled up on the end of her bed in a warm pool of light filtering through a broken slat in the shutters. The line of morning light just happened to extend from Druff's sleeping form, up across the bed, and straight into her eyes.

She got up grudgingly. Only the self-promise of hot tea forced her out of bed. Getting up early, while important when running her own business, had always been a matter of bribery.

As her frayed wool socks hit the floorboards, Druff uncurled with a lazy stretch. She'd slept in socks this winter to keep warm. There were days when she'd curse at her sisters. Not for real, mind you. She'd never *actually* curse her sisters. The coven had assigned Lushwood as her village. She'd been naive and excited then, but the years of long, cold winters had stacked up. The great Evermoss, the swamp of the West, extended from the northern peaks of the Fraentfrost mountain range all the way into the steamy jungles of Nesari. Her mother had always had the opinion that she hadn't worked hard enough at her craft. So when she asked for a placement, they'd given her an out of the way, small, quiet hamlet. She preferred that, really, not being responsible for too many souls. It was perfect, except for the long, abusively cold winters, which were objectively horrible.

Eshail put a few logs into the stove and flicked her wrist, setting it to flame. Some things about being a witch were the best. Her home was attached to the back of the shop. Usually, this wasn't a problem. She liked not having to trudge through dirty streets to her storefront. Also, anyone wanting to make trouble with the local witch knew better than to do so when the witch was present. Having her residence in the place where she did business and brewed gave her a sense of security.

Thumping sounded at the shop's front door. Unfortunately there were other times when an upset mother would wake her up or disturb her morning tea, in which she regretted a lack of separation between home and business.

"I'm coming!" Eshail slept in a threadbare cotton shift but had thrown on a long wool sweater that buttoned down the front. Pulling it tight, she strode into the storefront. The curtains blocked most of the sun. She generally didn't open before noon on weekdays; it was a mid-morning sort of sun. The pounding hadn't abated.

"Pussywillows, I'm coming!" With an unsatisfactory yank, Eshail remembered the bolt. Unlocking it quickly, suddenly apprehensive at who might be on the other side, she opened the door.

If her mood was already poor from the early hour, freezing temperature, and lack of breakfast, the woman standing before her worsened it. It was the stranger from the night before, clad in a brand new heavy brown coat stretching to her knees. The coat had stylish leafing embroidered down its sleeves. It was such an expense that Eshail doubted she could afford it even if she'd saved for years. The witch was suddenly conscious that her long sweater had several loose threads, moth-eaten spots, and a smattering of black Druff fur as he frequently napped in its wooly confines.

This led to a harsher-than-usual question: "What do you want?" She immediately regretted the question, as they both knew what the woman wanted.

The woman smiled, which was irritating. Then she bemusedly said, "I need to do business with you this morning."

"I told you last night, and nothing has changed. I don't *do*"—Eshail lowered her voice, looking around the street to see if anyone was near enough to overhear—"*love potions.*"

The woman nodded sagely. "Yes, well, I have other business with you."

Eshail blinked. This was entirely unexpected. She shifted back, opened the door further, and reached into the window to flip the sign from "closed" to "open" more forcefully than necessary. She kept the door open and left it to the woman to tempt fate by walking inside or leaving.

Unfortunately the stranger followed Eshail into the store. Between the long winter, an insatiable itch to create, and now this irritatingly pushy woman, Eshail was completely off-balance, and witches needed balance. She tried to regain her upper footing and moved resolutely behind the counter. Commerce and entrepreneurship were the crutches she needed to put herself at ease. The simple transactions of commodities available, haggled, paid, and received. This formula she knew well.

"What can I help you with today?" Eshail said in her syrupy, warm customer service voice. Even she had to swallow a smirk at how stupid the voice sounded to herself.

The infernal swamp take me.

Now that Eshail wasn't squinting into the sun, she could see the woman was just as well-manicured as the night before. While Eshail was positive she had a bedhead. Druff frequently slept part of the night on her pillow, creating a cat's nest she'd have to brush out the next day, a tangled mess she hadn't been able to tame yet. Her cheeks reddened at the intrusive thought and her imagined self-image.

"Well, I have other needs. Since you can't create a love potion—or is it give me one? I imagine you have several in stock?" The woman lifted a thin eyebrow into the air.

Eshail didn't bother answering the inquiry. She would offer this woman nothing of the sort.

"Ahem, anyway, I thought I could offer some trade. I'm headed west since I can't get what I need here." Another pause, fishing for an answer. "I have a wagonload of herbs and supplies from the East that I was hoping to trade and barter. Do you have other wares available that might be of use? Talin found a few of my wares interesting." The woman motioned to the coat. If Talin had traded her for *that,* she must have valuable wares.

The bad morning was getting worse. She'd be overwhelmingly excited to trade with the woman at any other moment of the year. She didn't often get the chance to get a shot at ingredients from the east. The problem, *her* problem, was she didn't have anything left to trade. In a month, with crocus breaking through the ground and the swamp coming back to life, she'd have plenty. Unless the woman was interested in cobwebs, she had nothing that would be useful today.

"What are you looking for?" She hesitated a second before adding, "What do you have to trade?" She wasn't sure she wanted to tempt fate by finding out what the trader had available. It would only make turning her away that much harder.

The traveling merchant looked like a cat with a fish. She lifted a leather hardback case that Eshail hadn't noticed.

"My name's Thayatesh"—*the damn Easterners and*

their unpronounceable names—"but you can call me Yates. Mind if I flip open this case? I've got samples of what's in the wagon. I've got heart thorn in here, and, well, you'll see. There's a lot of options." Eshail leaned in to look at the case. Heart thorn was hard to come by, and critical for a few of her primary potions.

"Why not, Thay-yat-tesh?" Eshail tried to use the woman's formal name, avoiding the familiarity of a nickname. Tried and failed. She felt bad enough to blush. "Yates, go right ahead."

The case flipped open with the click of metallic latches, revealing the cleverest sales tool Eshail had ever seen. The case held rows of vials held in place by a ribbon of stretchy fabric wrapped around the narrow part of each vial. Within each stoppered container sat a variety of the most cherished herbs in any Evermoss apothecary's inventory. Eshail couldn't help herself. She leaned forward, examining the leaves, roots, vines, and assorted fragments of animal parts.

"Is that a wompry rat's tail?"

Yates nodded.

"And, don't tell me that's drowfemeril? Is that all you've got?"

Yates produced an inventory scroll. It was marked up in a language Eshail couldn't read. "I think I have three." Her finger scanned the list of figures. "No, two packs full," she said, holding her hand up, mimicking the size of a loaf of bread.

Eshail was completely in awe. That much drowfemeril was a ransom. This woman carried a king's bounty on her wagon. She began thinking. She had nothing to trade for the ingredients, but she had some coins stashed away. She could quickly profit from some of these items, so using her savings wouldn't harm her long-term.

"How much for any of this?" The witch tried to sound nonchalant and keep her eagerness from her voice. If she'd known she'd be involved in this negotiation in the morning, she would have stayed up and cast a chant. She would have done something to sway the barter further in her favor.

"I'm more interested in a barter than a sale. What do you have available?"

Eshail cringed; it was hard to hide how empty her shelves were. "I don't have much at this time of year. As you can see, it's been a long winter." She prodded her brain, gazing from shelf to shelf. She had withered skunk root—an effective antifungal, even if unpopular due to its smell. She had cedar shavings, oil, and essence. No one would trade for something so ordinary. Her tea box held a few things, but just shavings of flavor. A bundle of wilted parsnips hung from a peg. She never understood folks' aversion to the white root. It had more flavor than potatoes. She'd planned a soup for herself if they weren't bought this week.

"I was hoping you had some hidden reserve I could view."

Eshail thought about her hidden reserve. Every witch had one. Hers mostly contained the one type of potion she would never trade this woman—that, and her stock of dragon's eye, the rare herb her sisters had ordered her to collect for their bicentennial coven casting.

With resignation, she gave her only answer: "I'm afraid I just don't have a reserve this year. What you see here is really what I've got available." She didn't have to fake the regret in her voice. It was a real shame. This Yates represented a once-in-a-lifetime opportunity that she couldn't convert.

Almost by magic, the case snapped shut. Yates smiled knowingly. "I see. Well, I will just have to go elsewhere. Unless . . ." Her voice upturned. Eshail would have grown hopeful if she hadn't already known what the woman would ask. "You have something in the amorous-inducing quality? If it's a matter of ingredients, I can find you what you need."

"I will not make, sell, or trade you any such potion. If that is all, I would like to return to making my breakfast." Eshail was proud of herself. Her voice only quivered a moment at the statement.

Thayatesh nodded. "Very well. I'm unsure why you Westerners won't sell me what I know you have. It's not illegal here. I will find someone if I have to travel the entire length of the Great Swamp. You need me. You need this deal. I see your empty shelves, the cobwebs in the corners, the sickly villagers coughing in the corner of the tavern. This village isn't healthy, and it will come down on you."

The woman had voiced the heart of Eshail's fear: that the season wouldn't break, and the hunger and illness that had been dogging them the last month would worsen. Everyone blamed the witch when the weather didn't turn, never mind that a witch's magic was for small things, small cures curated with great effort. Weather workings such as these were massive things commanded by the court mages of mighty kings and queens or whispered on the wings of dragons.

"I care for the people entrusted to me as well as I can. Times are hard. What's new? You take your Eastern ways with you. Even if I'm a humble hedge witch, I know better than to dabble in a bedeviled cause. Only fools chase an ill-formed goal like coerced love."

Eshail decided to do something risky. She looked up, caught Thayatesh's eyes, and used Witch's Sight on the woman. It was one of the most intrusive powers in a witch's arsenal and frequently had unintended consequences. After all this, she wanted to know the Easterner's plan and what motivated her.

Eshail could immediately see the discomfort in the woman's expression as her gaze focused. She saw the desperation behind Yates's extraordinary request in a split moment. As she concentrated, trying to sense the root of it, the power flickered and surged. A loveless, political marriage for . . . someone. It was unclear who, but Yates wished to change the wretched fate of someone she loved to something *different*.

"Stop."

This time, the harsh refusal wasn't Eshail's. The woman fled of her own accord.

Chapter 3

The shop was looking more dour than ever. Druff sat, judgmental, leg lifted in the air on the main counter where Eshail organized sales. As the season had extended, her mood and will had slowly eroded. Witches were attuned to the land and seasons, and she seemed particularly so. She'd get up later, sit on her stool, and watch the townsfolk pass by. It was easier to justify shutting up shop when it got dark early. And since her ingredients were slim, she didn't even work at night brewing anything new. She was a witch of the spring; she loved nothing more than gallivanting across the swamp, gathering herbs and ingredients.

Eshail had things she could have, would have, done if she'd been more ambitious. She could have fixed the window sign and brightened the colors in her advertisement—which just seemed like a spring activity. She could sweep the cobwebs. But that would disturb the industrious spiders that shared her home. What she really should have been doing was mending her clothes. The state of her morning robe had been embarrassing. She could be cleaning her dishes, giving the cauldron its annual scrubbing, or working to further purify some of the potions she had left in her secret stash.

Thayatesh had been right. Every witch kept a stash

for an emergency. Her trade wasn't the most accepted in the known world. Witches were needed in the countryside, where the scientific doctors peddling stitches and snake oil were less prevalent. She could admit they did *some* good but were as likely to drill holes in your brain as give you a little butterbur to soothe your headaches. They also didn't know one way or another for women's needs.

Her stash was the stash every witch kept: those things needed for a swift exit and a restart in a new location. A potion that provided stealth, a lattice of safety, and a charm charged with quickness. Tarwa, her sometimes mother and sometimes coven head, had sent a bottle of translocation. One of the rarest potions their coven could concoct. She'd been grateful to that crusty old witch, even if they'd never gotten along. Eshail had been the youngest adult in their region, and Tarwa always acted like she couldn't care for herself. Translocation would move a witch from one place to another in two heartbeats. Three, if she took Druff with her, which, of course, she would. They were tough to brew, and the ingredients were found only once every decade. These treasures were untradeable keys to a witch's survival.

Yates kept popping into her head because the woman had at least three ingredient variants needed for the base of translocation: heliotrope, yebamante, and prismgrains. If the Eastern Empire hadn't rid themselves of witches, they could have had the most potent logistical tool any army had ever encountered.

Eshail, if she'd been a good witch, may have been out in the community, doing her best to soothe the cold and touches of flu prevalent in a late-to-break winter. She'd always been nervous about illnesses though. A stupid quality to have as a soother, to be fearful of illness, but she watched the flu take their first mother to the nest, to the existence beyond life.

Her birth mother had been lost during Eshail's

arrival to the world, a problem witches were at the forefront of combating. Her father hadn't been known, and she'd been taken in by the village witch as most of such a fate are. Her first mother, the witch, Yaventis, was everything a person could want in a mother. Patient, kind, and warm. Eshail's childhood was full of speckled sunlit days of harvesting and cozy nights brewing. She'd been a sheltered ten-year-old, much too young to lose a second mother. Tarwa had been old even then, one of the heads of the coven. The woman had traveled weeks to take Eshail and deal with her mother's household.

She'd been so grateful to see Tarwa walk up to the village. Witches didn't generally have children, not in the traditional sense. If they did, it usually resulted from an unfortunate event that hadn't been avoided. Something ill-fated. Most witch children were a result of the decision to bring an orphaned child in or to steal a child from a circumstance they wouldn't survive or a circumstance they shouldn't have to endure. Eshail didn't know the details of her origin story but knew she wasn't the first child Yaventis had raised.

The local village children had told her she'd been abandoned, and the local tavern owner had taken her in. He needed another maid to serve patrons. She'd almost given up hope when word came to the tavern that a woman was looking for her. The sight of the brown, patched, travel-stained dress and Tarwa's greased hair—saturated with malice oil to keep the flies off—was the most welcome sight she'd ever seen.

The melancholy was getting to Eshail. She only daydreamed about Tarwa when she thought about long-forgotten days and only did that in the last two months of winter. Muttering to herself, she decided she needed to snap out of it. A list always helped.

Eshail had one extravagance beyond the necessary needs of her craft. Every witch had a cauldron, large or small. They all had vials, twine, and a list of spells. What few of them had was a chalkboard and a passion for lists. She'd stumbled upon a hill made of slate in the swamp, and with a crazy amount of effort, she'd hauled two large pieces of the stone home. She then glued them on a board. Then, with an arduous weave of mending, she'd smoothed it into a clean writing panel.

Tarwa was known for her chalkings. She made substantial temporary murals for her village to celebrate holidays and meaningful moments. Early on, she'd taught Eshail how to conjure multiple colors of chalk from almost any soft stone.

Eshail tried to knock herself out of the hollow she'd fallen into by erasing the depressing stock list. She no longer needed to keep track of what she had—her stock was so low she had it memorized.

Today was going to be about what she wanted to do in the next year.

"Happy New Year's Druff!" The cat gave her a look as though she'd lost her mind, then calmly returned to his bath to ignore her antics. She didn't care; spring promised rebirth and a new year. Villagers may celebrate in the heart of winter, but every witch knew it should be celebrated in spring's first blush.

Part of her knew it was dumb to pretend winter had ended. To declare spring's arrival without evidence, but to her senses it was past due. So she was going to pretend, if nothing but to lift her spirits.

She began to write the rat's nest of thoughts she'd been having, each loose thread she'd woven over the winter tugged at a real need for the village, a contingency she wanted to plan for, or an opportunity to bring in more profit. The list was made of the mundane: tinctures against infection and bloat, a potion that would stop the burning of the heart, headache brews, congestion looseners, general antidotes to the poisonous snakes prevalent in the swamp, and a compactor that would seal up the worst of a digestive flux. She drew up a list of those things with a touch more magic and a touch less simple apothecary.

She needed a potion of lust—not love—that made her a pretty penny over the years, as those who needed a performance boost sought her out. She'd make sure those buying that potion knew she'd know if it were applied to an unbonded partner. Charms of finding and mending were popular among the village mothers with small children. Each charm would need to be charged in pure moon water from the basin of the Everspring she'd found in the swamp. As soon as things thawed enough, that would be her first stop.

Druff smacked his lips as he watched her write "Everspring" on the board. He loved drinking from the pool, the greedy critter. The last category was one that she hesitated to write down. It was the greatest magic she could do. Her skillset, currently, was very narrow, but Tarwa had warned her that if she didn't practice, she'd never have the skill to grow her repertoire. This was the area that she felt the most cursed. She could charm a lost sheep back to its flock, even if it'd been missing a week. She could craft a mend that would almost reweave her long sweater into something brand new. These were minor magics.

In her major magics, she had a perfect grade in a potion, which she'd never agree to allow anyone to use. Her stash was full of the results. As Tarwa told her, she couldn't let her skill slip. A witch didn't know when they'd enter the great dream and pull the possibility of a new spell, charm, or potion from the very fabric of the nest. So her cache was full of pink love potions. An entire floor-to-ceiling rack of pink burbling odorless promises of ardor and adoration. She absolutely despised it.

She loved her secondary aptitude for greater magic almost as much as she hated her primary skill. Druff resulted from her first attempt to find a familiar. He was a grimalkin, a cat familiar that would be her companion to the end of his days. The spell to call a familiar was something some witches spent their whole lives trying to master. The power had come to her on a cloudless night she'd spent with the moon. She could help an ordinary person find a remarkably faithful furry companion, or someone with a magical aptitude could follow the complete rites and have a decent shot at obtaining an actual familiar.

Not only was this a fulfilling endeavor, but it ensured that most traveling witches and hedge mages sought her out as they passed through. They would consult with her on their familiars, or ask her to pull a companion for them. She enjoyed the company and the comradeship and tried to pick up at least minor magics in trade. It's how she grew her vast knowledge of minor magics. She could cure almost anything that was non-life threatening.

The bell at the front of the store jingled, and Eshail turned around. She half expected the Easterner again and was disappointed when it wasn't her.

Eshail paused, cataloging her disappointment. She didn't want to see that woman again, but some of her was still clearly disappointed. Thankfully, the individual trotting in wasn't a goodwife looking for a cure or a farmer complaining about a sick cow. It was her closest friend in the village, Hedwarg.

The man leaned against his staff with two familiars close, Kipsini perched on his shoulder, and Sneit clutched to the top of his head. Hedwarg was the first person she'd gotten her familiar spellcraft to work on more than once. She didn't account this to her skill but more to his affinity with animals. He was a druid of sorts, maybe not in the old ways. She doubted he could *talk* to trees, but he listened well. The animals appreciated that more than any other skill of his.

Kipsini was a black-bellied sparrow, common as any little brown bird but sharp in her commentary. Sneit was a black squirrel, uncommon to these parts. He was a runt, tiny compared to the giant brown squirrels in this area of Evermoss. Both creatures were gluttons for snacks, and Eshail wasn't sure if it was her familiar spell or the promise of unlimited treats that kept them close.

"G'afternoon. You hear what the wind has been saying?" Leave it to Hedwarg to cut straight to the topic of his choice. His yellowed teeth smelled of the mint he constantly chewed. It was the middle of winter, and he still had a sizeable stash of it. He was a great source of swamp knowledge and wares; the man lived off of harvesting from the wild.

"I'm not sure what you're talking about." But Eshail had a sneaking suspicion that she did. She reached under the counter and snagged a couple of seeds out of a bowl she kept for this purpose. She stepped forward, holding her palm out for both of the animals, who greedily snatched the seeds out of her fingers.

"They'll grow fat if you keep spoiling them." Hedwarg gave the admonishment he'd given every visit. They shared a smile as she held out another seed. His face grew serious as he broached his topic. "Swamp-sister, have you met with the Easterner yet?"

Eshail held out another seed, contemplating her answer. She didn't look him in the face when she lied. "What Easterner?"

Chapter 4

They'd been friends too long for her ploy to work. Hedwarg went right for the heart of the matter. "Don't deny it. Do you know what that dark-haired witch hunter did? She went straight for what she thought was the next possible source of magic in the village: me. You could have given me some warning, you know?"

Eshail looked down guiltily. "I'm sorry. I didn't expect her to do that. Any idiot here knows you'd not be able to fill her request. I'm the only witch outside of Tarwa that has a chance of having what she wants."

Hedwarg was about as magical as a rock. What people mistook for mysticism was just a scientific understanding of the world and an eccentricity that preferred a sparrow and squirrel to human company. She'd speculated on some druidic powers, but he'd given no hints beyond his unusual companions and uncanny ability to navigate such a dangerous swamp.

"I don't understand why you don't take up her offer. I've always wondered about your rejection of love magic. What is it that's got you this adamant? If the winter was a little hungrier, or the food stores a little more stark, I'm not sure the village would let this traveler continue her journey unscathed."

His statement shook Eshail's core. The idea that the city would descend into lawlessness to rob a traveling merchant, even if they *were* an Easterner, was frightening. A rejection of order at that base level led to witches hanging in the square. Had she misjudged the state of Lushwood so severely? Were they that close to the brink?

Eshail whispered, as though doing so would make it untrue, "Do you think it's that bad?"

On Hedwarg's shoulder, Kipsini chirped, demanding another sunflower seed. Eshail mechanically reached out, watching the sparrow skillfully split the husk and swallow the heart of the seed.

Hedwarg let out a long-suffering sigh. "They love you because you feed them their favorite seeds, you know? I don't understand how you can be so smart yet so dumb."

"Thanks," she said sardonically, giving Sneit a nut she'd saved for him.

Hedwarg leaned back. His hair was its normal unkempt tangle. Most of the villagers were used to him, but his appearance, and often odor, could be off-putting. The man just didn't care what others thought, so it always surprised her when he knew what people were thinking before she did. He'd tried to wave her off of pursuing Evelyn years ago, which she should have listened to. This was one reason, among many, that she listened now, as he began to speak. "If the winter keeps lingering. I don't know what any of us are going to do. We need relief soon, or things are going to become dire."

"That's the thing when I read the leaves. It tells me spring is here, that the bulbs will be blooming any day now. Crocus should be breaking through the soil as we speak." Yet the words were ash in Eshail's mouth; her fortunes had been saying the same thing since the previous month.

"And yet when I walk the swamp, there is snow and slumber. It's as though the very ground we walk on has been told to sleep, the skies told to remain crisp." She knew the truth as he spoke it. She even felt the spell on the land, the desire to remain inside, cozy and warm.

The long winter was unnatural. Hedwarg knew the land, and she knew the portents. He knew enough not to accuse her of such great magic. This wasn't a charm for a rainy day. This was a work that disrupted the very turn of the seasons. A grand witch of yore might accomplish it, but the world hadn't seen one in a thousand years. If they still lived, they slept deeply. It was well beyond the skillset of a simple hedge witch, even one as talented as herself.

"You may need to rethink your answer to this woman before she moves on to the next village. She may be our one chance to help us outlast the grasp of this weather."

Some of Eshail wished she could agree with her long-time friend, that she could assure him she'd be reasonable, that love potions were something that she could compromise on for the good of the village and her safety. But they just weren't. He read her answer in the set of her face. Sneit looked up from his nut, giving her a mournful look.

Hedwarg's smile saddened. "Normally, I don't mind your stubbornness. I even admire it sometimes. This, though, this is a dog with a bone that nips when asked to share. You're being unreasonable." The last sentence was said with care. Eshail's heart lurched painfully as his simple request ran straight into her iron resolve.

She thought about what to say, the careful argument she could lay out. The logic and disgust for her art. She hadn't told anyone before and didn't think Hedwarg had a firm understanding of love. She hadn't met anyone who understood.

"Hedwarg, have you ever drank a love potion? Have you seen its effects on someone?"

He answered quickly, "No, I haven't. They are a

rare sight. I've not met any with your skill." Both of his animals had stopped cracking on their treats and watched her, waiting for an answer as though offering their own judgment.

Eshail nodded. Most folks didn't know what they were asking for when they wanted a love potion. The truth was, most witches couldn't brew love. What they could brew was lust or a potion of persuasion, something that could tip the scales—an elixir to give a nudge when they were already looking for it. Love potions were something else altogether. In her opinion, love fell into the dark arts.

Love potions were a compulsion. A love potion didn't tip the scales. It removed them all together. Free will was chucked out the window with the wash water. A person under the spell of a love potion had no willpower to resist the pull of blind adoration and lust. Some witches could make a love potion with unique ingredients, circumstances, and practice. Her love potions, however, were her prime skill as a young witch. The spells that she wove with them were long-lasting, life-altering, and destructive.

"Imagine waking up and falling completely in love with me."

Hedwarg smiled at the thought. The man reserved his love for nature, for the things that creep and crawl and grow. He didn't care a wit for people, and the only reason they got along was because she had the same reverence for the Evermoss as he did.

"Imagine that you give up everything that makes you you: Kipsini, Sneit, and even Sssers. That you'd be willing to sit in this shop and operate the front door every day for me."

"I love you dearly, but that's not a future for us."

Eshail made her voice cold. "I could make you." She stepped closer, almost threateningly. "I could force you with one of my potions. Make you fall hopelessly in love with me so much that you'd rather die than not be with me. You would give up everything that you hold dear just to be able to spend your life with me. You'd be content never to go into your beloved swamp again." She used a cantrip for the day, pulling shadows toward her face. "I could have every villager in my thrall. Every. Single. One. It would take"—her voice dropped gravely low—"a drop each to have them wrapped around my finger, a cup for a stronger soul, a pint to control every aspect of their lives. I could do it and brew fast enough to keep it up. And then the village would be mine."

She'd gotten to him, she could tell. Hedwarg took a step back, afraid of her for the first time in their friendship. She dropped the evil glamour and returned to herself. "And so you see, Hedwarg, why I'm unwilling to give anyone that power. I don't want it. No one should ever have that type of power over another being."

Shaken, Hedwarg whispered, "Then why do you brew them? I've seen your stash. You have dozens of love potions down there."

She gave him a rueful smile. "You've never met Tarwa. My mother would beat the crap out of me if I let my greater magic skills atrophy. You know how witches' magic works."

He didn't, not that intimately, but she knew he'd be too embarrassed to admit it. Her dismissal did its job. They chit-chatted a bit of the afternoon away, chipping away at the wall that had sprung up between them from the fear that her explanation elicited. They'd be okay. Hedwarg was a good soul, and he'd forgive her eventually for being more dangerous than he ever suspected.

Eventually, he pled apologies, needing to help Sssers, his third familiar, find dinner. The orange and black striped snake was blind in one eye and had trouble catching its own meals. He tended to upset the villagers, so the snake typically stayed in the swamp when Hedwarg visited

Lushwood.

Hedwarg's drop-in made Eshail nervous. If he'd been putting two and two together, the rest of the village wouldn't be too far behind. He was a kind soul who would take her word for what she said it was. Many in the town, especially those she'd struck a hard bargain with or whom she'd had to turn away in moments over the years, wouldn't be so kind in their interpretation of the situation. If this mysterious stranger stayed in the city, touting the fact that she couldn't get what she wanted from the witch. Well, one or both Eshail and Hedwarg's reputation would end up ruined—and it was possible they'd be killed for it.

Eshail knew this was the life witches led. She'd watched her first mother and Tarwa run from the villagers they kept within their care. This was the other side of the coin: if one had the power to heal, it was believed that one had the power to deal death. If she had the power to enforce love, she also had the power to implement hate. She sighed; for a moment, Eshail just wanted to be average. A baker. A wife to some unambitious farmer, popping out the next generation of peasants.

"May the nest forgive me such thoughts," she murmured askance. The only one in the room to hear her was Druff, but they both knew that was enough. She'd put her intention into the world, and it would manifest. She set her shoulders and resolved to talk to the one person she wanted nothing to do with: Thayatesh.

"You coming with me, cat?" Druff was perched on one of the empty shelves. He liked being up high to observe everything, especially when Hedwarg's two companions were about. Eshail secretly thought Druff would made a friend with one of the eight-legged folk that haunted the ceiling of her shop. The cat just looked at her, not as a familiar, but as an ordinary, judgy cat who had much better uses of his time than to follow her around all day. She shrugged, bade him goodbye, flipped her sign to closed, and went looking for trouble.

Eshail went where most travelers found themselves resting: the Toadsprigen Inn. The cobblestones were mucky with wet snow and mud. She pulled her sweater tighter. The town looked shabbier than usual, with the clouds washing all the color out of the world and the cold bite having had stripped paint off the walls of the buildings. Signs on rusty hinges squeaked in the wind. The streets were empty. Everyone was inside conserving energy. The only people about had business and kept their heads down. Not that anyone met the eyes of a witch in the winter anyway. In the winter, a witch in your house meant disease and death.

Witches were fair-weather friends. When spring was in full swing and births were plentiful, everyone wanted to talk to the witch. When it was nearing harvest, and they wanted a good crop, they'd stop and ask her about a possible charm. During the winter, though, the only reason they needed to visit a witch was for ill-omened happenings.

Eshail walked like a duck, letting the rain roll off her back. The inn was several blocks away, but outwardly it always put on a cheerful front. This was why Talin was the nearly unanimous vote for mayor when the last mayor died of Winter's Breath Fever a few years past. He kept a clean inn, sold non-watered-down wine, and always put a merry step forward—fine traits for a mayor.

The Toadsprigen's thick windows offered a warm glow against the dreary weather. The scrolling of flowering vines on the shutters still held their vibrant colors. Eshail could even hear the pluck of a lyre on a nameless tune. She paused outside the door, bracing herself for the encounter. She wasn't much of a people person. She preferred Druff. Generally she stayed away from the tavern because it usually held more people than she was comfortable with. With resignation, she pushed the door open and was immediately inundated by smells: unwashed bodies, baking bread, perfume, spilled ale, sage over the door, and a meaty stew.

Nauseated, she stood on the threshold, trying to be unobtrusive as she scanned the patrons. The Easterner was nowhere to be seen, but this didn't stop Talin from spotting her. He stomped over, brows knitted together. She didn't need to have Tarwa's mind-gleaning skill to know he was upset.

"I don't know what you said to that woman, but you blew this village's biggest possible deal in the last ten years." If she could have seen his aura, it would have been storm clouds. Alas, she didn't have that skill either.

"I did nothing," she started with a lie, but her brain knew it wouldn't stick, so she stumbled forward, "I did nothing but tell the woman I had nothing for her. This is the truth, Talin. You've seen me turn folks away. It's been a hard winter on me too."

His face softened a bit. "I know it, I know it." He was a good soul, one of the reasons she'd voted for him. "She was just so sure that you had what she was looking for. I know she's a stranger, but I'd started hoping things were looking up."

"Thayatesh left then?" She'd butchered the name, but he got the idea. "I thought she'd be staying for a while."

"Me too, but after visiting your shop yesterday, she muttered something about needing to move on. It's some weird quest she's on. I traded her a bit for that coat, but it was for nothing that will last us."

Eshail nodded, trying to hide the relief she felt. If the woman had given up that easily . . . well, she hadn't been in the village long enough to stir anyone up. Hedwarg's anxieties had been an aberration among the village. She'd be safe.

Her shoulders, which had been knitted up to her ears, started to uncurl. She took a deep breath as she realized the danger had passed.

Nothing prepared her for a messenger bursting through the doorway and careening into her and Talin. The three of them stumbled in a soggy mess into a table. The lyrist stopped, and the guests' murmuring halted. Everyone stared at the newcomer.

The young woman—Ry—was a frequent messenger to Lushwood. She had fiery red curls and piercing eyes. Many men, and a fair number of women had crushes on the muscled runner. She was adorned in traveling wools and held a strapped letter and package carrier she hauled from village to village along her route.

"Mayor Talin, we have an emergency. There's been a gully rush, and there's a wagon stuck. The driver's got a possible broken leg, and the position's about to be completely washed out." At that statement, Eshail knew that every bit of peace she'd assumed just moments ago was about to be extinguished.

In a soft voice, she asked, "Was the driver an Easterner?"

Ry looked at her, astonished. "How'd you know?"

Chapter 5

Talin, being the good citizen that he was, sprung into action. He began pulling together anyone with a set of muscles to help with the rescue. Gully rushes were dangerous in the Evermoss. They occurred when natural dams broke and were overwhelmed with spring water. The ground hadn't completely frozen, and the soggy build up must have overwhelmed the dam. Gully rushes could drain out a shallow lake in minutes and wash out roads, stick people in quick mud, and trap folks, gear, and animals with swift-flowing debris and the suction of the muck. Usually this didn't kill anyone. A broken bone or five was the extent of the initial damage. What killed people were the snakes and poisonous leeches that were attracted to such events.

Even Eshail didn't understand how the animals knew that a gully rush occurred. She'd talked to Hedwarg about it once. He'd muttered about the vibrations of the ground but, she thought it was nonsense—what did a snake know of vibrations? Either way, they'd have to pull Thayatesh, her horses, and her wagon out of the mud quickly, or every living being would be dead or dying in a matter of hours.

Eshail couldn't escape the inn. The door flooded

with people running in and out to gather supplies and help. She wanted to watch the excitement, even if she wanted nothing to do with it. Eshail hid at a corner table, away from the madness.

This didn't save her from Talin. The man had a knack for knowing people.

"I'm going to need you when we bring her back. I'll have Chester set the bone if we need to but you'll have to bandage it right." Eshail began to protest, but the look on his face stopped her. "Besides, we both know that she'll have a few snakebites. There's nothing my crew can do to help with those."

Eshail closed her eyes. He was right. She was the only one who had a chance of defeating multiple snakebites. Most in the village could deal with one or two, but several bites from the watery snakes inhabiting Evermoss would be a sure death to anyone but a witch. Hedwarg may have had a few solutions, but she would be the only sure bet.

"Make sure you grab her cargo too. I'm running low on supplies. I might need it." Eshail could hear the exhaustion in her own voice.

Talin put a hand on her shoulder. "You're a good witch, Eshail. We can always count on you, and I know it: this moment will pass." His words were a balm on her fears, and she felt her tension release. She *had* made a home here, and Talin considered her one of their own. *This* was safety.

"Thank you." Eshail's eyes met Talin's, and in that moment, all the communication they needed was passed in that heartfelt look of gratitude.

He departed with his rescue party, muscles and levers, ropes, and the city stretcher in hand. She watched them go, silently wishing them luck. No one deserved to die alone with the snakes and gators—not even an Easterner.

Eshail left the tavern to return to her home and business to prepare for the fight she could sense coming. Her mind took inventory of what she knew she had on hand. She had a couple of minor anti-venoms worked up for an emergency. Most of the locals were smart about avoiding snakes, and most of the snakes didn't bother with healthy humans. Every year, an adventuring child would unwarily stomp into a nest or try to capture a snake, only to be bit in retribution. She always had a few vials on hand for those moments.

Eshail's mind spun out, an unraveling mess of yarn. The woman would need care, and she'd need to stay in the village. Usually visitors, unless they were family, were quick to move on. Lushwood was a rarely used stopping point for a minor trade route. It wasn't equipped to host anyone long-term. They never saw Easterners. It was too out of the way. Most Easterners were afraid of the swamp and thought it malevolent—the source of witchcraft. Whatever would come next tonight was bound to be a unique experience.

Eshail had almost mindlessly walked back to her shop. She stopped at the front step, wiping her muddy boots off her entry mat. At first glance, she didn't see Druff, so she called to him: "Druff, I'm home. Going to need you, *mei fasciliear*."

The words held a tug of magic for a familiar. Hedwarg had no magic. His beasties stayed initially because of her calling and then because he'd bonded with them. Druff was a creature of a different sort. Together they were magically bonded, and both were better for it. Druff shimmered into being by her feet and rubbed up against her legs.

His presence was reassuring, but more importantly, his proximity would boost the effectiveness of her craft. The first task was to get the fire going and some hot water boiling. If she had to extract venom, she'd need fresh linens to clean the wounds and soak up the poison. She threw a couple of logs on the coals in her fireplace, the fire flaring almost instantly.

Satisfied the fire was well on its way, Eshail cast about for her cauldron. It was empty, as was prescribed. One of the first rules of the swamp: one didn't keep sitting water in the house. Even in the winter, insect larvae, long dormant, could awaken in the warm temperatures and grow into the biting and stinging bugs the swamp was known for.

She considered conjuring water but thought better of it. It was better to physically collect some from the local well than to waste magical energy before she knew how much she'd have to expend on the Easterner. Druff wove, almost magically, in and out of her legs as she walked down to the well in the square west of her shop.

The only other woman in the square was performing the unenvious task of washing. With her sleeves rolled up, she was rubbing out clothes on a washboard in the frigid air. Her knuckles were red and raw from the effort.

"Good evening, Eshail." The goodwife sounded tired. "You need a bucket?"

It always surprised Eshail when the townsfolk knew her name. She knew them all, of course, but she was always surprised anyone took the time to remember her given name and not just think of her as "the witch."

"Hi, Mauve. Yes, if I can just sneak in, I need some water for healing." She tip-toed between the laundry piles in various states of washing and began cranking the wrench to pull the water. Awkwardly she tried to make conversation above the noise of the crank. "It's an odd time to do laundry, isn't it?"

Mauve, a mother of three, wore the clothes of a drudge, fitting for wash day. "Aye, the littles had a bit of the stomach aches. They threw up over everything, I swear, twice. Honestly, though, I just wanted a break." She gave the grin all mothers do when successfully escaping for a few moments of peace.

Eshail nodded in understanding. "I can give you something to settle them?" The bucket had dipped into the bottom of the well, and she'd reversed her crank, bringing the heavy load back up.

"Thank you kindly, but they'll be fine. If it persists, I'll seek you out. It sounds like there are more pressing needs for your skills . . . ?" Mauve gave Eshail an appraising look. It was an odd time of day for her also to seek water.

"That Easterner seems to have fallen fate to a gully rush. Talin organized a group. I'm just preparing for the worst."

Mauve winced. "That bad, huh?"

"We'll see." They fell into silence as Eshail turned the crank. She could feel the woman's eyes on her. Most of the village's women were curious. The men were always business—*I need this or that*. They sometimes wanted more, but most didn't dare cross a witch. The women, though, were curious. Witches used women's magic, an easing of the world, a comforting touch. A witch's magic was not of steel and fire but wood and herb.

Eshail almost released the pull on the bucket when a third voice joined their two. "Easterners are trouble. If you have any trouble, you come to the council. We'll help." Eshail's ears burned at the familiar lilt. She continued to pull her bucket up while slowly turning her head as though attempting not to startle a shy bit of wildlife.

Evelyn stood with a red nose and cheeks, soft blonde hair curling around the delicate features of her face. Her nose was upturned, just like Eshail remembered, unique and unusual. Although she'd long memorized Evelyn's features, it'd been months since she'd seen her in person.

The herald of the council, Evelyn, stood a little straighter upon Eshail's examination. She was guarded in a way that made Eshail sad beyond words.

"It's good to see you, my friend," the witch spoke softly, emphasizing the word "friend." She returned her gaze to the crank to bring the bucket up the last couple of yards.

Evelyn was the head of the city council, a position known as the herald. She and Eshail had been fast friends, both apart from the rest of the villagers, both lonely. Eshail had mistaken their friendship for something else and had finally worked up the courage to be honest about her feelings last harvest.

Silence sat between the two. Mauve hummed aimlessly, utterly oblivious to the tension between the two.

Finally Evelyn spoke, "It's good to see you too, friend." The words were warm, and in the moment, all the frustration, disappointment, and awkwardness between them evaporated. Eshail pulled her full bucket onto the ledge and turned to Evelyn.

Eshail extended a hand for a shake. "Well met, herald."

Evelyn reached back. "Well met, witch." It'd been their inside joke: Eshail the lowly witch, and Evelyn, the prestigious herald. They'd always acted as though they were meeting for the first time, since people were usually surprised by their friendship.

Their friendship hadn't returned to what it was. If it had, they'd have hugged. Eshail wasn't going to press; a little distance was probably best for both of them. "Thanks for the support. This winter has been rough, and an Easterner won't make things easier."

Evelyn nodded. "It has been a long winter, but we'll make it through. Spring has not once missed its turn." Evelyn gave her "councilwoman smile," the one she had to wear for the village. Eshail nodded, remembering a time when she was in the herald's confidence and she wouldn't reassure Eshail—she'd share the worry.

"Good evening." Eshail bobbed her head in goodbye. She carefully left the square with her bucket in tow. Things weren't completely repaired, but she walked with a lightness she'd missed all winter.

Chapter 6

When Eshail returned home, her hearth was warm, and despite the fears of the last couple of days, her heart was healed. Things were on the mend with Evelyn. With the herald on her side, the Easterner couldn't possibly use the village against her. This was *her* home.

At first, Eshail had been in a whirlwind of activity. She set a cot out in her workroom, piling blankets and pillows on top. She unfolded her doctor's table out in the main room, draping fresh linen over it. The table had tall legs and could raise people to a certain height, which made it easy for the witch to work on any wounds or illness. She suspected if the Easterner survived, she'd need it.

The bucket of water was divided, some set aside for later, the rest sat in a pot, boiling to sterilize her tools and bandages. Her stitching kit was laid out, along with a few emergency drafts: anti-venom, anti-infection, and some wound cleaner. She was woefully unprepared to deal with a significant trauma. Only fools tried to travel this time of year.

She paced her now cluttered storefront. The waiting was driving her crazy. Eventually, she stopped hovering by the windows, watching for the clash of cartwheels on cobblestones. She set herself in her reading chair. The oversized cushions surrounded her petite frame in a hug of comfort. She'd put the chair in the main sales room to act as a place for an old bitty to rest if she was waiting for a curative. Eshail used it mostly though. In the evenings, she'd curl up with a book, the chair's red fabric overstuffed with cotton and wool.

Her pot of water had started boiling, so she removed it from the heat. No part of her wanted to make the cold trek back to the well because all the water had evaporated. The witch opened a book, a love story. She'd read a fair bit of them that winter. She set a cantrip for light, stretched her feet on the plush footstool, and pulled a blanket out on her lap. As soon as she settled, Druff climbed onto the footstool, snuggling into the blanket pooled around her feet.

She was several chapters in when the story had turned dark. One of the main characters was a bonedust witch that had been bent on crafting a reanimation curse. The words spooled out before Eshail, and she drifted off before she knew it.

Hours later, by the coals of her fire, she woke groggily to a thumping at her door. For a disoriented moment, she couldn't imagine why someone would be hammering so loud, and then all the memories flooded back. Druff had jumped away, anticipating her dumping him on the floor. She set her book down, unlatched the door, and stepped aside as Talin and three burly townsfolk barged into her shop. They carried a moaning woman, soaked through from a cold rain and covered in muck.

"Took long enough," Eshail commented as they put Thayatesh down on the doctor's table.

"One of the worst gully rushes I've ever seen. She's got half a dozen snakebites that I could see, and her right leg may be broken." He pointed to their makeshift splint. Between the cloth wrap, she noted severe purpling. She'd have to clean up the leg and rebrace it. "What do you need from us?"

Eshail took a quick account. The woman was covered in mud, and it was hard to tell how many snakeholes she had in her skin. This was more dire than she expected.

"Were you able to save much of her supplies?" Eshail looked at Talin. The supplies were going to be essential to Thayatesh's survival.

"We got some, not much. Most of it was ruined, covered in mud." Talin told her, distractedly trying to hold the Easterner on the table as she moaned. Eshail's heart sank.

An idea popped into her head. The woman had the traveling case. Everything had been well strapped down and in waterproof jars for travel. "How about the case?" She mimed the case's size.

"Ah yes, Chester found that. It was intact, covered in mud, but the case protected the bits and bobs." Talin looked at her blankly.

With an exasperated tone, she instructed the man on what came next, "Well then, get it for me. Do it before anyone else starts breaking into the ingredients. If most of her wares are gone, the least we can do is save her life with what's left." Talin still looked at her blankly, his mind catching up with her words. She used a tiny bit of mind magic to impress her next sentence: "Get it *now*. It's her life." The dash of magic did the trick.

The mayor turned to the men who'd helped him bring the woman in and said, "Go, run. Get the case." His command was unmistakable, and the three men dashed off, leaving Eshail's store in a jumble.

Talin bit his lip, looking at the moaning woman. Eshail could tell his desire to help warred with his desire to have nothing to do with what was ailing the girl. His heart won out. "Anything else you need help with besides the herbs?"

She looked from him to the woman. He was a good man, but she'd have to strip the woman down to examine her for bites. As she looked at him and weighed his worth, she realized that he was exhausted. Talin, normally fastidious, was covered in muck. Deep bags sat under his eyes. "Find me a woman or two to assist. Someone used to wounds who can treat scrapes and bruises. I will need some help, but no one of the rescue crew. You're all tired and much too dirty to be of further service tonight."

Talin instinctively tried to run a hand through his hair to fix his straw-colored mop, only to get halfway there and realize his hand was still crusted in mud.

The man blushed and stammered, only just realizing how gross he was. "That's probably for the best. I'll go arrange for help and get cleaned up." Eshail absently waved him off, already moving on to the problem at hand.

Talin made a quick exit. Eshail drew the curtains tight and flipped her sign to "closed." Looking at the woman, she felt nothing but compassion. Thayatesh was unrecognizable. Her skin was caked in mud, and her hair, once meticulously prepared to frame her face in curls, was greasy and dried in stringy, dirty clumps. Her face twisted in pain, and the fine coat she'd bought from Talin the night before was nothing but mud and ribbons.

She started peeling away layers of clothing while scraping as much muck off the woman's body as she could. Her mind shifted into the cold, detached mode she reserved for patients. She was focused and determined to save the woman's life. It didn't matter that she was an Easterner, that she hated witches, or that she was an utter fool. She was Eshail's job now, and the witch would do her best.

Eshail's mind noted when Evelyn slipped into the room, clean and calm. The witch nodded professionally; they'd worked together on several emergencies, and the two women fell into a rhythm. Evelyn always knew what Eshail needed next, what to hand her or prepare without a word. They were partners in a dance to save Thayatesh's life, and it was hauntingly beautiful.

The witch put a new water pot back over the coals, soaking bits of linen in hot water. She began scrubbing, wishing she'd asked Talin in what position they'd found the unconscious woman so she'd know where most of the bites were.

It didn't take long to figure out, though, as one side of her body was covered in leeches—a sure sign it'd been sitting in water for a prolonged period. She got a bowl of water and dumped some salt she had into it, stirring to make it dissolve.

Eshail's mind calmly noted that the mud may have saved the woman's life. She hoped it had masked the woman's presence from the predators while waiting for rescue. Overall, for the hours she spent in the swamp, helpless, Thayatesh was lucky to be alive.

She handed off the salt water to the herald to remove the leeches. Any native of Lushwood knew the basics of leech removal. For herself, she went back to cleaning the woman's body. She peeled back plastered-on clothes. The mud caked on like a thick glaze.

"You're going to need a lot more water for this," Evelyn said in a kind voice. Eshail felt overwhelmed; she needed to find the snakebites, but Evelyn was right. She needed to get some more water.

"I've got Yin outside. He has quick feet and can run and get us anything we need." This was why Evelyn was the head of the village council. She was always a step or two ahead of everyone. She was a planner. With Yin sprinting to the well to bring more water, Eshail returned to work. She didn't have time to be gentle. It was time to scrub.

Thayatesh's skin showed a raw pink as another layer of dirt and mud fell away. Eshail found the first bite, two angry lumps right on the shin of her left undamaged leg.

They were puffy but not very deep. It was obvious that the crusted-up remnants of her pants had taken most of the impact. The second bite was much worse. It was mid-thigh of her injured leg. The closer the bite to the core, the quicker the venom acts. She marked the spot with a bit of blue chalk. No one had arrived with the briefcase yet. Ideally she could mix a tincture for the snakebites to counteract the venom. She only had enough innate magic to stop one or two bites from turning sour.

Eshail weighed the situation. She had a stored reserve of magic, carefully curated over the last three years. The woman could be covered in snakebites, enough that she was already a lost cause. Or she could have these three alone, and quick actions could save her life. She needed her magic for emergencies and greater workings. Thayatesh moaned again, eyebrows knitted together. Eshail's heart gave a tug. No creature deserved this fate.

"Fine, you stupid woman. I'll do it," Eshail murmured to herself.

"It's the right choice." Evelyn had been silently watching her.

"Maybe, but we might still lose her."

The ever-righteous herald said, "Even if we do, it's the *right* choice."

Eshail looked up at the woman's determined eyes. "I know, alright. I *know*." She started weaving magic to stabilize the bite closest to the woman's torso.

Evelyn smiled her smile that lit up a room and made birds sing. "And that's why I love you." Evelyn's words were meant to be warm—a promise between friends. Eshail's heart gave a bitter pang as she returned her efforts to Thayatesh. She'd wanted Evelyn to say those words and mean it as lovers did, but the woman only had platonic sisterhood to give. Eshail was determined that their friendship would be enough; it'd been a long winter without her friend.

With a sigh, Eshail brought her cold, magic-soaked hands to the flesh of her most hated enemy and drew out the poison. She let go of her frustration and angst. It wasn't Evelyn's fault she didn't return the witch's feelings—she was built differently. Nature was like that.

The red line that had crept up toward Thayatesh's heart slowly began receding. A spark of purple magic pulled it down to Eshail's fingers. Poison floated in a globular ball above Eshail's hands, white and red and frothy. She strained with her intention, pulling it out, until a pop attested to her success. Before she lost concentration, she grabbed a dirty rag and grabbed the poison ball out of the air before it dropped onto the defenseless woman.

She looked at Evelyn. The herald had returned to her task without a word. Eshail was relieved. Many townsfolk historically didn't react well to true displays of magic. A wave of exhaustion assaulted her for a moment.

She ignored it. There was no time to be tired. Four hours later, the two had rebandaged the leg, used the delivered case's contents to cure a half-dozen other snakebites, and fed the woman some broth full of an anti-fever agent. Evelyn and Eshail had managed to get some decent clothes on her unconscious form and sent Yin for help. Talin, who had much improved in hygiene, came in with several other folks to help relocate the Easterner to the pallet set up in the workroom. The woman slept peacefully, surrounded by clean blankets, Druff on her stomach, and with a soothing juniper and eucalyptus vapor misting from a pot nearby.

Talin left with a nod to the herald and witch. He knew how hard they'd had to work. Once the rest of the men had left, Evelyn and Eshail sat on the floor. They were too dirty to sit on real furniture. The two leaned against each other, exhausted.

"It's done." The herald stated with her normal directness.

"Indeed."

"You think she'll live?" It was the question of the night.

Eshail thought about it momentarily. "If the Nest Mother wishes it, she'll live."

Evelyn didn't respond. This was the way of the world. Hard work of this sort frequently didn't pay off. It took Eshail a moment to realize the herald, whose head rested against her shoulder, had fallen asleep. Soft snores were her only company as she thought about the day's insanity.

A year ago, she'd dreamed of this moment. Evelyn and her working hand in hand, and the herald falling asleep against her. Now she was numb, tired, and glad they'd repaired things. Eshail took a deep breath and exhaled the last of her bitterness. With her acceptance came sleep. The witch began lightly snoring with a smile on her face. Her dreams were warm.

Chapter 7

Eshail aged as witches did. Wise beyond her years in the experience of sickness, death, and heartache. While also being young in connection, love, and communication.

She woke up stiff. Her heart immediately betrayed every boundary she'd drawn around it as she found Evelyn snuggled into the crook of her shoulder. She looked down on her former crush and instantly regretted falling asleep propped up with Evelyn. Eshail burned with the need to pull away while also not wanting to. Her cheeks reddened with the inner conflict.

The Easterner moaned loudly from the other room. Eshail, regretfully, started to maneuver herself out from under Evelyn, who apparently was a heavy sleeper. As she adjusted, she got a full whiff of the herald's hair. It was all rose petals and vanilla scented. Pure heaven. It would be easy to pluck a hair and use it in a potion—no, that would be truly evil in nature. Eshail dismissed the intrusive thought as soon as it popped into her head. Instead she leaned the herald against the footstool, surrounded by blankets.

Thayatesh was still unconscious, but the numbing agents had worn off. When she'd come into care, in addition to the bites and the leg damage, the woman had also sustained some potential frostbite. Eshail carefully picked up her hand and unwound the bandaging, checking her fingers. She held her breath as the last layer came undone.

"Oh, thank the Nest Mother!" Eshail whispered. The woman's hands were nipped, with a few blisters indicating a worse frostbite, but she'd keep her fingers. Her examination continued- checking the snakebite locations. Several were puffy with a mild infection, but thanks to the hard work they'd done before, none had the tell-tale angry red lines extending from the wounds.

The woman's leg looked worse. No bones seemed to be splintered, which was miraculous, but the witch wasn't sure Thayatesh hadn't fractured her leg. Large, deep bruises circled her knee, and swollen patches of purple indicated a few impact spots. It would be a while before she'd walk around without a crutch.

Eshail put on some water to heat and began examining the herbs she had on hand. The Easterner's case contained numbweed, which was good. She'd need it. Tea. More Eucalyptus. Eshail took her chalk and began tallying the ingredients until the teapot whistled. She stared at the pot momentarily, forgetting what she'd been doing before her inventory had started.

"Will you take it off the heat already?" Thayatesh asked shakily. Eshail blinked, staring at the woman's clear, brown eyes.

She hadn't noticed the eyes before. Thayatesh had the eyes of all Easterners: dark brown, soulless orbs— people whispered. Eshail saw irritation.

"Yes, muckwood, hold on." She put her piece of chalk down and donned her hearth mitten, grabbing the metal teapot with the protective barrier. She set the pot on a trivet. The whistling started to decrease in volume immediately.

Eshail grabbed two delicate tea cups and grew self-conscious under the Easterner's gaze as she prepared an herb mixture for the woman. In the front room, Evelyn had started moving around as though she, too, would get up. Eshail poured Thayatesh's cup to steep and grabbed a sturdier mug from the inn. Knowing Evelyn, she'd want to charge off into her day.

The witch kept busy, placing the tea leaves in her and Evelyn's respective cups and pouring in the water. The stranger watched Eshail the entire time.

"I think yours is ready, Thayatesh, although the water is still hot," Eshail stated, finally working up the nerve to look at the Easterner again. She caught a wince at the woman's name. "I'm sorry, am I still mispronouncing your name?"

Thayatesh reached out as Eshail handed her the tea cup, wincing as she tried to sit up. "Yes. I'm just not used to hearing someone with your accent try to say it. You can call me Yates, if that's easier."

"Yates." Eshail tried out the name while sipping her black tea. "I think that suits you better."

At this point, Evelyn had joined them. The normally immaculate herald was still covered in grime, with her hair in a wild, messy tangle.

"Good morning, herald," Eshail said with a smile, thoroughly enjoying the dishevelment of her friend.

"Good morning, witch," Evelyn responded saying *witch* harshly, in line with their joke. They both broke out in a grin.

"Are the two of you . . ." Yates's face screwed up, looking for a word. ". . . paired?" It was evident that she found such a state distasteful. The Eastern Empire tolerated such pairings about as much as it tolerated witches. Another idiotic Eastern way of thinking.

"Eshail *wished*," Evelyn blurted out with a smile. Eshail was embarrassed at first. When they'd awoken, the dregs of her emotions still simmered, but then Eshail laughed. It was true: she had wished it. But if they'd moved to teasing her about it, their friendship must be well healed.

"You? You're almost as stinky as a fishmonger. I don't think I'd pair with you well, *herald*." Eshail mimicked a haughty noblewoman's voice, smiling. Their friendship had sprung up between each other in full form.

"A fishmonger?" squeaked Evelyn in mock outrage.

The Easterner watched the two, keeping her own counsel, which was fine by Eshail. She didn't want to hear what the woman would have said anyway.

Eshail sipped her tea, noting the way Yates shifted in her makeshift bed, wincing. All in all, the woman had a leg beat to a pulp, multiple snakebites, bruises everywhere, and mild frostbite, but . . . Eshail's magic had done the trick. She'd stored her power for three years. Three long, miserly years to save this woman's life. The worth of saving a life was a heavy one, which was why the act had been so costly. Preserving life was the Nest Mother's most favored use of power, so she knew she shouldn't regret the expenditure. But she did.

She had planned to cast a finding spell to help her seek and add to her greater talents. To unlock a primary skill with more use and push her from a young witch into true adulthood.

She'd never admit it out loud, but she was disappointed. To have to use her magic on a woman she didn't like, from the Eastern Empire, a country she actively hated, and for, in her estimation, a genuinely foolish decision to leave the village. Employing her stored magic for that bordered on a crime to witchhood.

Yates yawned. "What was in this tea? I'm getting tired again."

Eshail answered with what she hoped was a reassuring smile. "It's alright. You're tired because you almost died last night. The tea does have a sleep agent to help you rest, but you really need it." She left off the part that using that much magic had drained the woman's own energy stores. She *should* sleep like the dead for the next day or two.

Yates looked at her blankly and nodded. Her lack of argument was wise. Eshail suspected Yates was feeling her misadventure: "I still can't believe I'm safe. That I'm alive." Eshail reached forward as the hand holding the teacup wavered. She plucked it from the injured woman's fingers, noting it was almost empty. Any second, and the Easterner would be down.

"Just get some sleep. I'll keep you safe," Eshail found herself saying.

"*Thank you,*" came one last, surprising yet heartfelt comment before Yates's head returned to her pillows. Druff trotted up as though he'd been summoned and hopped onto the bed, leaning in to the woman's legs. His purrs, she'd found, had healing qualities of their own.

"She out already?" asked Evelyn.

"Yes, so it seems."

"Did you see she didn't move her legs in that entire exchange?" The observant herald pointed out, a touch of concern in her voice.

Eshail quickly replayed the morning tea and realized she was right. Her mind raced across all the possibilities.

"I don't *think* it's what you're worried about. She didn't break her back, as far as I could see. I would guess it was a paralytic from the snakebites on her legs." Eshail looked at Evelyn's worried eyes and said with more confidence than she felt, "It'll wear off. She'll be walking around in a day or two with a crutch."

Evelyn nodded, taking the explanation at face value. Eshail kept a lid on her anxiety. She suspected what had happened but didn't want to jump to conclusions. A nugget of worry wormed in her gut—worry and guilt. If she hadn't had the best intentions when using her magic, it's possible the poison on the initial bite hadn't fully cleared Yates's system. The world's magic relied on intent and power, as did most things. If her intentions weren't pure and she'd let any of her feelings toward Easterners into the act . . . she was *sure* she'd been focused on healing.

Druff had moved to the counter, waiting for his breakfast. He examined the two women sharing tea, and his disapproval surpassed the species barrier. He sat, licking a paw, ears akimbo in judgment. It felt like the Nest Mother herself had descended and found her unworthy. Which she would be if she'd let her own intellect interrupt the healing magic.

Eshail mechanically fed Druff from his kibble jar. She didn't have it in her to go into the basement. He huffed but bent to the task. Evelyn began preparing some toast and pulled out a jam jar. The woman was efficient and diligent. She'd been fancied by most of the village and had passed into her twenties and thirties unclaimed. Now Eshail knew why.

Many have suspicions, a secret love that wasn't meant to be. A summer abroad at her cousin's could only mean marriage and widowhood. In this part of the world, it was not customary to remarry after losing a husband. The other rumors grew darker. But the truth was simple: no person could enchant the woman. She was as untouchable as the moon and perhaps more beautiful to those around her for it.

"Would you like some more tea?" Eshail found herself asking with a smile.

Evelyn looked up with clear hazel eyes. "More tea would be lovely." There was a trust. Not all townsfolk would willingly accept tea from a witch's pot for fear that she'd bespelled it. She could admit that not all witches were honest. Common folk might have small justifications for their fear.

Eshail first tipped the hot water into her teacup,

refined into the shape of tulip petals. They were one of her most cherished possessions, gifted from one of the Wanderer Folk after she'd cured their dogs. Then she poured a larger helping into the mug from the inn. She plunked the little balls containing tea leaves into the cups for their second steep and decided it was a good moment to use the last of her honey.

"That first cup was delightful. What is in it? I taste a bit of cinnamon, and something else, a toasted nut perhaps?" Evelyn called as she pulled the bread slices out of the pan.

"You've got two out of three correct. Care to guess the third ingredient?"

"Well, there's something sweet. Not honey."

Eshail nodded, pulling her nearly empty honey pot down from the shelf. She knew Evelyn liked her tea as sweet as possible, so she'd traded the wandering folk for the secret third ingredient last summer.

"Is it sugar?" Evelyn asked in a voice that knew she was wrong but couldn't grasp what was missing.

"Kind of." Eshail turned around with a smile. She'd been disappointed when she couldn't test the ingredient out on her friend when their friendship had collapsed. The packet had sat unused in the back of her pantry. "I've added just a hint of brown sugar."

"Ah yes, that's unexpected and delicious. You wouldn't have some more for this second cup?" The herald's eyes were warm as she continued, "*Thank you*, by the way. I know that couldn't have been easy to obtain."

Eshail bowed her head, knowing that her gift had been well received. "Of course, if you keep coming over for tea, I'll feed it to you all summer."

"You minx. Is this how you lure the townsfolk into your evil lair?" Evelyn accused with a laugh.

"Oh no, you've seen through my evil ploy."

The two chuckled as Evelyn handed over a piece of

toast covered in apple jam.

"Seriously, though, I was going to offer to have one of the boys stop by with supplies. I want to ensure that this Easterner isn't a burden to you. I know you don't want to hear this, but probably best she stays here for at least a couple of days."

Eshail paused in her bite, startled by the abrupt turn in conversation. Her shock must have been evident as Evelyn rushed forward, "She's not going to heal overnight. Even my untrained eyes can see that. You're the best there is on caring for the sick and wounded." She conveniently left out that most of Eshail's healing practice in the village over the last five years was on pets and farm animals. "I was planning on stopping by so that I can check on her and make sure you've got everything that you need."

Eshail weighed the woman's words. She did *not* want Yates living with her. An Easterner didn't belong in a witch's home, didn't deserve a witch's hospitality, and she didn't want her digging around in her cellar, finding her stash of potions. The thing was, Eshail *wasn't* the best suited to take care of the sick. She was the one folks went to in an emergency; she came to their house, gave them medicine or brew, and left. She was very good at leaving and letting folks heal in their own time.

The denial of this ask died on her lips as she looked at Evelyn. That was the thing about heralds. Not every village had one. Not every community could tolerate their presence. Only some of the people with herald potential did it right. Heralds weren't the mayor; they were just another part of the city council. They were one simple voice—but a voice that commanded. They represented what was possible. Evelyn had a way about herself; if she believed something could happen, she looked at a person or group in a way that made the task no longer an option but an expectation.

All of Eshail's internal complaints and objections

looked petty in the weight of Evelyn's judgment, and she'd already taken care of the complex arguments of cost, lugging water, and the danger of being alone with the Easterner. She'd even thrown in that she would be personally checking on the progress of the woman, which Eshail wanted to avoid admitting did have a bit of weight in and of itself.

Before she could stop herself, Eshail heard the words escape from her mouth, "I can keep her here. But she *is* an Easterner, and I'm a witch. This will be difficult to do alone, so I want her gone when she's on her feet."

Druff sat on the counter, his sensibilities affronted. He turned his head in insult. At some point, he'd picked up on the idea of "side eye" being a superior form of judgment, and he used it constantly now. His body indicated that she was not *alone* in watching the woman.

The beaming grin Evelyn gave her, smile lines wrinkling around her mouth, was worth the payment. Or at least that's what Eshail told herself in the moment.

"Thank you." Evelyn reached out and took her hand. The words were low and genuine. "I know you've got many important tasks to perform, and she's going to be a distraction. I know you'll take good care of her, and we both know that may not be true of other households in the village."

The words chilled Eshail. She had dark thoughts about the Eastern Empire, but she'd never hurt someone over it. For a moment, her consciousness twinged. She'd never *consciously* hurt an Easterner.

The two friends caught up over their tea for a few minutes. Then Evelyn left. The frantic evening and shared morning turned quiet. Eshail was alone with a sick, sleeping stranger and her cat.

The witch mulled over Evelyn's words. That she couldn't trust some of the others in the village. Eshail's stomach cramped with worry, wondering if she was safe either. Then again, she wondered if Evelyn should be trusting *her* with the woman's health either.

Tarwa always insisted work was a good cure for worry. With that philosophy in mind, she returned to cataloging her new cache of supplies.

Chapter 8

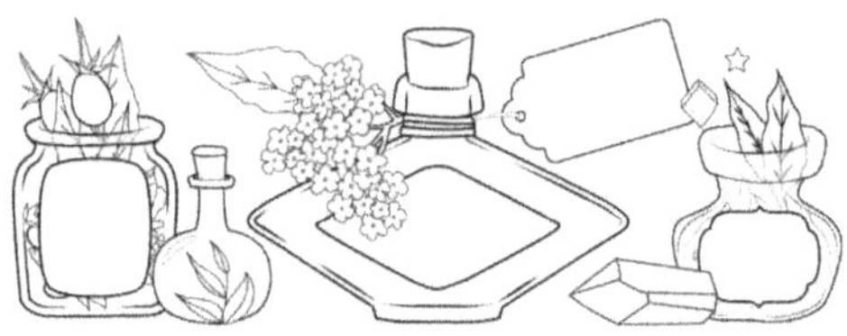

It took a long week before Yates was on her proverbial feet and mildly coherent. Eshail used a couple of the vials from the briefcase to help. She was careful not to use too much, only enough. She didn't want to make use of rare Eastern plants, but local supplies were nonexistent.

Thankfully, the feeling in the woman's legs returned on the second day, just in time for her to become conscious enough to start noticing. Eshail'd fobbed off the lackluster movement as the aftereffects of a nasty bite. The Easterner bought it, but she still wasn't so sure.

She'd moved the woman, mainly out of guilt, into her bed. It was considerably more comfortable than the wooden slat pallet she'd erected in the workroom. Evelyn had been faithful to her word. Toad? Todd? One of the village boys had been bringing food and water twice a day, even if Evelyn herself hadn't found too much time yet.

"Druff, is it me or is this the worst?" She waved toward the workroom. She stuffed a sweater full of extra laundry to use as a pillow. It was lumpy and hard. Druff gave her a slow blink. He'd been irritated with her. He'd been sleeping with Yates, which she viewed as a betrayal, even if she knew he was simply trying to heal her. For her part, she'd been so off balance she was frequently forgetting to feed him on time.

"What's the worst?" came the lilting voice of her guest.

"Awe, cattails in the water. You're awake?"

"Yes, and I have ears that work even from here," Yates said acerbically. Now that she was feeling better, the woman became noticeably grumpy about being locked away in her room. She was bored.

The worst part of the situation was that the Easterner was about to get much more bothersome. She was starting to heal fast, and with a crutch, she would be cleared to walk around today. "Well, welcome to the world of the living. It's nice of you to join us."

"Am I alive? I feel like I fell into a vat of fire plumb, and the parts of me that haven't simply given up for dead just *hurt*."

Eshail's eyebrows stitched together. She wasn't sure what fire plumb was, but it was concerning that some of the woman's body was still numb. The numbness initially pointed to the cold conditions she was found in, and it now pointed to severe issues in her body's web. She walked into the workroom, skirts swishing, and looked at Yates's face. It was sweaty from illness, but her dark brown eyes were completely clear for the first time in a week.

"So you *have* joined the land of the living?"

"I guess? I certainly don't feel very good. And my right leg, I can't"—Strain was evident in her voice—"move it very quickly."

Eshail moved to the bedside, knelt, and prodded at the leg—the one that had had the nasty snakebite on her thigh. The one she'd used her magic on the most. She'd assumed it was just a normal venomous Fenlow. No red line had appeared after the healing magic. The bite could have been a juvenile Red Death Adder. This was possibly a lie she told herself but brushed it aside.

"Can you move your toes?"

The woman strained, and her toes slowly curled on themselves.

"I know you were bitten by at least one Red Death Adder, possibly two. I managed to get enough of the venom out of you to save your life, but it's possible that it was not enough to save the complete mobility of your leg."

"How long until it possibly returns?"

Eshail toyed with the response. It was likely the leg would stay disconnected, but there were things they could do to improve the chance her life web would reconnect. Witches' lives often depended on not overpromising hope.

She saw the fear in Yates's eyes. Losing mobility was life-altering for a merchant.

"It is"—She meant to say "unlikely" but didn't— "possible that feeling and mobility can return." She immediately regretted her choice of words at the spark of hope in the woman's eyes. "It'll be hard work, and you'll have to take the brews I give you, and work on walking, even though it hurts. We'll have to use much of what's left of your stash." This was the truth. "Is this your mother's foot?"

"My what?"

Some things, it seemed, didn't translate well for Easterners. They didn't have the concept of the Nest Mother, who watched over all, and the All Mother, the source of life itself.

"Your primary foot, the one you kick with?" Eshail thought hard about how else to explain it.

Realization dawned, and Yates nodded.

"Well, that makes trying to heal your web even more important. Do you have feeling in your right arm?"

If the arm was also having issues, it meant the life web on that half of the body was disrupted, a more severe problem.

She wiggled her fingers. "I can move my fingers fine, but it *hurts*." Eshail looked at the hand. It had the most frostbite blisters. The pain probably didn't mean anything worse than that.

"Well, that's good, as long as they're mobile. I assumed you were lying against the ground on that side since it was more frostbitten. This is a good sign."

The woman looked down at her leg. Layers of bruises had started to heal. Black had turned to blue and blue to yellow. It was gnarly but mending.

"How long before I can walk on it?"

"That depends."

"Depends on what?"

The witch looked Yates in the eyes. "How high is your tolerance for pain and difficulty?" She said it with a challenge, adding a bit more incentive. "I don't know much about those from the Eastern Empire, but I imagine rich merchants, like yourself, don't have to endure much hardship or pain." The gauntlet was thrown.

Eshail watched as Yates's back stiffened with the prescribed insult. "I'll manage fine." The words were cold.

"Good, some backbone. This will serve you well." Eshail walked out of the room and waited for Yates to come out. "There's a crutch against the wall. Make sure you're using it."

Eshail used a cantrip she could only cast in her house. The Seeing Eye. She watched as Yates leaned against the wall and closed her eyes in frustration. Eshail saw a self-pitying tear leaking out of her eye. The witch was unmoved. The Nest Mother helped those who helped themselves.

Sure, Yates was in a tough spot, but the village had stepped up and cared for her. She would leave this experience with her life, which she was lucky to have. If Eshail had been a little less humane or the village a little smaller and without a witch, the stubborn merchant would have been long dead by now.

Eshail turned off her Seeing Eye and waited. A few

minutes later Yates awkwardly stumbled out of the room, clad in some of Evelyn's castoffs. They stood there in silence for a moment.

"I understand if you're unable to help someone like me. The Evermoss filth runs deep."

Eshail wasn't sure exactly what the insult had been, but she knew it was one. Anger flared. "I helped you with the heart of my magic, and I didn't have to. You should be grateful for your life. You dry landers are all the same, skin deep. You take, not understanding why." Yates's face went white at the talk of magic. She didn't respond, some part of her brain probably registering that she'd insulted a *witch*, a soul stealer with access to powers she didn't understand.

Eshail turned her back and left. Her mind was in turmoil, and Druff followed, rubbing against her leg, trying to ease her discomfort. She shouldn't have lost her temper on a woman who was infirm with a broken web and facing long-term mobility consequences. It was unbecoming of a witch. She couldn't help it though. The resentment of losing three years' worth of saved magic had been building all week, and the woman's lack of gratitude rubbed her fur in the wrong direction.

It was better she separate herself and return to the business of healing a body.

It so happened that Evelyn's visit would turn the conversation around. The herald had been stopping by the last couple of days. Eshail was sure if it'd been a busier time of year, she'd be by less frequently, but after helping everyone recover from the rescue and salvage mission, there wasn't much to keep a herald busy while everyone waited for the weather to break.

Evelyn had walked in, soft knocks announcing her arrival. "How's our patient?"

"She's awake. You can ask for yourself." The mood was apparent in Eshail's clipped tone.

Evelyn reached out, putting a hand on Eshail's

shoulder. "That bad, huh?"

Eshail didn't bother to respond, just waved the herald toward the back room. "Go ask the ungrateful sandworm *yourself*."

Evelyn marched into the back room without saying another word. Eshail didn't try to listen, but it was impossible not to hear the murmur as the two women talked. The murmurs got louder, and voices raised in a matter of minutes. Evelyn was less patient with stupidity than Eshail, which is probably how she became herald. She was good at browbeating the council into action when they wanted to sit on their laurels.

"You let that filthy witch put poison into my body, and now we're all surprised it doesn't work, right? She probably did it on purpose." Eshail winced. Those last words hit too close to her fears. "I'm from the *East,* from the sacred lands. You've defiled me, and I'm anathema."

"*You* came here seeking magic, and magic is what you got, you Mother-forsaken hypocrite. That woman worked on you for hours to take the poison *out* of your body! I've always pitied your people, living in the desert, a land forsaken by the All Mother. Now I know the truth. You're just a bunch of fools. If it weren't against *our ethics,* our *heathen ways,* I'd dump you back into the swamp and let the snakes take you."

Eshail had lived as most witches did, at the fringe of the village, as a pseudo-outcast. People didn't like things they didn't understand, and magic was tricky that way. Few were like Hedwarg who understood enough not to be fearful. Evelyn's words, though, made her wonder if she'd underestimated the village. If the herald thought she was one of them, a critical part of the village, then maybe she wasn't as close to getting run out of town as Hedwarg had suggested.

Nothing but silence answered the herald's last words, and after a few minutes of it, Evelyn came stomping out of the bedroom.

"She's an ungrateful whelp, isn't she?"

Eshail only nodded. Druff even seemed to nod.

"I'm half tempted to make true on my threat. I know what resources you used to save the woman's life. It wasn't nothing—not this time of year, not in a witch so young."

This brought Eshail up short. How could Evelyn know of the ways? Did she? Or was she just misinterpreting the statement? For a moment, she thought to act like a squirrel and run back up her tree in isolation. But the prospect of being able to talk to someone who *knew* and could understand her grief was too great. She dipped the tip of a toe into the water.

"She doesn't understand. Few people do." She waited, seeing if Evelyn would take the bait. Eshail studied Evelyn. The woman's mouth had been set in anger but was replaced by a concerned softness as her eyes searched out Eshail's. A faint scent of vanilla, rare in these parts, brought the image of the two of them snuggled up on the floor. Eshail blushed, warm thoughts bringing her back to that moment of connection.

With a soft voice, Evelyn asked the question Eshail had hoped for but dreaded the answer: "How much did you have to use? How much time have you lost?"

A lump had been knotting in her chest, and the acknowledgment of her loss loosened it. Her eyes teared up; she couldn't help it, and for a moment, the words caught in her throat. Evelyn saw it all and reached forward, wrapping her arms around Eshail in a hug. For a moment, the witch leaned into her, enjoying comfort from another human, a rare bit of luxury for one such as herself.

"I lost at least two years, maybe all three, of power. I'm not skilled at healing; it takes a lot of power to do what someone gifted might do delicately." It was a lot. It would take her that much longer to unlock her next skill, and the only way she could build up the reserve was by using the skill she had—the skill she detested.

"I will help. *She* will help. There is a debt here." That Evelyn stated this was the power of a herald. They saw a thing that needed doing, and they could move physical and imagined mountains to make it happen. They had a bit of magic in themselves to motivate, move, and inspire. Eshail allowed herself to believe the woman for a moment, then she leaned in a little more, and inhaled her scent.

Then, the moment's vulnerability caught up with her, the fear of the humanity she was meant to serve. She pulled away.

"If the Nest Mother wills it." Eshail turned their conversation to bigger problems. "We've got other things to worry about with the winter lingering."

A flash of hurt ran across Evelyn's face at the abrupt change of tone, but she was astute enough to know when to take an exit. "Yes, actually, I need to go. Rumors are floating around that a group is forming to take on the heart of winter. We're discussing whether we want to add to the expedition." Eshail nodded. An expedition meant heroes from the cities would investigate the cause of the prolonged winter. Likely several groups would venture into the mountains to confront the frost dragons.

"That sounds important. Let me know if you need any assistance from the town witch. In the meantime, I'll try my best to get this one moving."

"Will do." The herald was all business now. The moment was over. "Torad will come by with some water in the next candle mark." Without a backward glance, she was gone.

Chapter 9

It'd been three long days of nothing. Eshail was grumpy. Even Druff had started avoiding her. Intellectually she knew she was being unreasonable. Yates hadn't asked to be saved. The woman had been a complete fool to leave Lushwood during one of the first spring rainstorms, when the ground was frozen and floods were likely. Gully rushes weren't exactly predictable, but it was the most optimal time for one. Of course, the Easterner wouldn't know the ways of the swamp. The woman was from the desert and had as much swamp sense as a babe. Eshail's mind made these excuses for her, but even still they didn't break through her stony resentment.

It only made her more pissed off that she couldn't reasonably blame Yates for her loss of power. And if she were truly honest with herself—and she was trying hard not to be—her guilt over Yates's slow-to-heal leg didn't help.

Evelyn had promised retribution or at least some repayment for the debt. The village coming to help. But so far, the herald hadn't been back.

This irked her too. Evelyn had given her hope that something could be salvaged. But with each minute ticking away without a plan or movement, she fell deeper into melancholy.

Hope was like follymoss, which grew where the tips of trees met the clouds. It might be real, but it was so untouchable. Yet people made decisions, even lost their lives, trying to harvest the moss. Everyone knew what it was and the magic it was capable of, but no one had seen it personally. Hope was like that; it was desperately hard to touch unless it was real.

Evelyn's power as an orator and a bender of wills was such that she could sow inspiration and hope without even thinking about it. Eshail knew this and had seen it working for years.

"Will you stop your self-pitying and moping already?" Yates crutched into the main room. Eshail had been absently stirring her tea, trying to avoid the woman who'd taken over her bedroom.

"Excuse me?"

"What do we need to do to fix this?" Yates waved at the room with her crutch, including Eshail in her wave. "I'm going to pull out my hair if I have to stay cooped up in this shop one more moment with *you*."

"You're not prize company either." The witch couldn't help the retort. A solitary creature, she was not used to having someone *in the way* every moment.

The Easterner snorted. "Well, at least you're honest." She hobbled over to the tea kettle and poured herself a cup. With a crutch, she could get around reasonably well.

Eshail was curious. "Why do you care?"

The merchant turned, a thin eyebrow raised. "Wasn't it you and that herald of yours that told me I had incurred a debt?" She leaned against the counter, crutch propped up. Yates blew on her tea, attempting to cool it. "Do you know if they could save any of my stock?"

"No." Eshail was being petty and short. But she felt like it.

"Is that no, they weren't able to, or no, you don't

know?"

"I don't know. They got me your case the night of the accident, but I don't know what happened to the rest of it. Talin hinted that it'd been lost, but I haven't confirmed since the weather turned."

Eshail'd been pinned to the store for weeks now. It was too much. She needed to be in the woods, in the Evermoss. She was out of balance, which impacted her mood more than she wanted to admit.

"Then go and find out."

Eshail just looked at her, shocked.

Yates's face softened, realizing orders weren't going to win the witch over. "Please. I know my quest doesn't mean much to you, but I invested a lot in that stock. If it's lost, my journey is done." Yates's last words were spoken with a depression that matched—perhaps even beat—Eshail's. For a moment, the witch looked outward instead of at herself, and her empathetic nature kicked in.

"Fine, yes. I will check. You stay here. I'll send Hedwarg over to watch you."

The Easterner nodded. They both knew she didn't need Hedwarg to watch her. It was a babysitting exercise. Eshail didn't trust her.

With a whirlwind she obtained her thick sweater, cloak, and hat. She stood by the counter, giving Druff a moment to hop onto her well-padded shoulders. With the cat firmly in place, Eshail left. The weather was overcast with the type of clouds that misted cold rain for hours, soaking everyone venturing outside. She took a deep breath. The moist air smelled like freedom. Eshail's spirits lifted almost immediately.

She headed over to Talin's tavern, Druff calmly clutching her shoulders, tail wrapped around her neck, which was the easiest way to keep him close in environments in the city. It was the type of day Hedwarg would spend over a mug of ale at the Toadsprigen, and

Talin would have knowledge of the state of the wagon's supplies.

Her boots clacked against the cobblestones, and she nodded to Mauve. The goodwife gave a smile and nod in reply. Eshail's wide-brimmed hat bobbed at each step.

The tavern was full. Talin was behind the counter taking orders, so Eshail found Hedwarg in his favorite spot: a tiny booth meant for two. The wildman had spent several winters carving scenes of nature and animals into the wood of the booth's frame. He'd marked his spot.

Eshail approached the booth, steeling herself for bargaining. Although the man was her friend, he was notoriously hard to obtain a favor from.

"Good to see you in the world," he grunted. Kipsini gave a more welcoming head bob and a chirp of greeting. Sneit popped his nose out of Hedwarg's pocket, sniffing the air as though he could summon a treat from the witch. Eshail couldn't help but smile at the squirrel's antics. Druff snuggled closer into her neck, trying to disappear to avoid upsetting Hedwarg's companions.

"My apologies, friends, my snacks are back at the store," she said with genuine regret. Sneit stuck a tiny paw out of the pocket and waved as though all was forgiven as he returned to his nap. Kipsini bobbed her head as though she was just a regular bird and did not understand the witch.

"I feel like you came here for a reason besides taunting my friends?" Hedwarg was unimpressed.

"Can you babysit the Easterner? I need to get out for a while. I wanted to investigate the gully rush."

"There's nothing left of the woman's stock. Talin's crew checked."

"I figured. It's just"—Eshail took a breath, letting go of her embarrassment—"I'm unbalanced. I need to walk in the woods a bit." It was an argument the not-druid would be particularly susceptible to. She tried not to look at him too pathetically.

Eshail moved her gaze from Kipsini to Hedwarg's eyes. Few looked him in the face, just as few looked her in the face. Hedwarg's hair was long, greasy, and clumped, sometimes braided. Today it held a twig, and it looked like Sneit had stored an acorn in a patch. His eyebrows were untamed bushy caterpillars. He brought his mug of ale to his mouth, took a sip, and studied her. Foam caught in his mustache.

Eshail searched his grey eyes. They were the hardest to meet. His eyes were like looking into a lake so placid it reflected the perfect sky. He was quiet and odd but very deep.

"I'll do it." The words came between the furs of Hedwarg's overhanging mustache.

"That's all? You'll do it?" she asked incredulously.

He smiled in his way, mustache quivering in amusement. "Sometimes you just have to ask a friend. Besides, I can tell from here you *are* off-balance, which serves no one."

Druff rubbed against her ear causing her to twitch, telling her to take the gift.

"Thank you. I'll be back tonight." The stoic man nodded. Eshail followed Druff's advice and, with a nod to Talin, left.

Chapter 10

Eshail had already grabbed her harvesting basket, traveling pack, and boots on her way out of the shop. She left Lushwood, and her feet grew lighter with each footstep. The weights on her chest lightened. She walked, the ground underneath her changing from cobblestone to gravel to the packed mud of the main route out of the village. Lushwood sat on a prominent knoll in the swamp, and as the road dipped down into the watery landscape surrounding her home, she began to smile.

Once they got into the wilderness, Druff jumped down and raced ahead, his lithe form hopping on logs and stones. He'd scout and find lovely patches of greenery or roll in a nice dusty bit of dirt under a fern. The cat was very good at scenting out a rare blossom. Not that she expected to find anything blooming yet. Patches of snow sat on the ground. Pools of water were still edged with ice. Stubborn as the mole in her garden, winter held on.

There were still things that could be harvested. Being locked in her house for two weeks inspired her to think creatively about harvesting. The first stop was a silent sassafras tree. She'd harvested from it in the fall and wanted to check on its healing progress. Strips of the bark could be ground and used to ease the aches of age and help with chamber pot burns. It wasn't something she'd often use for folks, as it had detrimental long-term effects, but it was good to have in her armory.

She patted the tree, thanking it for its help. The wound was healing nicely. Ready to move on, she spotted Druff, calmly licking a paw, sitting on a downed branch from the sassafras tree. Eshail couldn't believe her luck. She petted Druff on the head and then shooed him away. She began stripping bark off the branch and laying it in one of the cloth wraps she'd brought to separate her finds. Once she was done, she carefully placed the wrap in her basket, making sure not to drop a scrap of bark.

They moved on. The next stop was the maple tree grove. Maple trees were common around the village, but one area had a large concentration. The town took advantage of it, putting taps in to collect sap. The operation was communal; anyone who wanted sap could collect some as long as it was only what their family needed. A grove keeper tended the trees and gathered the overall harvests. The grove keeper also understood that Eshail's work required a little more than everyone else. The witch repaid the keeper with charms to prevent disease and promote growth.

Eshail had two glass jars in her basket. She found the first collection bucket fairly full of sap and filled a jar. The other she left empty. She needed spring water if her meanderings made it there. Druff led them deeper into the lowlands.

Lushwood got its name from the tree groves surrounding the rich soil of their knoll. Druff led her down into the swamp, and her carefree skipping through the forest became more cautious. Not that Druff would lead her astray, but it was important to stay alert; the swamp held many kinds of curiosities and dangers.

The cat nimbly leaped onto dead logs and daintily balanced on rocks and twigs. He was putting on a show of grace as Eshail's boots sucked into the wet soil and she struggled through the bramble as a mere human.

Druff brought her south and west toward the southern trade road. It was an odd direction for him to go. They usually avoided the people on the road if possible. Long ago, she had learned to trust the cat when he was determined to lead her in a particular direction. Familiars had their own sort of magic.

Eshail pushed through the dense underbrush. This trailless, cross-country journey would likely have been impossible in the summer. It would have been full of choking vines, nettles, and poisonous plants, and the foliage would hide sink pits, snakes, and other unsavory swamp treats. In the winter, though, the mud was more solid and easier to traverse. Most ground cover had died off for the season, so nothing was hidden. Soft squelching met every footfall.

It was always curious to Eshail why the snakes in the Evermoss never deeply succumbed to the brumation cycle—their version of hibernating in the winter—as they did further from the swamp. Hedwarg had his theories, Tarwa hers. Eshail didn't think anyone knew, but she was practical. She'd found a stick as she walked. Her skirt was loose, and the splayed stick was ready. She watched for sleeping snakes.

Thankfully she'd also worn her sun hat, as the first snake to find her hadn't been where she'd looked: on the ground. Instead it fell from a tree branch, hoping to catch her unawares. She shrieked, an unwitchly act, as it flopped harmlessly off her overbrimmed hat and onto the soil before her. It was an aggressive hunter; it struck out at her legs, getting tangled in her skirts, which were designed for that purpose. The outer layer of the dress was loose-knit, perfect to get snake fangs caught. The snake hung mostly helpless by its fangs as they sank harmlessly into the multiple layers of her skirt.

Eshail tapped it lightly on the head with her ever-present snake charm. The snake instantly stopped struggling and collapsed. Now that she was relatively safe from its harm, she examined the creature. It had a black, brown, and yellow mottling that gave up the species. Formally, they were called Guisvaek's Revenge, which was an odd folklore tradition. She had her own translation of names—in her head she called these snakes *camouflaged bites*. They waited, almost perfectly hidden, and then attacked with ferocity when their prey ventured near. They could be deadly. Their bites *hurt*. They were some of the most dangerous snakes in Eshail's opinion. She'd stepped over one when she was new to the village and had it stuck within her underskirts. She still had a few scars and a healthy respect for the snake's bite. They were admirable, if irritating, predators.

Bringing out a vial, she milked the unconscious snake for its venom before throwing it back into the woods. It'd regain consciousness within an hour if a hawk didn't eat it first. If she'd had a use for its body, she might have harvested the creature, but although she'd lived by the swamp for most of her life, she'd never been one too fond of snake-based magic. Venom was vital in making various antidotes, but the Nest Mother could keep the rest of the snake.

She kept moving forward, snake crisis adverted. Ahead sat a small stream. She wasn't familiar with this part of the Evermoss, but she suspected she knew where Druff was taking her. The ground was muddier. She sank down an inch, each step sucking at her feet as she stepped forward. Rutabulum was found on most of the trees, a fluffy, friendly-looking moss. She took her harvesting knife and cut a bit from the bark of a swamp oak. She'd been resisting cutting any until her return; each harvest added to the weight of her pack, but she needed to procrastinate.

Druff was leading her to something she didn't want

to see.

The cat rubbed against her leg to reassure her that he'd never harm her. "Not bringing her harm" didn't include "painful things she needed to confront," unfortunately. She rubbed under his jaw, feeling his silky fur against her hand. She forgave him. Some things were meant to be.

They resumed the journey. The clouds had started to break, allowing sunlight to pass through. The forest was quiet without the rustle of leaves. The only sound was the dull smack of her feet patiently moving through the muck. Her mind wandered.

Each season had its own look, feel, and taste, which made this journey strange. Fall had left them long ago. The leaves were gone from the trees and had biodegraded into the moist soil. There *was* snow, but it no longer dominated the landscape in its attempt to sweep the mess that was nature under its white cover. Fall was over. Winter was over. But it wasn't spring. Eshail saw no signs of the crocus, no curls of leaf trying to break through the soil. She even moved a bit of debris that may have sheltered a hopeful seed, but to no avail. Nothing poked through the ground. The trees also were devoid of buds. By this time, there should have been the first blush of foliage—and twitters of birds migrating back to their summer homes.

The swamp was silent. No insects had crawled from their cocoon or transformed from larvae. *Slurk smack.* Her boots steadily followed the cat until they reached their destination. The beaver dam—she could verify the rodent's work—*had* broken. It looked like it'd been an old one that rotted away. The ground she'd been walking on had been the bed of a small lake, saturated and damp. She could close her eyes and imagine the lake peacefully sitting and the crack of the last branch holding the dam in place.

She followed the outflow, a deeply carved divot in the landscape, down toward the trade route. The road's best season was typically winter when the swamp firmed up. The spring was the worst as everything thawed and rain worsened the mud. There would be spans of a month or two where it was impassable by wagons, and only those sure-footed, like Ry, would attempt the routes between the cities. Eshail walked down the slight slope, following the washout; twigs and branches and whole trees littered the tiny stream that still crept down the gradient.

The gully rush had been significant. The stream had always existed; it'd been the source of the lake. It wasn't until Eshail got to the road that she saw the scale of the rush's impact. The road wasn't damaged; it was gone entirely. They'd have to send out several crews to fix it once the ground thawed and traffic restarted. The road between Lushwood and their southern network was impassable.

She tried to imagine the Easterner alone on the road when the outflow hit. The woman was lucky to have escaped with her life. Druff kept padding southwest as though the incident wasn't the purpose of his journey. Eshail followed, still in awe of the damage extracted. Trees bent to the ground, pushed by the rushing water. She scrambled down, following the water's flow.

Eshail found the remnants of Yates's wagon three hundred paces from the road. It'd been crushed against a tree, split in two. The wagon itself was non-salvageable. The axle had snapped, and even the valuable parts—the wheels and bench—were splintered. When she'd talked to Evelyn, the herald had indicated that they'd grabbed what little wasn't ruined: the case with its small samples and a sack of wheat. Eshail'd considered doing her own evaluation in the heat of the moment; rescuers didn't tend to be thorough.

Surprisingly—or not, actually—there was little of the cargo left. Only a couple of dashed boxes with contents mixed together in a sludge. Eshail could sift through the muck and get a bit of usable leaf if she could tell what it was. Druff was further down in the washout, sitting on a rock, watching her sort through the mud. Snake tracks were everywhere. There must have been some scent they'd been attracted to.

Eshail wasn't sure what Druff and the Nest Mother wanted her to find. The wagon could be disassembled for firewood, but with the forest around the village, they did not need it for firewood.

She remembered the case of samples, the sheer volume of wealth that had been lost. Not so much for an Easterner; most of the herbs were fairly common out east. Here, though, the caravans rarely came west. The herbs were scarce enough to be used for any magic or compound.

"Druff, what do you want me to find?"

He may have been her familiar, but he was first a cat. He sat atop a broken piece of wood, demanding she engage her brain to think through the problem. The gully rush had brushed everything downstream. What was in the wagon? Herbs, seeds, leaves, bark, all things botanical—things she could leverage to make any number of potions.

She still didn't get it. Eshail looked at her cat. He looked back. She could feel the irritation through their mental link. She wished for a bond in which he could speak to her more directly. Tarwa indicated that could possibly be achieved as their connection grew over the years, but it wasn't something that young bonds could manage. Eshail guessed that she probably wouldn't want to hear what Druff had to say anyway.

She started a sacred spiral, starting at the seat of the wagon. She examined the ground, moving out in an ever-increasing spiral. This was a typical charm of searching. With each step, she examined the ground. A needle of dread poked the back of her brain. There was something important that she was missing.

Her eyes caught the edge of a barrel. She knelt and

started digging around the rounded corner. The part above the ground was intact. It was possible the rest was as well. The mud was thick, the ground saturated and cold. She was used to it. Digging for roots in the swamp was an effort she was well acquainted with. She put down her collection basket and pulled out one of her most precious possessions: a small metal spade. Most witches didn't like to use metal, but she'd never had a problem with it. She'd carved out bits of intention, soil loosening, delicate finding, and a wish for luck, among other hopes. It was her good luck charm and her favorite implement.

However, her digging skills were woefully inept for the task. A shovel would have been preferred. Inch by inch, she became more assured that the barrel was intact and potentially sealed. She compromised on a complete removal and just concentrated on clearing the end. If she could open it, she could remove what was in the barrel without excavating the entire thing.

Druff watched patiently. Eshail pried off the top, eager to discover what had survived.

"The water-forsaken Easterner! Why would she bring this poison into the swamp?!" She tried to close the barrel as soon as the seal had been broken. Her hands shook with the shock of what she'd found, though, and it took a couple minutes. The barrel contained magic. Harsh, red, Blight magic. Poisonous seeds that would destroy the Evermoss. The same biologic that had created the Great Waste separating their countries. Her breathing was shallow as she contemplated the doom sitting next to her feet.

Eshail was not happy. She was shaken to her core. The Easterner—that *monster* had shared her hearth, her home for *weeks*. She'd been breaking bread and preparing tea for someone capable of murder, of mass extension in the Evermoss. No wonder she'd felt so *unbalanced*.

The sun was going down, and the swamp was

getting cold. She continued her searching spiral, even though she was losing hope in finding any more intact debris from the wagon. Anger-fueled, she kept at it, using every last bit of daylight she could. If there was more of the Blight, if any of it had escaped . . . it was too horrifying to think about. She wasn't too worried about making it home. The road would be easy to follow in the moonlight, and she had Druff. He'd never navigated her wrong.

"That has got to be it. She wouldn't have been foolish enough to bring more than one of those barrels into the swamp."

Druff was silent, padding along next to her. He was no longer leading.

She gave up, eventually. She had to. Her feet burned, her dress and arms were caked in mud, and she knew she had at least three leeches attached. The night creatures would start to come out. She could deal with most of them when prepared. But she hadn't intended to be out this late. She checked the barrel lid, assuring herself it was tight. She'd return with help on the morrow. Eshail caked it in mud just to be sure, gluing it further in place.

Tomorrow, she'd get Evelyn to come out with a contingent, and they'd dig the whole nest-forsaken atrocity out of the mud.

It was time to go home and demand some answers.

Chapter 11

Eshail had considered leaving her basket but thought against it. If the Eastern fool had brought the Blight to the Evermoss, she didn't want to leave her finds within its grasp. Each step she took home on the packed road sent twinges up her legs; she wasn't used to a path so hard. Druff moved along with her, weaving effortlessly in the brush. Moonlight was the domain of black cats.

When Eshail reached her home, she left the basket outside on the porch in quarantine. She'd need to examine it closely for contamination before bringing it near her garden in the back or within her home. It'd been right next to the barrel when she'd cracked it.

The neighbors would wonder, but they knew better than to touch it after the Kontor boy was infected with poison sumac when he tried swiping some herbs she had drying on a line.

"Where have you been?" It seemed Evelyn had relieved Hedwarg in watching Thayatesh. Eshail didn't bother answering. Instead she walked right past Evelyn and straight into the workroom.

"How many barrels of fennis seed did you have on that wagon?"

The stranger, the interloper, gaped at her, eyes wide

in fear. "Fennis seeds? What are you talking about?"

"The sealed barrel I found in the remnants of your wagon was full of *fennis seeds*."

"T-two, there were two of those barrels."

Dark words came out of Eshail's mouth in rage. The room went dark with her intention. Eshail's eyes turned blood red. She'd unlocked a talent in an instant. It didn't happen often, but it could occur under extreme stress.

Talents were sometimes uncovered when great emotion or need presented itself in a moment of passion. In this moment, this skill was one of the Witch's Wrath. Thayatesh's face turned red, then blue, the breath of life being sucked from her lungs. Eshail was angry enough to kill, and she was about to commit murder.

With a slap, Evelyn saved them both—Thayatesh's life and Eshail's soul. The sound echoed in the shop. Druff stood, back arched, hair on end, hissing. Yates coughed, but Eshail's ears rang with the blow. As her hearing returned, the room was still quiet. Everyone was waiting for her explanation. Evelyn eyed her with a wariness and a touch of horror that hurt but that she deserved.

Teeth clenched against the anger and panic, Eshail tried to explain, "I only found one barrel. I pried it open, and it held fennis seeds." The two women looked at her blankly, oblivious to the repercussions. "Evelyn, this is the source of the Blight—the Everdream. If those seeds take root, the Evermoss would fall."

Evelyn's face paled. The Blight had created the Great Waste, the desert lands that separated the Evermoss and the Eastern Empire. Eshail had to figure out how to stop the atrocity from affecting her beloved home. The Waste had once been a lush forestland, hearty and full of life. Now it was a harsh desert dominated by dunes.

She had been thinking of the next step with each mud-squelched boot step on her way back to Lushwood. They'd have to return with a more considerable contingent of villagers; they'd have to do a full circle of the gully rush and find each infected root, the actual width of the possible infection. It was likely that it would be hopeless. If the seeds went out with the floodwaters, which was conceivable if the barrel was broken, then there wasn't a chance of genuinely stopping it. As it was, they'd have to identify where the infection was and cull it as completely and as soon as possible. Then set up a barrier to quarantine the infected part of the swamp from the rest.

The Prime witches placed spells on the land during the last war, separating the desert from the swamp generations ago. Building a barrier against the infernal plant took a monumental amount of energy. The effort cost the Prime witches their lives, but they saved the Evermoss.

The two caravan routes from the East were guarded, and wagons were thoroughly searched with magic. No one stepped out of the desert without being decontaminated.

"What do we do?" Evelyn, the *herald*, asked *her*, the hedge witch. Evelyn was supposed to know. "Eshail, what do you need?"

The anger drained out of Eshail. This was *her* problem to deal with. Even Hedwarg wouldn't be able to set up a barrier. This was a physical and a metaphysical problem. They would need everyone available.

These seeds weren't normal. They were tainted with dark magic. The fennis plants that grew from them would invade and envelop the local wildlife and foliage until nothing was left. Then, in a cycle, it would all turn to dust, drying up the land and scorching it until nothing was left. It was sinister magic of the desert and sands.

Eshail's mind started racing again, and she started rambling, picking up a piece of chalk. "We need to gather every able-bodied villager tomorrow and set up a circle search grid." She started making a list on the left side of her chalkboard and roughly sketched out the search pattern. As she made tick marks, she filled in the details: "The individuals should look for signs of the Blight. The soil will be off-color, normally red. Think of the red sands of the desert. Curls may form in the dirt, as though we're in a drought and the mud is drying on the surface. I don't know how long it takes to start affecting the plants. We haven't seen it in three hundred years. Without intervention, it'll look like a magical malevolence once it takes root. You'll be able to see it in the very air. Depending on its magical affinity, it'll make folks feel physically sick, and a hopelessness will creep into their souls."

"It takes a couple of weeks, so it's too soon," Yates spoke softly. The two Lushwood citizens looked at her with surprise.

"You *knew*? You knew, and you willingly brought this into our land? Into the Evermoss?" Eshail had to take a breath as the wrath came forward.

Yates's voice was small. "I did not know."

Eshail used her Witch's Sight to see the truth.

"Ram Sesat sealed the barrels for delivery to the Near Reach. He didn't tell me what was in them, and I didn't ask. You don't ask things when a Ram tells you to do something."

"How did you get through the border sanitation stations?" Evelyn asked about the logistics of it all. If the stations weren't doing their job, that would be a bureaucratic problem.

The woman swallowed. "I crossed the desert by a different route."

If Eshail's Witch's Sight wasn't active, she wouldn't have believed the woman's words. Be that as it may, they were true. She saw a desert route in the woman's eye, not along the oasis to the north and south but along pillars of obsidian sticking out of the desert. She saw a long, perilous trek.

"Impossible. You must tell me how you tricked the decontamination magic." Evelyn's voice was stern. "Or I'm going to lock you in the stockade and send you to the Truthseekers on the Border."

Yates shook her head in fear. Eshail let the woman sweat momentarily, opting to wait before coming to her rescue.

"She's telling the truth. I see a third way through the desert in her mind, with obsidian pillars marking the way."

"Look, I had no idea the barrels contained the Blight." *Truth.* "I would have never taken that across the sands if I'd known." *Truth.* "I was on a mission to bring back a piece of magic to save a dear friend." *Mostly true.* "I'd heard rumors that Eshail was one skilled in that type of magic, but if I didn't find luck here, that I should continue to the Near Reach, where there are less reputable magic users that could help me." *Truth.* Everything that counted was true.

"What type of magic were you seeking?"

Yates gave Eshail a side look and asked if she should disclose the truth. Eshail didn't think she had much choice in keeping her secret. Evelyn was tenacious at ferreting secrets if she felt something threatened the village.

"I needed a love potion. She—my friend—needed a love potion."

Evelyn's eyebrows raised. "And you thought Eshail could provide that for you? How in the Evermoss would she be able to give you that sort of magic?"

Eshail saved Yates's explanation. "Because it is my magic of Skill." Everyone knew that young witches had a primary Skill, but most didn't discuss it. It was private; even among witches, it was kept secret. People tolerated witches because they did a lot of good. Who else were folks going to turn to when they needed someone to heal their ailing child or grandmother? Mortality due to illness was much lower in villages with a dedicated witch. That didn't mean that the villagers weren't still scared of magic. It didn't mean they knew their Skills might not be in baby reaping, hexing, or weather cursing. So few asked, thankfully, since some witches were cursed with prime skills in an unsavory art like her.

"Oh."

And there it was. Their newly repaired friendship was wounded again. The unfairness of it all twisted in Eshail. She *hadn't*, and would never, use a potion like that on Evelyn. But for the woman, she could see that that sort of magic would be the ultimate betrayal.

She was a witch, but one that could manipulate feelings, especially those such as love. Who could trust her? She'd never dose Evelyn, but she'd be lying if she said she'd never thought of it on a dark night. It'd been a lonely journey. Thoughts were a very long way from the action though.

Eshail used a technique she'd seen Evelyn use. She distracted the group with the next actions that needed to happen: "So, step one, we set up a search party to identify where the infestation may have spread. Evelyn, you will need to lead that. We must find every trace of the Blight in the swamp, or it will destroy us. I'm going to be working here to send some messages." That was a light explanation for what she'd be attempting. She needed to burn the last bit of her magic to call for help. Tarwa would know what to do.

"I'm going to need some supplies. Can we get Hedwarg in here? I will need him to dig me up some specific ingredients that will be fairly hard to find this time of year." Eshail began scribbling a list on a scrap of paper.

She handed it to Evelyn. The woman pivoted perfectly. "I will get Hedwarg here as soon as possible, and Talin always keeps a stash in his cellars, so we'll open them up too. Nothing is as important as stopping the infestation in the Evermoss, and I can use Ry to spread the word. She's back in town for her weekly drop-off. We'll have what we need."

Good. The herald understood the scope of the problem. Now, it was a matter of getting everyone else in line.

"Let's meet the searchers in the southern town square at dawn. I'll be there to help describe what to look for, but I'd appreciate it if you could organize their search pattern."

Evelyn nodded, acknowledging the ask.

"Once you clear out, however, I need to turn to a bit of magic to aid us." Eshail focused on the business of things. Evelyn straightened, her eyes resolute. She was the town herald and would take up the mantle of responsibility.

"I'd like to help." Yates's voice was regretful. Eshail read all the guilt and mourning in the woman's mind and then snapped off her Witch's Sight. She didn't want to empathize with the woman who may have single-handedly destroyed their home due to negligence.

"We'll see." She put what hardness she could muster into her voice.

Evelyn left. She had a lot of door-knocking to do before the night was over.

Eshail gave Yates the cold shoulder, sitting in her front room with the coals of the fire and Druff's cozy form to keep her company. Her mind raced from problem to problem. She needed to call a greater coven of minds. This problem was the most significant danger Evermoss had faced since the Great Blight that'd destroyed half the world. This wasn't a problem for a junior hedge witch. It required minds much more remarkable than hers. She calculated the moon phase, the ingredients needed, the magic she had left. There wasn't an easy way to open up the communication lines. It was going to take everything she had. Possibly everything she ever wanted.

The guardians of the swamp, the four witches that stepped in after the Prime witches perished constantly travelled from problem to problem in the Evermoss. It was impossible at any moment to know where they were, which was why communication magic was needed. Like healing, however, this was a weak magic for Eshail. It would take everything she had. Her best bet was to reach out to Tarwa—at least she had a connection to her mother.

"Druff, I'm not sure I'm strong enough."

Her familiar sat on the arm of her chair. He turned his face to hers and, for once, didn't act like the cat. He headbutted her face, leaning into the gesture. He would be there for her one way or another. She just wished she felt more confident that this was a problem she could solve. Her résumé was absent of swamp-saving references of this scale.

Night enclosed the village of Lushwood. The townsfolk hurried to their doors at insistent knocking. Women's faces held determined lines, and everyone oiled their boots. In the morning, they would be ready. They would heed their herald's call because they knew what was at stake.

Chapter 12

Angry voices filled the square. Talin had quickly erected an essential piece of stage work used as a platform for festivals. He stood as the mayor, trying to calm the worried groups of people. There were no rumors; they knew exactly what had happened, but they didn't know the details of their job in this mitigation plan.

"Quiet, listen up. We need to band together." Talin's voice was ignored. Folks were angry and fearful.

"SHUT UP!" Evelyn used a belly roar. The crowd quieted instantly. "Everyone, please listen to Eshail."

Pink-faced, Eshail moved to the podium. She stepped up, and, seeing all the faces, she opened her mouth to speak. She'd had a speech prepared, but nothing came out. Her words froze in her gut. Dozens upon dozens of fearful faces looked up at her, waiting for her words, and she couldn't speak any of them.

Someone coughed.

A slight murmur stirred through the crowd.

Evelyn raised her eyebrows as if to say, *Well, go on already*.

Eshail needed to tell them to search for the Blight bloom, what to look for, and why.

"Is it the witch's fault?" a voice called out. She

couldn't tell from whom.

This was what she was afraid of, the village turning on her.

"She brought it here, didn't she? The barrier is failing."

Anger and fear ran through the crowd, about to turn mob.

Evelyn finally realized what had happened and shifted nervously to speak up, but a dull *click-clack* sounded on the cobblestones before she could. It was loud where the crowd wasn't. Eshail looked to her right and found the Easterner clacking toward her on her crutch, a determined look on her face.

"This wasn't the witch's fault. This was mine," the stupid woman called, limping closer to the crowd. Their anger turned to the Easterner, the person more of an outsider than the witch. Part of Eshail was relieved. The other part was worried the crowd was going to erupt in violence.

She found the courage she lacked for herself, defending Yates. "I have seen the truth. This woman was set up. So before you rip her to pieces, know that she's got the best description of Blight in our village and is willing to help." The admission was hard, but Eshail had replayed confronting Yates all night. Her magic had revealed the truth: Yates was as innocent as Eshail herself.

"We have to band together to dig out the infection from our swamp, and even then, it may not be enough to stop it. This effort alone won't be enough." She had their attention, and the people waited for her, following her words quietly. "I will call upon the Guardians. We're going to need magic to contain the poison. This is the responsibility of witches: the protection of the people and the land. Right now I need search parties to work within the pattern Evelyn put together. Those adept at herbology will work with me and Hedwarg to find specific plants that I need to call for help. The winter has been hard on everyone's supplies, but we need specific ingredients for a great working."

The best thing Evelyn had taught her was to give people actions to accomplish. That way, they wouldn't dwell on hysteria.

"Searchers with me!" Evelyn called.

"Herb finders with me!" Hedwarg bellowed, and everyone sorted themselves out.

The night before, Yates had helped make several copies of the ingredients Eshail needed for the herb searchers. Eshail and Yates joined Evelyn's searchers.

Evelyn looked across her group, eyes as hard as iron. "Okay, you're going to be looking for off-color areas, a sickly green or red color. You will find it in the mud, possibly working into plants. We have merely days before it'll be too big to stop; we must identify every infected area." It might already be too late, but Eshail and Evelyn decided to hide that from the village, at least for now.

Evelyn continued, "Each search unit will have these yellow and red ties to attach to stakes in any identified area. We don't know how bad the infection's going to be. The second barrel washed away in the gully rush. We will have runners follow the flood down until we find the second barrel of infection. Eshail," she emphasized the witch's name, "provided us with a charm of finding so we can locate it. I've sent Ry to notify the neighboring villages to send help. So the next fastest runner in town, Kleopa, will follow the charm's direction. Are there any questions yet?"

Eshail waited to see if there was more about what the Blight looked like.

"I want to add something." The crowd's eyes turned to Yates. "If you shade your eyes, you can see a soft glow around the Blight. Remember, it's not just a physical infection; it's got a magical component. If you catch it from the side of your eye, in the periphery, it'll sparkle like a distant firefly in flight. We've lived with the Blight for a long time in the East. I wish this on no one." The words were sobering and heartfelt.

"Thank you for that." Evelyn redirected the crowd to her, not wanting them to dwell on the source of the insight. "Any questions?"

"What should we do to it when we find it?"

"Right now, simply mark it. Whatever you do, please don't touch it. Don't try to burn it or move it. These things were tried in the Great War and failed. If you get it on your person, you may spread the infection, so *please* be careful. We need to go about this methodically and coolly. After all of the Blight has been located, Eshail will work with her sisters on a method to treat the infected areas."

Eshail began moving, trying to exude confidence that she did not feel. She didn't have a method of dealing with the Blight. The best her ancestors could do was sacrifice the Great Waste to the magical plague. Her stomach turned in anxiety.

The villagers continued with Evelyn, working through their questions, forming search groups, and getting their marching orders. Hedwarg had taken his smaller group directly out of the city. The only ones remaining were the mothers and fathers watching the littles and those too infirm to go out in the cold swamp.

Yates and Eshail watched as the last groups left.

"Now what?" Yates asked, leaning on her crutch. The wind swept through the empty town square.

"Now's the hard part for me," Eshail said glumly.

"What are you going to do?"

"I have to call my mother."

Eshail's statement didn't open the door for questions. It was a simple inference from her tone that calling her mother wouldn't be pleasant.

Yates hobbled as quickly as possible after Eshail. "What must you do to call your mother? What is 'calling?'

Who is your mother?"

Eshail walked faster. She didn't want to answer any of those questions. Tarwa was the woman who'd taken her in after her first mother died. She'd treated her at best as a pupil and mainly as a nuisance.

"You Easterners don't like witches or magic. You may want to go with Evelyn or Hedwarg or help with some of the littles."

The hobbling stopped. Eshail continued at a brisk pace back to her store. The only thing she was looking forward to seeing in the house was Druff.

The first order of business was pulling out the village cauldron. For her daily potions and spells, she used her first mother's cauldron. It'd been one of the few things that had survived her death, and she cherished it. However, a spell web this large needed a more significant tool. The village had given her a large one when she'd first joined the town. Lushwood was deep in the Evermoss, and new flus, poisons, and bugs were always crawling out of the swamp. They'd wanted a witch prepared.

She kept the cauldron in her cellar, and it banged against her knees as she used two hands to lift it up the narrow staircase. Once she got it upstairs, she dragged it out back. It was too large for her hearth. Instead she placed it on an iron frame.

The witch started piling up wood. The sky was fair, belying her mood. She was surrounded by empty trellises and dusty herb beds. The large cauldron sat like an uninvited guest in the midst of her garden on its iron frame. A fair amount of heat would need to be applied. She needed a solid bed of coals to heat the large, thick cauldron.

Eshail stacked the wood under the pot, ensuring the heat would be evenly distributed across the bottom. Most problems in spelling occurred due to the incorrect circulation and uneven application of heat. The Nest Mother was all about balance, and the worst thing a witch could do was unbalance a spell.

Eshail wasn't terribly proficient in message spells, and part of her dreaded having to attempt one so important. There was also a significant amount of anxiety associated with Tarwa.

She had added the sage to the fire, causing it to smoke, when Yates came out the back door and into her garden.

"What can I do?" The set of the woman's jaw was harsh. She didn't really want to help or participate in the magic but felt obligated to be a part of any possible solution to the Blight. Eshail looked at her, the sternness in her face, and nodded approval.

"I need you to keep feeding the firesticks at a steady rate. It's important that the fire hit the underbelly of this pot evenly, and it takes poking and feeding."

Eshail began filling the pot with water, waiting for it to boil. She then went inside to collect her intentions. She patted Druff on the head; his long whiskers tickled her hand.

"It's been a long time."

The familiar leaned into her hand, rubbing his cheek against it.

"Do you think she'll answer?"

Druff stopped and looked into her eyes. He gently squeaked and put his paws on her chest, hind legs still sitting on the countertop. When he looked right into her eyes, the connection between them was most substantial. She sensed that he was telling her not to worry, to do human things, and everything would be alright.

She nodded, mostly just trying to soothe her friend. Her stomach roiled. Things would be however they might be. This was the way of the world.

Eshail went back outside, taking a deep breath to calm her nerves.

She approached the cauldron and waved Yates

away. "Add only as necessary. Depending on how well—or not—this works, we may be standing here for a while." The sun had come out as though to mock the direness of the Evermoss. Eshail straightened her shoulders, lifted her chin, and began.

Yates backed away, wide-eyed, with some kindling in her hands.

Eshail typically wouldn't perform something like this in front of a non-witch, but she wanted to throw the woman's perception of magic off. She wanted to show a spell in its most mundane form. She walked to the pot and looked at the water sitting in it. She smelled the faint bit of sage. She pulled out a piece of paper Ry had delivered to her a few months ago. The top of the envelope read, "To Eshail from Tarwa." The seal was unbroken.

Eshail spoke, "Nest Mother, hear my call. Please connect me with Tarwa, my mother of childhood. Bring my thoughts to her and her intentions to me." She dropped the sealed letter into the boiling water and watched it grow slick and wet. She waited. Her intention was in the wind. Now it depended on the fickle wind to take it up and deliver it.

Message spells were easy in theory. Carried on vapor, sage's smoke, they were a sacrifice of connection combined with intention. She added her power to fuel the working. The connection to the source of her stored magic had to stay open as long as the spell was active.

Yates waited, expectant.

Eshail sat on the ground, getting a stick and poking at the logs under the cauldron. It was going to take a while. Steam curled out of the pot. Half the struggle was keeping her mind focused and on the task. The other half of the challenge was truly intending on connecting with Tarwa, a person she mostly tried to avoid. Eshail cleared her mind, thinking of the Blight and the need they had. She ignored the Easterner.

"That's it?"

Eshail blinked. They must not teach Easterners basic manners. Or the common sense that it was unwise to distract a witch mid-spell.

"Yes, we wait."

Yates paused, picking up on her annoyed tone. She continued with her questioning anyway, curiosity driving her forward. "I thought magic was"—she seemed to think for a word that wouldn't be insulting—"*more*. I thought there'd be more to it."

Now Eshail was irritated. She didn't know why she wanted this dimwitted nose-bushed bat waddle to be impressed by her magic, but she did. She stood up, careful not to rock the cauldron and ruin the casting. She held the fiery twig that she'd been poking at the coals with and turned to Yates, pulling a glamour across her face.

"You want something sinister?" She pulled at the mid-morning shadows, which began collecting in the creases of her face. She elongated them, casting a darkness on herself.

"You want something powerful?" She sent a spark of energy—nothing much, but it caused the tip of the stick to glow brighter, casting a mirage in the air. She moved the tip of the stick closer to Yates. The woman drew back.

"Something wicked?" She removed the stick and stepped close to the Blight bringer. She stretched out a hand and reached out with a shadowed fingernail to trace a line down the woman's cheek.

To Thayatesh's credit, she didn't flinch. She held Eshail's gaze.

"Am I interrupting something, child?"

Eshail cringed, letting go of the glamour and turning her attention to the cauldron. In the curling vapors above the pot was her mother's pockmarked face. Taciturn, warped a bit from all the brews through the ages, the woman hadn't changed a hair since Eshail had last seen her.

"Good morning, mother. I've got a dire situation here in Lushwood. We need your help."

The witch was unfazed. She looked at Yates, eying the woman. "First, you must tell me, who are you sharing my gazing with? You've never brought someone else into our circle."

Eshail had been trying to put her body between Tarwa and Yates, but it hadn't worked. "*This* is the Blight bringer, the cause of our doom."

"Blight bringer? That does sound dire." The elder witch was all business. "If she has brought the Blight to the Evermoss, why is she still alive?"

Leave it to Tarwa to go straight for the kill. Yates took a step back, her wonder replaced by fear. As it were, Tarwa could curse her even from a great physical distance.

"I read her. She didn't intend it. It was a whirlwood trap." The analogy was adept. The whirlwood tree branches were whippy and coated in a light poison that attracted and killed insects. It was a suitable defense mechanism, but hunters frequently used the branches to create and set traps for bigger game. It wasn't the whirlwood's fault.

Tarwa's eyes moved back to Eshail. This was a good sign for Thayatesh's life expectancy but not great for Eshail. "You're reading now? That's an improvement. We will have to discuss this advancement when I arrive."

"When will that be?"

"How long has the Blight infection been in place?"

"We likely have a few days before it sets. But it may have taken root already. I've got the village herald in a search spiral with most of the village."

"I will be there tonight. It is concerning that the chimes didn't awaken the coven. We will consult, and I will arrive." The last words were spoken on the wind as Tarwa shimmered out of existence. Eshail knew she needed to conserve her power to make such a trip.

"That's it?" Yates asked yet again.

Eshail looked at Yates and said, "That's never it. We must build a gate. Today. Also, I need to brief you on a few things about my mother, or you'll end up in a stewpot." Tarwa was low on patience, and . . . it was possible some things they whispered about witches might be true.

Chapter 13

A gate was easy enough to build if a witch had been in place for a few years. A couple of years ago, Eshail had found some young saplings and woven the tree trunks together, molding them into the frame needed. Easy enough. Eshail's problem was that a weaved gate required a bit of care and pruning, things that she was not terribly motivated to do, especially when a working gate near the village meant Tarwa could just pop in for a visit.

She'd figuratively and literally let the village gate go to seed. Which meant it wasn't salvageable for their purposes today. Her intention of allowing it to overgrow removed the location's focus as a travel point. They'd have to find a new clump of trees that could be quickly coaxed into some semblance of a moon step for witches.

Eshail knew where a grove existed, but it wouldn't be easy to manage. Yates had insisted on coming along, and with a tight brace and her crutch, the woman could manage a decent stride. The two walked through the woods. It was a cool day; the sun was out, but its warmth was weak. Winter still held on tight, which might have been their only chance in this fight against the Blight. The fennis seeds wouldn't find it easy to take root.

"Why do you hate your mother?"

The thought was thrown out between the two of them haphazardly. The best defense was sometimes a good offense. "Why do you want a love potion?"

"I told you, to save my friend from a loveless marriage."

"Friend?" Eshail sensed the duplicity of the statement. There were too many emotions for this to be about only a friend.

Eshail took a slight detour around an Adder den. The woman followed admirably. The swamp wasn't a good place for someone who was unknowledgeable and broken. Yates had insisted though.

Yates tried again: "My sister, okay. She's about to be trapped in an arranged marriage if I can't do something about it." This had the smell of truth.

"That's unfortunate, but what would a love potion do?"

Yates sidestepped the question, with a counter, "And your mother? Why don't you like her?"

Eshail waved the stick she used to fend off snakes in front of her face. The stick removed clumps of webs that had formed between the trees. She disturbed their daily chore, but it was either the stick or her face. She preferred the stick.

A leech had uselessly attached to her boot. She flicked the stick down, removing the slug-like form and flicking it into the woods.

Awkward silence sat between them before Eshail simply stated, "You still haven't answered my question."

She'd thrown down the gauntlet. The Easterner might be able to fool herself into thinking her motivation was pure. She was only moving forward for her sister, but there was a more profound truth. Thayatesh was silent. The woman crutched along.

Eshail was leading them to a small island in the swamp. It was the only place outside the village that consistently had young, secondary, bendable tree growth amenable to gate building. The island frequently got wiped clean by the natural wildlife. It was dangerous, but she figured they'd be okay with the frost still in the air. The ambient magic of the place would make the gate easier to form, not requiring to draw as much from Tarwa.

"A love potion is the only way to save her from the loveless marriage. The guy, he's nice enough. Handsome, charming, rich, all the things she should want in a husband. I love my sister. I would do anything for her." Eshail had used a cantrip to detect the truth of it. Yates believed every word. She loved her sister above anyone in her life. "I take it you don't feel the same way about your mother?"

Eshail sighed. "Tarwa is complicated. I'm not sure she even loves me beyond my potential. I'm honestly not sure I've even felt that kind of love about anyone. Well, maybe Evelyn."

She clamped her mouth shut. This is why witches were of few words and spoke in riddles. Their mouths were not always under their own control. Sometimes a truth slipped out, sometimes a personal truth, and sometimes a truth of the universe. Words had power, and with a will and a word, that power was irresistible. The Easterners claimed to have no witches within their borders, but this didn't mean they didn't have their own magic.

Yates's eyes darted to her face at Evelyn's name, but her words were about Tarwa. "I gathered Tarwa was a hard woman from my brief interaction with her. Surely, though, a mother loves a child?"

"You're attractive enough; I'm sure your sister shares your family traits. Couldn't she just find a more suitable companion? Someone she loves?" Eshail countered with offense again. She didn't want to talk about Tarwa. They'd all be exposed to the woman soon enough.

"You didn't answer my question," Yates said with a smile.

This was the problem with these tangles; a rule applied could be leveraged against the speaker. Eshail relented, knocking another spider out of their path, "My first mother died when I was young. I still remember her warmth and the aroma of her pots. Sometimes I think that if I could but create the smells of her cauldron, then maybe I'd have a strong enough link back to her to see her again. As it is, I barely remember what she looks like anymore. Tarwa, well, she's a mother of sorts. I am forever thankful that she rescued me from the fate the village I lived in had for me. Tarwa, however, is not exactly my mother. She is *the* mother, sure, and she raised me. That is all."

Yates digested this news. The honesty was out in the open. Eshail had spoken truths to this stranger that she'd never said out loud in her life.

Sometimes truth begat truth. "My sister's love is not allowed in the East."

Eshail frowned. *Is not allowed?* What did that even mean? She stopped walking, unstoppering a flask of cleansed water to take a sip. She silently examined the woman over the water bottle and then offered it to her. Yates took it greedily. Eshail used her spider stick to flick a few leeches off the Yates's shoes before they could climb any higher.

"I don't understand this forbidden love," Eshail said, focused on the leeches.

"It's easy to understand. You seem to have it. It's one of the reasons witches are outlawed."

Eshail looked at Yates cluelessly.

The Easterner finished the logic leap in a rush. "The love between women."

Eshail laughed.

Of course Eastern propaganda made out all witches to be lovers of women. She noticed Yates's confusion and quickly explained, "Witches aren't all that way. Sure, there are some, maybe even many, but we come in all types and with many differences. The West is an open place; no one minds whomever a person loves." Yates's nervousness around her *and Evelyn* made even more sense. It wasn't just a programmed hatred of witches—it was personal.

The tension in the air dialed down a notch, and a gully rush of words came out. "I'd heard, but I hadn't seen. I mean, I see how you look at the herald, but I thought it might be frowned upon here too. She didn't do anything with it."

"The herald and I are not to be. You understand the tragedy of having feelings for someone who doesn't return them. This surely is similar across cultures." Eshail corked the flask and set off, but it wouldn't be long before they reached the hill. "In this instance, it's not so much a tragedy as, well, I'm not sure Evelyn has a type of person she wants to pair with. She's a lone hunter. We're just friends." Eshail looked back at Yates. "Do you feel better for admitting it all out loud? I imagine the East has been a harsh place."

Their feet slapped the mud. "I do. My sister has burdened me with her feelings. I'm the elder, and it's my job to take care of her. This task seems impossible."

As the pieces fell into place, Eshail had a suspicion. "And so this love potion is for . . . her?" She snapped her fingers, sending an anticharm toward a swamp puppy. The gators normally didn't come this far north, turned off by the long winter and the cold. This one had a belly full of magic that kept it warm. Thankfully, the sting of the anticharm did its trick, and it swam away with lazy hips swinging side to side.

"Yes, she is to be married in a few months to her fiancé. He's a lovely man. All the things one could reasonably hope for in our land. Wealthy, smart, considerate. He treats her as a partner might, as an equal."

"But?"

"But she is unhappy. She told me she thinks she could be his friend, but nothing more."

"Yes, I see. Evelyn and I are like that," Eshail said, turning so Yates could see her smile, removing the bitterness from her comment.

"Our family—we both have responsibilities. Duty. This alliance would cement our place in the Empire."

Eshail thought about her next question as she wove around a mudhole that would have swallowed them both. Yates, unaware of the threat, stupidly put her crutch into it. The witch had to grab her arm to keep her in balance.

"I can't tell you what to do. You've set yourself along this path. But have you thought about supporting your sister instead of assisting her in ignoring her desires?"

"That would be impossible. There is no way to support her back home." Yates's words had a confidence to them, a finality that made Eshail sad.

Another swamp puppy came wading up. This one, Eshail had known since it was a pup. She reached down to touch its scales. Thayatesh froze, clenching her jaw against a scream. The woman hadn't seen any of the gators until now.

"You have nothing to fear. This is Fluff. She's a friend." Her hand dipped a little lower to the pool the gator was swimming in, lightly rubbing the scales and the weave she'd done between the ridges. Every time they crossed paths, they reaffirmed their bond.

"Fluff?" The word was squeaked between tension.

"When I found her, she was a young thing half coated in tar and had recently eaten a chicken. She was covered in fluff. Very young and unbecoming of an alligator."

"I see."

"Relax, trust me. We haven't reached the dangerous part of this journey. I'm hoping Fluff can assist."

"How?"

Eshail turned her head, one hand still on the gator. "The one that guards our gateway island is hopefully sleeping. If not, I'm hoping Fluff's presence will keep it calm and sedentary."

Fluff had a touch of magic on her that she'd stolen from her mother, the grand dame of local firedrakes. She was the closest Eshail had ever been to something resembling a dragon. Fluff had none of the offensive firepower of her mother, but they did share a bond. One that Eshail was hoping to exploit.

She spotted another transparent web in their path from the corner of her eye. A giant mamt spider skittered back into its hiding spot in the tree as she took down the web with a wave of her stick. She watched it, making sure it was out of leaping distance. Its bite was ferociously itchy.

"You can hold back. I told you this might not be a good idea with your condition."

Yates seemed to contemplate the offer and shook her head. "I go where you go."

"You may regret that once Tarwa is officially here. With my stores at an all-time low, I suspect I will get a thrashing like I haven't had since I was a kid."

"Stores?"

"Surely you've noticed my store is fairly barren. You tried to play that to advantage in our negotiations."

"Yes, I figured it was just that moment of winter. Why would you be blamed for it?"

"You have little understanding of witches, don't you?"

"All of ours burned before I could get to know them." The joke didn't land.

"Two of Tarwa's daughters died by fire." Eshail couldn't hold the words back, even if they were a schism in their ability to connect. The history between their lands and ideologies would stay a breakpoint between them either way.

The comradeship their honesty had built wilted a bit with her comment. The two moved forward in silence.

The swamp had grown waterier, less solid, warmer. They were getting close. Their boots were getting sucked into the mud. She felt the tannin tinge of bitterness in her mouth. It stuck to her soul.

"My mother was also . . ." *effected by these attitudes.* The words choked in her throat. They'd fled more than one village when she was a child. Eshail didn't finish. She moved to take that next step but was held back by a hand on her arm.

"I'm sorry. I wish I could change the history between our people." Thayatesh stood, waiting. Eshail collected herself and opened her eyes to meet Yates's brown ones. Few were willing to open their soul to meet the gaze of a witch. What the woman said next was heartfelt: "I know it's not enough, but you've changed my opinion on witches."

It was enough for the moment, if not for the arc of history.

"I need to tell you what's next and what I need from you if you're still determined to help." She held up a finger, silencing Thayatesh's assurance of help. "Listen. Within the next span is a hill in which the local firedrake lives. I trust you know what a firedrake is?"

"It's a dragonling, isn't it?" Genuine fear shook the woman's voice. Those in the East were terrified of dragons. Rightly so too. The dragons had defended the Evermoss, their home, fiercely in the last conflict. They'd enforced the treaty dead zone, the Great Waste, between the nations.

"It is. I will not teach you more about their lifecycle." She thought of Fluff, floating off to her right. The fire belly that the alligator had inherited from her mother meant she was one of the few gators destined for a firedrake's—and possibly a dragon's—lifespan. It was the precursor to what was to come if she survived her gator childhood. "But the drake is deadly and, at this stage, not fond of humanity. What I need to do is weave a new gateway. The drake is dormant at this time of year, but it's close to spring. Or it should be. So I need you to be my lookout. I'm going to help you climb a tree." There was an old growth that dwarfed the other trees. "You'll be fine. The key here is I'll need you to blow this whistle if you see the drake stirring." Eshail reached into her shirt and pulled out a wooden whistle Hedwarg had carved for her a few years back. It was sharp and shrill, like one of the local water birds giving an alarm.

Yates took the whistle, putting the leather thong around her neck. "I can stand watch, although I'm not sure how we're going to get me in a tree."

"Trust me." Eshail gave a mischievous grin.

Chapter 14

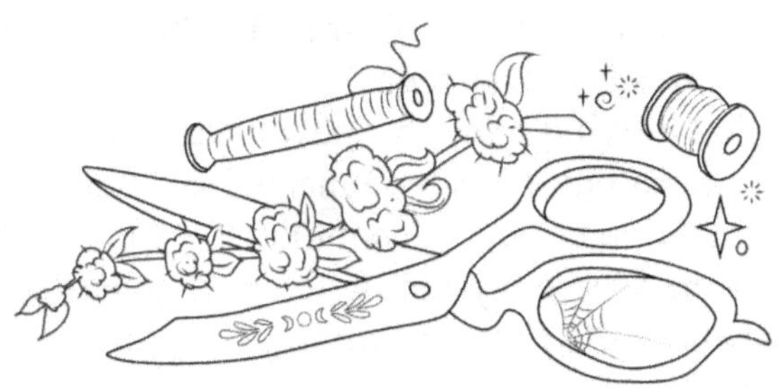

Eshail tapped the water in a pattern with her spider stick. She was asking Fluff to wait for her, and the alligator gave a snort. It wasn't a happy snort, but it was affirmative. The witch changed her navigation from head-on toward Firedrake Island to a parallel path, waving her stick in front of them to knock out a few more webs.

"Why are there so many spiders in the Evermoss?" The disgust was evident in Yates's voice. Eshail understood, as few do, the significance of the eight-legged swamp kin.

"It's the bugs."

"Excuse me?"

"You know spiders eat bugs, right?" She hoped Yates wasn't completely oblivious to the circle of life. At the nod, she continued, "Swamps breed insects like no other terrain. The Nest Mother welcomed spiders into her domain to control the outbreaks. In my opinion, spiders are the only reason we humans can survive in the swamp. You should see Hedwarg's swamp dress. He wears a hat of spiders to keep the mosquitoes off of him."

"I'm not sure I want to see that."

"Yeah, it's gross. I prefer my citron robe, myself.

It's good that you came through this time of year, or you'd have been sick with Yelet Fever and everything else." Eshail paused. Then, "We're here."

Thayatesh gasped as Eshail moved her stick to push back some secondary growth obstructing their view of the biggest tree Yates had ever seen.

"Is that a living tree? I've never seen a tree so huge. It rivals the tallest buildings in Dunesledge." Eshail gave her a quizzical look before she continued, "Dunesledge is where I'm from, where my family lives." Eshail didn't know much about the Eastern Empire, and she'd never heard of the city.

There were larger trees in the forest, but Eshail was only willing to share a limited amount of her Evermoss with the outsider. The woman had shared very little about her own desert home. She saw a water viper plop into the thin pool they were standing in, and she reached into her left pocket, grabbed a pinch of cinnamon, and murmured a charm to keep the snake away.

"It's old and perfect for what I need you to do. Let's get closer. Watch your step; there are some underwater roots here." There were no roots, but it kept the woman's attention on the ground instead of the tree. Eshail let a bit of her magic go to ask the tree to reconfigure for their purpose. It obliged as Eshail played up her caution, carefully stepping through the rootless water, calling out another viper swimming along even if it wasn't going to bother them. Yates was oblivious to the magic above their heads, so concentrated was she on the imagined danger at their feet.

"This tree is old, and I don't know its history, but you'll see how it was made as a haven. It will be perfect for you to watch the island."

They got close, and the old, shaggy bark of the tree wrapped around in giant clumps. The tree stood like a tower, and to Thayatesh's surprise, a natural staircase wound its way around, reaching up toward the sky.

"I'm to climb that?"

"Yes. There are even handholds as you get higher. Here, let's go up together." The tree's base was as broad as a small house, and each formed step was easy as they spiraled around. The shaggy bark was rough but provided good handholds against the trunk. "Just don't look out to your right until we're at the top." Eshail'd made that mistake a few times, getting dizzy from vertigo.

"This is incredible," Yates said heedlessly of her warning. She looked out as she climbed above the majesty that was the Evermoss. "It reminds me of the Watch Tower on the White Plains. Although you've got—maybe not a more interesting view but one that's more diversified." The White Plains, Eshail had heard, were beautiful, reflecting the colors of the sky, but barren, devoid of most life. Different perspectives, perhaps. She'd never claim a barren view more beautiful than the Evermoss. Then again, she'd never seen the deserts of the Eastern Empire.

"I imagine we've got more vegetation and more life."

"More vegetation, sure. I wouldn't be so sure of life."

Eshail raised an eyebrow. That was news to her. She made a note to revisit the nature of life on the high desert plains.

"We're almost there. There is another circle around the diameter, and we'll be in the nest."

Thayatesh looked up, and the tree continued, well above everything. Eshail was thankful Yates didn't question her logic. She was starting to experience a bit of vertigo, and she wanted them to be safely ensconced before explaining the rest of the job. One foot in front of another, the stairs were pretty smooth, but a gust of wind had kicked up. She clenched the bark against the tree with white knuckles. One wrong move and she'd be tumbling a hundred feet to the floor of the swamp.

"We're here, thank the Nest." Eshail turned the last bit of the curve and found the split in the tree trunk. Few folks, even those who spent their entire lives in the Evermoss, understood the great trees. Eshail loved them. The tree's first branching typically held a small world to itself. The branches diverged and created a cradle. With this tree so large, the cradle was ten feet wide with a pool of water and its own unique plants, all dependent on the tree for life. Here, so close to Firedrake Island, the cradle couldn't help but have taken on a bit of the fire magic that made its home here. This made this tree one of Eshail's favorite things to visit in the winter. The nest was warm, heated by a glowing, fiery drop of amber that hung loosely from a vine.

"This is pure magic."

Eshail smiled at the awe in the Easterner's voice. The Eastern Empire had tried eradicating all magic, including the great trees, from its lands. They'd sliced them down to make their cities and palaces. Nothing like this existed beyond the red desert.

"Isn't it?" Eshail watched the woman take in the nest. The warmth was glorious after the chilly winter day they'd spent hiking. Here, there was safety. Most of the dangerous animals in the swamp never made it this far up a tree. She'd only found one of the great trees infected with fire ants, and that one was far to the south.

"Don't drink the water; it'll make you sick. It's been sitting up here too long to be safe. That being said, you shouldn't have to worry about snakes or leeches."

Thayatesh still hadn't said anything.

Like a mother talking about their favorite kid, Eshail found herself babbling about this favorite place of hers. "These oases in the forest have been a source of comfort for many. If you have food, you can hole up here almost indefinitely. Do you see how moss has grown on the bark up here? You can siphon off enough water to sustain yourself by collecting the drips off it."

They stood in silence.

Eshail was letting the peace of the place fill her. It was the calming balm she needed before risking her life to bring Tarwa into the swamp. The walls of the nest blocked the wind as it gusted around the tree. She knew it was time and needed to get on with her mission, but she didn't want to. Tarwa was judgement incarnate, and Eshail knew in her heart she hadn't been taking her witchery entirely seriously. Her mother had a way of illuminating all of her shortcomings. She built her resolve; the Evermoss needed this. It'd be a day before Tarwa would be in Lushwood. She could—would do this.

Yates ended her reverie. "Okay, what do I need to do?"

With a sigh, she took Yates to the edge of the nest. "Do you see that burrow? It looks like a dark spot." The two squinted across the lazy river that snaked through the swamp. In the middle sat an island, peppered with scrubby brush and trees. At the southernmost tip of the isle was a built-up hill with a burrow deep into the center of the island. Eshail would be carefully working on the northern side of the island to construct her gate—close to the tree and as far from the firedrake's nest as possible.

"I see it."

"I need you to blow that whistle as hard as possible if you see movement there. I will be on the other side of the island, doing my work. I need a warning if the drake wakes up."

"You can't possibly hear this whistle from that distance."

"You'd be surprised how sound travels in the Evermoss. You're right though. There's a trick to this particular whistle. The bird it imitates is one of the most common in the swamp, and the warning will get picked up and transferred to me."

Thayatesh didn't understand how the witch could trust a swamp network of animals, but it seemed at this point she was willing to believe whatever she was required to live through the moment. There's a certain amount of natural magic to just go with when one is a hundred feet up in a secret nest in the sky.

"If you do blow it, make sure you start heading down immediately. It also has a way of calling a flock if you're not careful and don't know what you're doing."

They made their farewell. Eshail hoped that this risk was going to work. If she died in the attempt, the Easterner would be abandoned in the middle of the swamp, as helpless as a babe. If Eshail fell to the firedrake trying to construct the moongate, Yates wouldn't have a chance of finding Lushwood again.

Eshail made the trek down to the base of the tree quickly. She could move much faster without slowing down for questions, awe, or the injured leg. Whenever they got back, she would need to make a pain-relieving concoction. All of the pull from the suction of their boots in the muck would certainly cause Yates's leg to ache tonight.

She tapped the water, asking Fluff to close the distance. She would ride in on the puppy if she could manage it. A human swimming in the waters around the island were sure to create the wrong type of vibrations. The alligator snorted at the request but gave permission with a whiffle through its snout. She removed her boots. They'd interfere with the connection. All witches had some form of beast speak, to greater or lesser degrees. Her powers lay in that direction as a literal swamp witch, but she was weak. For genuine trust, she needed the vehicle of touch. She needed to feel the connection and the silent communication that occurred through twitching muscles.

Fluff's scales were warm, hot even. She wouldn't have to worry about leeches. They would stay away from the heat. She shifted her weight from the shore to the back of the beast. Fluff gave her the impression that she needed to hurry up already, that the drake mother wouldn't sleep forever. Once Tarwa was here, no creature in the Evermoss would dare cross one of the greater Guardians of the swamp. However, being a lesser witch of no consequence, she was fair game.

Eshail imagined she looked like a goddess of the swamp as the breeze pulled at her hair and her dress floated above the waters, her vehicle of motion swimming smoothly toward the island. She could feel Yates's eyes on her back. Distant though they might be, they bore into her. It was going to be an unpleasant task to weave the young aspen together under the watchful eye of the Easterner. She'd always had a keen sense of knowing when eyes were on her. It made most witches uncomfortable.

Eshail was trying to sneak by unobserved. Cattails surrounded her. The drake preferred a smoother flow, so it'd made its lair on the knoll in the middle of a current. The pace of the water swirled. The beast had magic to propagate and encourage the plant life on its island. It used the reeds to sift out the muck and floating debris and filter its water. Dragons were intelligent, thoughtful creatures, equal if not greater than humans. Drakes, their baser form, lived a more brutal life bent on survival of the fittest. It was a good sign that this firedrake was starting to purposefully alter her habitat. The beast still had a hundred years until it entered its metamorphic phase, but a rising intelligence meant it'd be calming down.

Eshail gave the command to circle behind the layer. It wouldn't be good to weave the moongate in front of the maw of the drake's cove. Fluff obliged, giving a faint warning to step lightly as the drake slept in the back of her den. They drifted over to the mushy shore. Eshail stepped off with a bare foot, sinking to her ankle in the gooey muck. The villagers said the mud was good for the skin, but she didn't see any of them venturing into the swamp without footwear.

Before her other foot removed itself from Fluff, the alligator gave a silent warning. It was going to swim away. It didn't want to be caught swimming in the drake mother's waters uninvited, but it would be back when she needed it; she just needed to call. She sent a grateful thanks through their link, then lifted her foot from her friend. She watched as Fluff swam away. She was alone.

Eshail took a breath, nerves clenching her throat. If it were for anything less than the Blight, she'd decline this task. She took a squelching step forward, briefly wondering how one could walk light-footed in such conditions, but as she got further away from the water's shore, the ground firmed up.

There were two main reasons why this drake's domain was the best spot for an ad hoc moongate. One was the ambient magic that swirled in the air. She could almost taste the magic, like chili pepper flakes floating on the air—it was the ghost of promised heat. Any workings would be more powerful here. The drake wove the magic of the Evermoss into its home. This magic would eventually help with its metamorphosis. The second advantage was that drake homes always had a plethora of young saplings. The drakes wallowed every few years, stripping down any larger trees nearby. The easiest way to spot a drake lair was to look for a grove of young aspens in an area that should have ancient trees.

She carefully stepped, still barefoot, through the knee-high tufts of grass toward the trees. They stood one to two inches in diameter, perfectly bendable. She paused momentarily, listening to the breeze rustle the leaves together. The leaves twittered back and forth, catching the wind. The deciduous trees leafed out in the heated microbiome despite it still being winter. She missed the spring sound of rustling leaves.

Eshail examined the trees, finding two clumps four feet from each other. She wiggled her toes, feeling the ground, the worms chewing on the detritus, the roots layered upon each other, overlapping and speaking the language of trees. She felt the sun beat on her face and took a moment to ask permission.

She was known in the swamp, and the dendron network snaked wide through the ecology. She waited patiently. The trees eventually concluded that it would be fun to experience a moongate and even better to meet one of the Guardians in person. The trees apologized upon sensing Eshail's disappointment caused by their excitement of meeting her mother. They'd given offense. She waved their unnecessary apology away, ashamed that her pride embarrassed the trees.

The work began. She reached as high as she could and pulled at the crown of the nearest tree, bending the flexible young wood to her will. She walked the branch down until the tip touched the ground and formed an arch. She wound the trunk around an existing tree, using a dash of magic to bond the two. She then took the tree she'd been weaving into and performed the reverse, taking its tallest branch and bending it down toward the ground on the opposite side. The process was slow; each bend had to be done slowly, or she risked the tree snapping. One by one, the trees were bent and woven. It took hours to get the initial framework in place, but she was happy with the result when it was done. The trees arched into each other, forming a matrix of trunks arched over other trunks. The smaller branches were hanging out at all angles. If left this way, the moongate wouldn't function properly, so the arch would need to be cleared of debris. Eshail started taking each branch and weaving them back into the trunks, creating a crisscrossing web of branches. This weaving took longer. Her personal store of magic was running low, so she had to rely on physical force and skill.

Her hands were raw, scratched from resistant branches that hadn't wholly agreed to their role in this magic. With the inner framework complete, she contemplated the last step. The top branches also needed to be woven in for a moongate to last beyond a few months. Right now, the arch looked frizzy, with diminutive tendrils snaking away from it in all directions. If left this way, the gate would function, but in a few months, the tendrils would form new trunks, and the gate would turn into the foot of a larger tree structure. At that point, the magic wouldn't flow in the suitable matrix.

Eshail stood, thinking about it. She didn't want a long-standing connection to her section of the swamp, which was one of the reasons she'd let her original gate go to seed. She wanted to take care of her village without interference. The only reason Tarwa had to make this trip was the severe nature of the biological weapon that'd been accidentally unleashed.

She stepped away. The angry caw of a red-winged blackbird interrupted her thoughts. She hadn't seen one when Fluff had floated her in. They commonly sat on the heads of cattails, offering their thoughts to anyone who passed by. She'd written their absence off to the time of day. Glancing around, she tried to identify the bird causing the ruckus, only to remember that she'd left Yates with the whistle that would mimic the red-winged blackbird.

Heart pounding, Eshail returned her gaze inward to the center of the burrow. Sure enough, a giant scaled head peeked out of the hollow, the drake's neck angling to give one of its broad, emotionless eyes a clear view of her.

"Pussywillows in a teacup!" Eshail swore, starting to backpedal. The drake's eye was bigger than her head. It watched her like a predator, contemplating whether its prey was worth the effort. After the long winter, she had no doubt that any prey would be worth it. She didn't dare look away. Her eyes were focused, and each step she took was slow and methodical, but inside, she was frantic. She didn't know what she would do when she reached the water. There was no escape plan without Fluff.

Chapter 15

All thoughts of the gate vanished as everything shifted to survival. Eshail had finished the basic build and enhanced the spot with a few charms to stabilize the connection, but she hadn't done anything more advanced to protect the gate's structural integrity. One blast from the drake and her work would be destroyed. She kept her eyes on the beast. It was less likely to attack if it thought she was dangerous, and the best way to show that was to meet its gaze.

She started sidestepping and moving backward. She was attempting to draw its eyes away from the aspen arch. The beast opened its mouth, letting out a deep croaking call. The noise reverberated through the air and shook the ground. It was not a good sign. The call was a warning for an intruder. Her feet moved more rapidly of their own accord. Each step took her closer to the bank.

The warning whistle kept going off. She wished she'd told Yates to stop once she realized she had Eshail's attention. There was no need to keep blowing it; that would only draw drake's attention to the old tree. No one wanted that destroyed, especially the vulnerable Yates at the top.

The firedrake inhaled. Eshail braced for the end. Was it going to be another croak or a fiery death? Suddenly she was blown off her feet by a gust of warm, meaty breath and the concussion of an up-close croak . . . from behind.

Eshail was launched forward, landing face-first in the reeds. She rolled on her elbow to see what'd been behind her, and the large mouth of a second drake towered above her. It was enormous, bigger than their drake mother. The beast was beached, and she'd almost backpedaled straight into its maw. She lay on the ground, only a few feet away from its toothy mouth. It inhaled and croaked again, answering their firedrake's call. Fetid, putrid breath blew past, pinning her to the ground for a second.

She lay helpless, mind racing. Eshail had no idea there was a second drake in the swamp. Her mind raced, searching for options as she waited for the end. Scraps of meat could be seen wedged between the monster's teeth. The drake eyed her, then tensed as though preparing to leap forward and finish her.

She tensed, ready to dodge. She knew it was a hopeless effort but wanted to at least try to live. The drake lunged, jaws snapping. She felt the whoosh of air as the maw snapped. It didn't hurt. She cautiously opened her eyes in time to see the beast snake on its way, as fast as possible, toward the mother firedrake. Its eyes had glazed over. Realization dawned on Eshail.

It was technically springtime—mating season. Her head shook. *But it wasn't quite spring yet—not exactly.* The beasts returned to their seasonal ritual once she'd gotten out of the way.

She looked toward the shore, wondering if she could spot Fluff. Her ride wasn't present, but on the opposite shore stood Yates. The woman had an arm raised in triumph. Eshail couldn't understand why. She looked back toward the now obvious male drake, rushing on its goal, mouth warbling in lust. On the animal's back was broken glass and a purple sticky liquid. She could sense her own magic. And she understood.

Her potion. Her *love* potion. The brief relief Eshail

felt at surviving was overshadowed by seething anger bubbling up at the Easterner, the *thief.* Eshail called to Fluff, willing the gator to her. It took time. A minute ticked by, but eventually, the puppy floated calmly up to the beach. The drake couple was happily distracted in their den, but Eshail wouldn't press her luck by working more on the gate; it was good enough. She calmly stepped onto Fluff's back, asking politely for a return to the shore where Yates looked much too pleased with herself.

Minutes later, Eshail stepped off the gator, releasing it of her charm and bidding it goodbye. Fluff floated back against the current. It wanted to watch the humans exchanging words. It was curious and lived for the drama.

"What in the hell did you do to that second drake?" Eshail already knew the answer, but she wanted to hear it from the thief's mouth.

"I used my sling," the woman said, holding up a piece of cloth she'd used as a whip-sling to send her ammunition against the second drake.

"And what did you put in your sling?"

The woman hesitated, evaluating her options regarding the truth of the matter. She seemed to decide on honesty. "I . . . used it to fling a love potion."

"You *snuck* into my cellar and *stole* a potion?"

The woman had enough sense to look guilty. "Yes, I took one from your store. I was going to take it back east with me. However, this seemed a better use at the moment."

Eshail combed through the last few weeks, trying to think of *when*. She hadn't left the woman alone. Had she done it in the middle of the night? When she was feeding Druff? It came to her.

"You went down there when I checked whether your cargo survived, didn't you?"

"Yes." Yates ducked her head in remorse. "It took Hedwarg some time to come by the store."

A small part of Eshail was grateful to be alive. She had mostly, however, given into a righteous rage. She'd offered hospitality to this monster and had been soundly taken advantage of. While she'd been feeding her, changing her dressings, and using what little supplies they had for healing charms, the woman had been scoping out her house. She'd been bent to the task of stealing a potion she knew Eshail was fundamentally against. The betrayal stung.

Eshail began stomping her way home, ignoring the amorous sounds from the burrow. The moongate was up, and the sooner Tarwa got to Lushwood, the sooner this Easterner would be healed and out of her hair. She paused, waiting for Yates to catch up.

She delivered her threat between clenched teeth. "Don't ever steal from me again. If I catch you doing so, I will curse you, your family, and your descendants. You will all slowly rot until you join each other in death." Her threat was the type that got witches kicked out of villages. Threat delivered, she stood, burning in anger, waiting for the woman's response.

They stood silently. Eshail's thoughts chased one another. Betrayal. Hating herself for starting to like the woman. Traitor. Stupidity for trusting her.

With no response to her threat, Eshail said in a calmer voice than she felt, "You stole from me. I don't know what customs are in the East, but hospitality is sacred in the swamp."

Eshail returned to the path home without waiting for Yates to respond. She set an unkind pace that would quickly bring them back to Lushwood.

She wasn't completely heartless. She wasn't going to outpace Yates on crutches. She wouldn't leave the woman to die in the swamp, even if the intrusive thought popped into her head to do just that. It'd been a while since she'd felt so betrayed, which grated on her. She hadn't trusted the woman. She didn't trust people. She wasn't sure why she was so upset. This should have been foreseeable, expected even.

A hand tugged at her arm hard, knocking Eshail out of her introspection.

Surprisingly, Yates didn't negate her responsibility. Much like the Blight, she simply owned it. "I apologize. It's my sister, you see. The world would be a truly bleak place if her fate came true without any . . . magical intervention." It hurt the woman to say magical. Yates sounded like she spoke most of the truth. She continued, "I used the potion I stole, and I'm going to need another one. I'll pay whatever it takes, just please."

Silence sat between them. Yates eventually started filling it with words. "You said I didn't understand the customs of hospitality here. But I do. It's just that I am desperate. You can't comprehend the expectation. The responsibility and duty I have to my family. People are not like me in the East." Eshail caught the truth, tenuous though it was. The hopelessness in Yates's voice made it true. The potion was not for her *sister* but for *herself.* Realization dawned on Eshail, the truth that had been eluding her during all their interactions.

"The love potion isn't for your *sister,* is it? Do you even have a sister?" Most common folk didn't know how to avoid a witch's gaze or how to dance around the truth. The Easterners, though, had been actively operating against witches for centuries. They likely knew all sorts of tricks to avoid the truth.

Each bit of the mystery. Yates's shock at the possibility of her and Evelyn and her derisive, *self-loathing* comments. The insistence that her sister *had no choice* because she had explored all options. That the man was lovely, just not right. It made sense.

"I do have a sister; she's ten. Retfait, my fiancé is a lovely . . . man." Yates's head drooped with the admission.

Part of Eshail's heart went out to her. She knew what it was to be a witch, to be part of the whole but separate. As a witch she had her sisters, her mother, and some grudging respect from her village. Eshail saw tears trace lines down Yates's cheeks and had to repress the instinct to tell her it would all be okay.

Thayatesh's voice was small as she continued, "Women don't love other women in the East."

Eshail snorted. "Obviously, they do. They just are not allowed to be, to live." She contemplated the situation and sat with the trifecta of anger, guilt, and pity. "I'm still not going to give you the potion." She pitied Yates but couldn't let her magic be used in such a self-tortured act. Not for something that was so core to her existence. "But I won't turn you over to the village council either. I have some thinking to do." The anger melted away in the light of compassion.

"Thanks," the meek reply came.

"For what it's worth, I do sympathize with your problem. I don't think there's a soul who's been born with our desires that haven't questioned their place in the world."

"You sympathize, but not enough to help."

Eshail didn't bother answering the statement. They both knew her answer.

No, not enough to help.

The first thing she would do was put a spell of binding on her potion locker. She should have done it before, but Lushwood was so country that she hadn't seen the need to lock everything away. No one would have dared go into her cellar and steal from the local witch.

They resumed their journey at a slower pace. Eshail went back to keeping up on relocating spider webs as they walked. There were a few instances on the hike where she'd left a couple for Yates's taller frame to walk right into. She felt a bit less vindictive. Being doomed to a marriage in which one didn't feel attracted to the other wasn't an ideal life outcome. Many ended up married to those they despised later, cheated on, or downright hated, but that should be the result of decades of interaction. Not something enforced by a lack of cultural awareness about those who preferred a different type of partner.

"At least I'll have an excuse for my mother to room at the inn," Eshail said.

"Excuse me?"

"Well, you're still too ill to be on your own. Plus, I've got to remove about thirty leeches from your legs. You'll still have to room with me, and my house can only support two people. Any more and Druff will be upset. Nothing's worse than an angry grimalkin."

"Your mother that bad?"

"Yes."

More silence hung between them. It would be dusk by the time they got back to the village. Her mother would port in at the highest rise of the moon for the night. Knowing her, she'd probably stay at the great tree, communing with the Evermoss, talking to other trees. She expected Tarwa at dawn.

"My mother is—I think the phrase you use is hard-nosed. She doesn't take dung from anyone. She owes no one anything. And she's judgmental as a scorned pitbull."

"This will be interesting." The Easterner winced as she stepped into a small hole with her bad leg. She was noticeably limping.

Eshail stopped momentarily, bending down to pluck a few leaves from a newly sprouted plant. She rolled them between her fingers, releasing the oils from the leaf. Bringing it up to her nose, she sniffed. Two plants in the swamp looked very similar. One would give a repulsively explosive result, and the other would act as a mild painkiller. Thankfully, they were both hearty. The leaf smelled sweet, as the painkiller would.

"Here, chew this. Don't swallow. Just chew it in your mouth. It'll help you feel better."

"You're not poisoning me, are you?" Eshail thought the Easterner was joking, but the statement had an edge.

"If I wanted you dead, I would have left you in the swamp."

With a shrug, the woman popped the leaves into her mouth and started chewing. The duo trudged along quietly, the chirps of the waterlogged forest their only company. Spring was trying to blossom. The insects were starting to return. When Eshail had communed with the trees, she could see they wanted to begin to bud. The spiders this far north were out; they were more resistant to the cold than most, but she could tell they were hungry. They spun their webs in desperate search for the first blossom of spring. Perhaps Tarwa would have some insights into the cause and progress of ending the long winter.

It would only matter, however, if they could stop the Blight. Eshail's expression soured at the thought. How could one simple Easterner cause so many issues for everyone?

"Why do you think this Ram Sesat sent a biological weapon to the Near Reach? Why use you as that vehicle?"

They plodded along, and the Easterner didn't answer for a while. Then, "I think he used me because I was desperate enough not to ask questions. I was going over the desert; no one goes that way. But I wanted to bring cargo I knew would be irresistible to a witch that would otherwise get stuck in customs."

"Were you going to return through the desert? That's wild. Attempting to go through once is crazy enough."

"Yes, well, to be honest, I didn't much care if I made it or not." Darkness clung to Yates at her statement. Eshail believed her. She could feel the hopelessness in her voice. "It's funny. Once I got into the desert, the terror receded. The place was peaceful, almost beautiful. Now I wonder if the only reason I survived with minimal interference from what lurks in the sand is due to the Blight in my cargo. It's all making sense now."

"Why return through the desert, though?"

"I wouldn't make it through one of the checkpoints with a magical potion. Just like the West checks for contaminants on those checkpoints, the Ram has conducted thorough searches for any magic that would infect the Empire."

"You all must really hate magic."

"We do." The words sat in the air. Eshail didn't know why they stung. This woman was an Easterner. Their hatred was fact.

"We?" Eshail tried to ask innocently but found herself invested in the answer. She didn't know what was wrong with her. This woman was a problem for her, the village, and the Evermoss. She wasn't sure Tarwa wasn't going to strike her dead once she met her.

"I don't know what I think anymore. Everything I've known my whole life says that you're the evil in the world. I have difficulty being near you, and living in your house has been almost impossible. It makes my skin crawl."

"But?" Eshail stopped to look at her companion. She removed another water flask and offered it to Thayatesh.

Yates let out the breath she'd been holding in tension. "But I haven't found you to be the monster I've been taught to see. Maybe it's a glamour." The woman gave a nervous chuckle. "Maybe it's just another indication that something's wrong with me."

Eshail wanted to insist that nothing was wrong with her, that it was her family, her culture, the East, that was wrong. She wisely kept her mouth shut. That was the type of revelation a person had to come to on their own. She couldn't force it, nor did she want to get mixed up in the ugliness that was Eastern Empire philosophy. This ultimately was a culture that wanted to burn her alive for her connection to the Nest Mother.

The rest of the trip home was made in silence.

Chapter 16

By the time they got into the village, it was dark. Days were still short and the summer solstice still distant. The streets were emptier than usual. The corner lamps on the squares had been lit, but no one was walking home from a friend's or making their way to the tavern for dinner. They walked along the cobblestones, Yates's crutch making a dull thump.

Eshail could almost hear the wince of Yates at every step. It'd been too hard a task for her body. Looking at her, she could see a feverish sweat had started. She needed to get the Easterner ensconced in her home and run to the tavern to pick up a quick dinner. Thankfully it didn't take too long to get to her shop. The front entrance was unusually dark. She didn't close the shop often.

Yates sagged gratefully against the side of the front door as Eshail fumbled with the key. She could count on one hand the number of times she'd locked the shop's front. She usually left it open even when she went on excursions to collect herbs and swamp finds. One never knew when a village emergency would occur, and Evelyn or Talin getting to one of her potions or antivenoms was a matter of life and death.

The door swung open, and Druff greeted Eshail on

the front counter. He'd spent the day keeping the shop.

"Good evening," she said, walking across the room to rub Druff's face in greeting. In response, he leaned into her hand, giving a loud, welcoming purr. She sensed his happiness at her return, as well as a faint bit of worry that she'd been gone so long with a stranger he didn't completely trust. She dismissed his worry with a pat.

"Why don't you lie down?" Eshail told Yates. "I'll bring you dinner."

Thayatesh gave a weary nod. The woman was exhausted, too tired even to make conversation. Eshail waited until she was wrapped in blankets in her bed. She felt her forehead and gave her a fresh glass of water, vowing to return, do a thorough bandage replacement, and see if she had enough feversbane to brew up something useful. Eshail left the woman tucked into her blankets.

Druff followed her out. He was inquisitive and wanted to know what the result of the day's work on the villager's part was. Without a limping companion this time around, Eshail took pavement-eating steps toward the Tavern. The village looked like a ghost town; only in a few windows did dim candles flicker. The chirps and calls of the swamp were loud, drowning out any noise that may have escaped from the array of residences.

She could sense—not in a sure way, but in the way an imagination runs wild—that people were huddled in their homes, by their fires, in their beds, trying to keep warm. She could imagine closing her eyes for a moment and seeing, like a mosquito, the heat signatures of all the warm bodies in their homes. She shook her head. It was time to confront the reality of what the Easterner had brought to her own home.

She bent down, allowing Druff to hop up on her shoulders. He tucked in between her neck and the brim of her hat, his reassuring warmth giving her the courage to enter the tavern.

She pushed in the worn wooden doors of the Toadsprigen Inn and was immediately assaulted by sound—voices. Her imagination had seemingly been wrong. The entire town was in the tavern talking. Their voices were an angry buzz. No one noticed her entrance, and for that small blessing, she was grateful. She wove her way toward the bar, hoping to get a food order in quickly and leave the mass of people to themselves.

She caught snippets of conversation, and none of it was good.

"What are we going to do? We'll have to move."

"I think we should burn her at the stake for bringing this plague to our home."

"She didn't know. The witch confirmed it."

"How do we know the witch was telling the truth?"

"How fast do you think it'll spread?"

Eshail had instinctively used a bit of glamour to make herself a little less intrusive, which was certainly the right call. Half the people seemed ready to walk down to her store, drag Yates out of her bed, and string her up on the edge of town. The other half of the tavern was simply worried about what the Blight in their swamp meant for them and their home. The only soul who'd spotted her coming in slid in next to her at the bar.

"You weave the gate?" Evelyn asked with a warm smile, apologizing for questions of business first.

"Yes, although it was a challenge. We have two firedrakes now."

Evelyn whistled. "Well, that's a good sign, right? Means we've got a healthy swamp." Theoretically she was right, the firedrakes wouldn't choose their portion of the Evermoss to live in if it was struggling ecologically. The two were likely still in ignorance of the Blight's infection.

Eshail flicked her eyes to the masses behind them and muttered, "You wouldn't guess it from the talk here. How bad was it?"

"The sooner we get Tarwa here, the better. It wasn't good. The barrel burst apart in the gully rush, and while some of the seed drowned before it could take root, we've got too many infected sites. And I'm not sure we've identified everything either. You know how quickly those waters flow."

Eshail winced. It sounded like the worst-case scenario. She nervously rubbed her hand along the smooth edge of the bar.

"What'll it be?" one of the bar staff, a teenager in overalls with a smart blue hat that Talin made all his employees wear, asked for the second time.

"Oh, sorry. I need three bowls of stew with lids. I'll return the stack tomorrow."

The boy nodded and darted toward the kitchen.

Evelyn leaned in, close to her ear, and whispered, "How's your patient?" Her breath sent a shiver down Eshail's spine. By the Nest Mother, she was lonely.

"Not great. She went with me today."

"Smart to keep her out of the village. Ruthers went over today but found your shop closed." Ruthers was a crusty elderly man who hated change almost as much as he hated strangers. He'd be the one holding the rope to lynch the Easterner if it came to a mob.

"Yeah, well, it turns out crutching through the swamp, barely recovered from a dozen snakebites, is a good way to throw someone into a relapse. If I don't bring her fever down, we may not have to worry about a mob."

"Have faith. This town isn't going to turn on you. They're not barbaric like that." Evelyn slipped an arm around her, and Eshail leaned into the warmth. She'd missed, more than anything, their friendship over the winter.

Eshail had come to peace that the strong, direct, and handsome woman was one of the Nest Mother's touched. Born to be friend to all and lover to none, born to move mountains and firedrakes. She was the best of them.

The tavern thrummed with edgy desperation. "Every witch burned at the stake had faith in their town at one point." The rebuke was harsh but true. *Evelyn* would never turn on her, but these people were furious.

"Here's your sack. The cook had me include some bread when she found out who was asking," the young man said to her, contradicting all of her feelings of distrust.

"Th-thanks," Eshail stammered. Blushing red in embarrassment, Evelyn gave her arm an *I told you so* squeeze.

"I think you're right in one aspect: keep the Easterner out of sight for now. Let's see what Tarwa says when she's here to survey the damage. If she confirms your sight that the Easterner was an innocent accomplice, I think the town will calm down. No one is going to blame the rat for the flea. And as much as sentiment toward witches changes, it would take a lot more guts than those found in Lushwood to accuse a Guardian of lying." Not just any Guardian, Tarwa. The thought reassured Eshail like nothing else.

"Thanks, Evelyn," Eshail said, looking back into her friend's eyes. They were kind and comforting, and they were all the things Eshail needed. She smiled with a twinge of regret and finally released her fantasies about Evelyn. They were friends, and it was more than enough. She slipped out of the tavern with her stack of bowls before anyone else spotted her.

Druff nuzzled her ear, offering a tickling reassurance with his whiskers.

The journey back to her house was uneventful. She walked quickly, trying to escape the tavern's angry buzz. The sack of stew swayed in her hands. It smelled good—carrot, potato, and the unending supply of onion they had. It smelled like the cook had dipped into her meat stores too. It was probably best to fill up bellies and send folks home.

No one would do anything too rash on a full stomach.

She walked into her house and sensed something was off—wrong. Immediately on guard, Druff hopped down to investigate, and she set the bowls of stew down by the door. Thankfully the stack stayed upright. She held her hands out, ready to defend or ready for a quick cantrip of protection. Her eyes examined the front room. Nothing had been shifted. For a brief moment, she questioned the uneasy feeling. A soft moan came from further in the house.

She stepped lightly and moved toward the workroom. If someone had been looking to make trouble, they would have kept searching until they found the Easterner. The workroom was empty. She looked in her bedroom and ducked her head into the garden. No one was present. The moan sounded again, and she realized the truth: the moan was from the cellar. Druff kept by her feet, his fur on end as he searched the house with her.

Grabbing the used latch, she tugged the cellar door open. The well-oiled hinges didn't complain. She sparked a minor cantrip of light and let her spark float down the stairs. The Easterner lay at the bottom of them. Druff sprinted down the stairs while Eshail squinted into the darkness. Yates was crumpled on the floor. Cursing, the witch climbed down the steep stairs as fast as she could without falling herself.

"What are you doing down here?" Part of her sparked a worry. Had the idiot tried to come down for another love potion? She hadn't had time to put a magical lock on her cabinet. She made a mental note to take inventory, regardless of the woman's reply.

"They . . . came to the door. They wanted me." Yates's words were frightened and disjointed.

"Did they say who they were? Did you recognize any of them?"

"No, I didn't know them. They wanted to kill

me." The words were slurred. The woman had lost what little consciousness she'd had with the proclamation. With nothing further to be gleaned from Yates, Eshail got to work. She snapped her fingers, lighting some of the candles she had set up for her inventory days. There was no way she could physically lug Yates back up the almost vertical stairs by herself, and right now, she didn't trust anyone but Evelyn to help. She sighed. It would be a long night trying to set up a pallet in the basement. Plus, she'd need to check for more wounds. Minimally, it seemed like her fever had either gotten worse or she'd hit her head. Either way, Eshail must be on watch duty, monitoring for abrupt changes.

"Druff, can you go to Evelyn's house? Fetch her when she returns home?"

The cat climbed the stairs, a study in grace. Eshail got to work setting up bedding in order to use the witch's cellar for its original purpose: a place to hide.

She whispered to the stone foundation, the spell that Tarwa had helped her set up when she first moved to Lushwood—the words of transformation, safety, and home. The cellar, ordinarily dark and cold, began to warm its features in temperature and ambiance. The stone shifted ever so slightly into a bed and a place to sit. A hearth grew out of the side, linking with the hearth above her head. The enchantments were too heavy a use of magic for her but not for her mother.

Tarwa would feel the pull of her magic's use. Feel the safety mechanism she'd insisted her daughter have woven into her home be triggered. She lifted Yates who'd invaded her life onto the stone platform. With a few trips upstairs, she grabbed blankets, pillows, and everything needed to nest. The last trip was for the now much cooler stew by the front door. Just as she lifted the latch for her final go, the front door burst open.

"Who dares threaten my daughter!"

The lamps in the house flared in alarm.

Tarwa had arrived.

Chapter 17

"Mom, it's okay. I'm okay."

All sources of light in the house had dimmed to the barest flicker. The place was thrown into shadow, and Eshail's lack of night vision at the moment made Tarwa look like an ancient goddess of swamp vengeance come to life. Her hair snaked away from her scalp, sticking up in serpentine locks ready to strike, and her nose bent like one unwilling to compromise a position. Her ears were craggy, large, and not as pointed as they'd once been.

"I swear by the All Mother I will end you. Come forth!"

Eshail was momentarily confused, not understanding Tarwa's words. The witch flicked her wrist, and a green miasmic ball floated in her hand. Realization of the situation hit Eshail as Yates had stumbled up the stairs, feverish and worried.

"Stop!" Eshail stepped between Tarwa and Thayatesh, where the putrid poison ball was about to be flung. "She's under my protection." This time, Eshail shouted the words, trying to break through Tarwa's deafness and general inability to listen to her daughter. The witch blinked in astonishment, her hand falling, the green glow fading.

"Eshailaesan, is that you? Are you okay?" Tarwa used her pet name for Eshail. It translated from the old tongue as "Eshail of my hearth."

For all that she sometimes, even often, hated the woman, the relief in her voice brought a tear to Eshail's eyes. For all her faults, the witch did care about Eshail. That was worth something in a world full of coldness.

"I'm alright, Mom. I'm okay." Druff backed up her statement by chortling and rubbing against Tarwa's leg. The old witch bent down and rewarded him by running her old, gnarled fingers along his head and spine.

"That's a good kitty." It was a rare moment of tenderness. It was short-lived, though, as the witch pivoted. "Why in the Evermoss did you set off my safety charm? Child, I thought I'd moongated too late. You could have warned me about the firedrakes too. Drakes!" She emphasized the plurality of the statement.

"I just got home myself not too long ago—" Eshail tried to get a word in, but Tarwa continued.

"This woman smells like one of those forsaken Easterners, and have you seen the shape of your shop? Don't you call yourself a witch? No self-respecting witch would allow her cupboards to be so bare. What would happen if a fever broke out in your village? You'd be roasting before the break of spring. I taught you better than that."

"It's been a long . . ."

"There are roots and supplies. You must have slacked off this summer, not collecting enough stock. This is shoddy witchery. Where's the town herald? I need to speak with her immediately."

Before Eshail could stop her mother, the woman was gone. It was typical of Tarwa to barge into her life, judge it, and leave without letting her explain or get a word in edgewise.

"Rotten fennel cakes! I hate that woman!"

"I heard that. I raised you to do better!" Tarwa called from the street.

"All Mother take you," she murmured under her breath. Tarwa was here, and the town would now coordinate with the Guardian. Eshail had effectively been sidelined regarding any importance in the town. This is what it meant to call in Tarwa. It was why Eshail had begrudgingly called her mother. The judgement, the righteousness, and the downright disregard for Eshail was bad. But Eshail had finally started to feel like her role in the village was respected, needed, and Tarwa would only point out her failings.

Perhaps it was better to be sidelined. The Blight had snuck into the swamp under her watch, after all.

Eshail purposefully turned her mind to a problem she could solve, to Thayatesh's illness. She shepherded the barely conscious woman back downstairs, which was at least a manageable problem to keep her distracted. She surveyed the cuttings she'd collected over the last few days and the remnants of Yates's case. Eshail was sure she could concoct a fever breaker and a restorative with what they had.

Restorative potions took time and resources. It was a bit quicker than rest and time spent healing, but no better otherwise. Eshail hadn't originally judged the Easterner worth the effort. Their trek through the swamp together had changed her mind. The woman had made some mistakes, but she was at fundamental odds with what her culture told her she should be. Eshail had compassion for that situation. She'd been in it most of her life. Plus, Yates had saved her life with the firedrakes.

A bit of codswallop, a pinch of stamin from a bachelor belle, and a base of feversbane. Eshail pulled the ingredients as if by magic. None of them were scarce outside of the time of season. It was a bit miraculous that Yates had brought just the right bits that she needed. Druff circled her legs. It was dinner time for him. She took her bone-handled belt athame and carved some preserved lamb for him.

The basement transformation included a spot for her cauldron. The hardest part would be carrying it downstairs. Her stomach rumbled, and she decided on the next task for herself. She'd venture back upstairs, grab what she needed, including the stew from the inn, and come back down. Tarwa's magic was particularly strong with the woman herself in town. She was unlikely to come back to Eshail's house. Not when the tavern had accommodations and was near the action.

The first floor of her home was cold and barren. Part of it was Tarwa's illusion. It was supposed to make the place look abandoned. It succeeded. All of the warmth of her home had been sucked out, and everything looked a little shabbier now. She wasn't quite sure if it actually *was* shabbier or if it was just poorly bearing the weight of Tarwa's judgment. Either way, Eshail vowed to make some strides in the overall showroom for her work. She went to the front door. Tarwa had kicked it open. She'd have to fix it when she got the chance.

Eshail reached down to grab the bag of covered stews from the inn that she'd left by the front door. The creak of a wooden board along the boardwalk drew her eye.

"Who's there?"

"I don't mean you any trouble, Miss Eshail," said the sweet sing-song voice of Edorm, the southern bachelor who came up last spring to preach his odd religion.

"What in the peat bog are you doing outside my store this time of night?" Eshail's mind raced, fearful that he'd been one after Thayatesh. Thinking quickly, she asked, "Do you need some medicine? Someone got an injury they need me to treat?"

The man was clean-shaven. He always was. She never trusted clean-shaven men.

"I'm here for the woman. Where is she?"

"The Easterner? Her? I think you must have scared her off when you ransacked my store earlier tonight." The man didn't deny the accusation. "She's probably halfway back to the East."

"Mind if I take a look?"

"I do, but I have the feeling you're going to look anyway."

He pushed in, his rough, homespun shirt harsh as it brushed against her arm. She hated his ilk with a passion. The man gave her house a once over, failing to find the glamoured latch to her cellar.

"Seems like she's left." His voice was feathery light, covering his dark intentions.

"Did you doubt my word?"

"I'm just looking out for your safety." Eshail could almost visualize the slime attached to the lie. "Can't be too sure of anything with these strangers about. Bringing their disease into our home."

"Last I knew, you were new to Lushwood too."

On his way out, he gave her a side eye and said, "Holler real loud if she shows back up. We'll be watching." The statement sent a shiver of dread down her spine that she tried to repress.

Steeling her voice, she looked him straight in the eye. "I think we've got more important tasks at hand besides watching the local witch. If she shows up, I can handle her. You know I have my ways too. Now get out of here. I want to eat my dinner and go to bed."

The man snorted and backed away from the door. Because of Tarwa, she didn't have a good way to secure it anymore. She dragged one of the dining chairs into the front entrance and wedged it under the door knob. Eshail made sure her shop sign said closed. Someone would knock loudly if it were an emergency, and she'd instilled in them just enough fear of being cursed by the witch that folks only used the privilege when they truly needed it.

Eshail took stock of her home. It'd been fairly empty before the trials of the last weeks, but now it had the look of being ransacked. It was time to move downstairs for the moment and give folks the image of abandonment for a while. She'd work with Evelyn and Tarwa if they needed her, but it was time to close the hatch and survive the storm—the spring storms they'd all been asking the Nest Mother for had finally come, just not how they wanted.

She piled her treasures in the workroom by the glamoured hatch to the basement: the cauldron, Druff's bowl, her roll of twine, her recipe book, and the dried rabbit's foot from Druff's first kill. She'd already moved her quilts and pillows. She piled it all in the cauldron and attached it to a long rope that wrapped around her shoulders distributing the weight of it. When it hit the basement floor, her strained back muscles relaxed, as did her mind. Everything was safe.

She took the satchel of her last ingredients in the store—not that it was much—and climbed down the stairs herself. She grabbed the hatch and closed it behind her, shutting out the outside world. The act had a finality to it, a shutting off of the village she'd spent the last several years watching over, of the people she cared for and yet was set apart from.

Moaning brought her back to the moment. She still had a patient to care for, and she'd brought her mother to save the Evermoss and Lushwood. That had to be enough.

She stored jars of water in the cellar in case of emergency, and she broke one open, pouring some contents into a cup for Yates and in her cauldron for the potion she would brew. She held the cup in front of the woman's lips, wetting them. Yates's hands instinctively reached for its rim, drinking greedily. She was dipping back into unconsciousness but still had some awareness.

"We're going to get you healed and get you back to your people."

"I can't go back," Yates murmured. "He's waiting for me."

"We'll figure it out, one way or another."

Yates snuggled back into the blankets, eyes still shut. A spark of something lit in Eshail's heart. A protectiveness for the woman she almost killed for a second time in the swamp. She watched her manicured eyebrows twitch and reached forward to brush some hair out of her face. The hair was silky smooth. Thayatesh leaned instinctively into the touch for a heartbeat and then let out a snore.

Druff jumped on the bed, purring as he kneaded the blankets. The familiar curled into the crook of Yates's knee. His bit of magic would be put to use; his presence would help stabilize her. It was an unusual gesture for him, but one he'd made consistently for the woman. She longed to question him why. He normally reserved his magic for herself, Tarwa, Evelyn, and someone on death's doorstep. Interesting.

Chapter 18

Tarwa's spell of safety set the cellar up to be completely functional for riding out a storm figuratively and literally. Her cauldron sat above stones that emanated focused heat for brewing, casting, and cooking. It was smokeless and contained—a greater magic many masters of their craft pursued. Eshail couldn't manage the magic herself.

The hedge witch fell asleep stirring the latest brew. Eshail'd had trouble sleeping, so after a while she had stayed up all night making poultices, bindings, and potions to help Yates. It'd been a long night. She'd set a kettle that gave off an aroma of chamomile and lavender, which put healing moisture in the air. The concoction worked too well, as she had succumbed to the slow blinking of her eyes and the quiet burble of water.

"Eshail, you there?" She woke to the words spoken in Yates's Eastern accent. The air had dried as the kettle's water had evaporated. Eshail's eyes were crusty, and she rubbed them, trying to remove the granules that threatened to seal them shut.

"I'm here," she muttered, unsure if she was conscious. "Give me a moment." She wanted a year. She wanted to return to before this stranger entered their village, dumped Blight-forsaken contaminants in her swamp, and before she had to call her mother. She said what any good witch would say, despite her mood: "How are you feeling?"

"I feel like you kicked me down one of the great sand dunes, and then I was eaten alive by scorpions."

"Not too bad, then." The woman's groan made Eshail feel a little better. "You know you owe me."

"I am grateful you've been taking care of me."

"Not for that. Evelyn is technically paying me to help you from the village's assistance fund. You owe me for having to bring my mother here. All Mother help me. It's going to be a long spring."

"I'd say she's not that bad, but I do have a vague memory of her trying to kill me last night. Did that really happen?"

Eshail nodded. "Yes, and it's so much worse than that." Yates raised an eyebrow at something being worse than getting killed. "You can't feel it—the pressure. The ambient magic has increased a thousandfold. Part of the reason you're so sore is that you're healed. Muscles and skin knitting together that quickly causes the soreness. She has that effect. My work last night, with her power in range, is so much *more* than me alone." It also meant that the swamp would be forced to change over into spring.

They needed it, and Eshail would have to take advantage of every spring moment because it was possible when Tarwa left that the land would return to winter. The woman was one of the four Guardians of the swamp. Eshail wasn't sure there wasn't anything she couldn't do. She was powerful, the most powerful witch Eshail had ever encountered. She was also as remote as a single mountain. Eshail had wondered, growing up, if the power Tarwa held in the land had caused her detachment or if she'd always been that way. She was as immovable as a boulder and just as unfeeling.

"I don't feel the magic," Yates said uncertainly.

"But I can feel my leg." The wonder in her voice had been worth Eshail's overnight efforts. "This is a good sign, yes?"

With a month of Tarwa's ambient impact, the villagers would be healthier than anyone living in a swamp had a right to be. Tarwa typically roamed the country, staying longer in villages with recent outbreaks of swamp fever to teach them how to control the sources of infection better, care for the sick, and she used her aura to stop it from spreading. This winter, however, had been extended, and outbreaks had been virtually nonexistent. The Blight was the biggest threat of the moment.

"We need to get up and check in with Evelyn to see if there's anything that's needed."

"Like breakfast?"

Eshail couldn't help but smile. The woman's appetite, even while sick, had been insatiable. Her skinny frame must have suffered coming across the dunes.

"I'm sure Talin will have something available for us to snack on."

Eyes clear, Eshail looked across the empty firepit. Yates lay on the pallet, pillows stacked up behind her head. The woman's cheeks were almost gaunt. One problem with accelerated healing is that it chewed through the body's energy reserves. Yates wasn't the confident merchant that'd barged into the witch's store demanding a love potion anymore. She looked scared and lost. Eshail moved to sit next to her.

"It's going to be alright." Eshail could see the words had little effect.

"That man wanted to kill me."

"You heard that too, huh? He was just afraid of what you'd brought. Tarwa will have the village calmed down by now. It'll be okay."

Eshail could see the next words left unspoken. *And after we deal with the Blight? What will I do?*

"It's still going to be a while until you'll be well

enough to travel, whether back east or in hunt of a love potion. Take a couple of deep breaths with me." Eshail led Yates through some breathing exercises she'd used on kids and adults who were in stages of panic. "Let's concentrate on the now. On the next step in the swamp. This step will be onto a stone firmly embedded in the firmament. There's no sinking, no worry, just another step. We'll get up and go to the tavern and check in with Evelyn and Tarwa." The thought of seeing her mother in full engagement mode with the village sent a trill of anxiety down to her gut. "And we'll get a task we can accomplish. That's all we need to worry about right now."

Whatever fate haunted Thayatesh, it could wait. In Eshail's opinion, it was unlikely she'd even make it back to the Eastern Empire. Worrying about a distant fiancé wasn't worth the energy when they were about to be overrun by the Blight.

Eshail watched as Thayatesh kept her eyes closed and focused on her breathing. Some of the creases in her face eased, and her shoulders lowered. Then again, Eshail didn't know much about promised hands. It wasn't a common practice in the Evermoss. Sure, folks may arrange a meeting or push young people together in the hopes that they catch each other's eyes. But forced marriage? That wasn't the way of the wetlands.

They both climbed slowly up the stairs. Thayatesh, because her body was stiff and sore from rapid healing. Eshail, because she'd slept crunched over on the old stone paving. Druff followed, limber as a kitten, taking the stairs in a hopping fashion that no cat had a right to master. As far as Eshail could discern, the cat had spent the entire night curled up on Yates. It was a wonder. He didn't tolerate many people touching him, much less show them that kind of affection or care. For all that he was a familiar, he was still a cat with a cat's fussiness and peculiarities.

The two didn't bother stopping in the shop.

Everything of consequence had been moved downstairs the night before. Yates didn't need the crutch, but she moved slowly in the daylight. They'd managed to sleep through most of the morning. Eshail would have been embarrassed at her idleness, but that was one thing Tarwa had never criticized. She could almost hear the old crone's voice: "If your body needed that sleep, then who am I to judge you taking it?"

The thought brought a smile to Eshail's face. Perhaps it wouldn't be that bad. The last time the two had seen each other hadn't gone well. She'd fought tooth and nail for the right to safe keep her own village. Tarwa had wanted her to be an apprentice, to follow her footsteps into power. Eshail wanted nothing of the sort. She wanted to strike out on her own. Eventually Tarwa had relented, the coven giving her Lushwood. Her mother had reluctantly set her home up.

The last time they'd talked in person, Tarwa had pressed Eshail hard on an apprenticeship. On pushing her powers. It might have been tempting except Eshail knew she wasn't that talented. They were both disappointed when her primary skill revealed itself to be something as useless as a love potion. Eshail knew she didn't have the natural talents to follow in Tarwa's footsteps. That path was one of disappointment and heartache. At least as Lushwood's witch she'd get to stand on her own, make a home for herself.

Rain fell from a dreary sky. Eshail was sure that elsewhere in the Evermoss, the rain fell as snow. It was a toss-up whether it was the infraction of the Blight or her mother's presence that caused the anomaly. Her boots, still crusted in mud, clonked heavily against the hard stones leading to the tavern. With each step, she felt right into her soul. She wasn't made for the surfaces of man. She was meant to be in the woods. With a long sigh, she kept walking. This time, Thayatesh kept pace easily. Druff padded daintily along, slowing himself to stay even with them.

People were out in the day time, Tarwa's presence already doing its work. Some folk kept their head down, en route to their next piece of business. A father tossed a bit of mop water out into the street. Kids ran along, releasing the pent-up energy the last several days had given them. Ruthers leaned against the side of a building, shielded from the precipitation by an overhang. He eyed them but didn't dare bother the two during the day with so many witnesses. Edorm stood across the way, nodding his head in acknowledgment that she'd won the engagement. The two gave her chills. She'd make a point to talk to Evelyn and have the herald handle the men.

Eshail grabbed Yates's arm, pulling her closer. They'd calm down once Tarwa started actively dealing with the Blight. Any fool would quickly come to realize that pissing off the Guardian that was saving the village by harassing her daughter was foolish. She moved a little faster, Yates's arm clutched tight.

Before long, they found themselves before the tavern. Thayatesh hadn't spoken a word on their journey, just one step in front of another.

Eshail remembered when she'd finally gotten the courage to tell Tarwa she wanted to be on her own. She'd shaken like a leaf that night, stuttering over her words, waiting for the denouncement that never came. She'd looked up and found an avalanche of disappointment painted on her adoptive mother's face—disappointment and weariness.

Within a week, Tarwa deposited her daughter in the northern town of Lushwood. The crone had made one last attempt to convince Eshail, but it'd come to naught. Eshail had received an empty home and a flock of people to care for, completely alone. It'd been hard the first couple of years, but she'd gotten by. Tarwa had only spoken through letters and a rare communication spell.

On the initial drop-off, Tarwa had set up her wards and the escape in the basement, but other than that, the old crone had been a distant memory of kin on those first couple nights. Eshail only found her absent mother in her workings of magic when she took a moment to remember who had taught her the weaves, the will, and the intention.

Thayatesh brought her out of her musing. "We're here. Are you ready to go inside?" The stranger-turned-friend gave her arm a squeeze. "It'll be okay. I'm here for you."

Eshail took a deep breath and let go of Yates's arm. "Are we ever ready to face our mothers?"

"By the sands to the mouth of babes, you've got me there. Sadly, it must be done regardless."

The two women stepped into the tavern. The place was warm as always, but it was lacking the chaotic mess of patrons and bar staff. It was packed but orderly and quiet. Eshail spotted her mother's handiwork immediately. Tarwa and Evelyn were seated at one of the larger tables, a map of the Evermoss stretched out between them, and neither looked up as the two entered. Eshail felt a twinge of anger. Her mother knew she'd come to the tavern. She would have known when she'd left her house.

Eshail walked over to the table and sat down with a loud thump.

"Hey, Eshail," Evelyn said softly, already adapting to Tarwa's preferred quietude.

"Good morning, Evelyn. How's it going?" The map was marked up with blobs of black, which she could only infer were Blight-infected swamp spots. Looking at the expanse, she winced. There were many blotches along the reported gully rush.

"How do you think it's going? We've got a Blight infection that's hit one of the minor arteries of the swamp," Tarwa's harsh voice interrupted. "Is this the one that you've been nursing back to health? The source of our infection?"

"She—"

"I am," Yates said firmly, sitting at the table. "What can I do to help?"

Tarwa eyed her suspiciously. "You caused this on purpose?" The witch had engaged her insight skill, examining the woman.

"I didn't even know it was part of my cargo. I'm deeply sorry this infected the Evermoss. I would have never intentionally brought the Blight across the desert. It is a curse that shouldn't be visited on any land, much less one as rich as this."

The witch snorted. Being appeased didn't make her any happier. They still had a massive problem on their hands. Once interrogated and found innocent, Thayatesh was of no interest to Tarwa. Just another Easterner dirtying her swamp.

"There's nothing the two of you can do to assist. This will take all my energy, and possibly the help of another Guardian, to deal with everything. You"—She looked at Eshail, eyes piercing—"have left your shop and this village in a sorry shape. Spring has followed me here, and you need to take advantage of it and fill your stock. The contingent dispatched to end the winter may or may not be successful. Do not let your stores get as empty again." Tarwa leaned back, looking down her nose at Eshail. "You may have been useful had you apprenticed to me. As you are, though, there is little you can do. I'll be by for dinner."

With that, Eshail was dismissed. Her only solace came from Evelyn, who mouthed the words "I'm sorry" back at her as she stood to leave. Tarwa was here, and Eshail's role in helping with the infection was effectively over. Tarwa had addressed her as Guardian of Evermoss and elder of the coven. She'd been admonished to get her house in order.

Eshail turned and left. She was numb. The emotion built up to meet her mom, to possibly confront all the feelings they'd never talked about, was erased in a dismissal that both diminished Eshail as a person and confirmed that her mom was still disappointed in her lack of aptitude and unwillingness to follow.

Chapter 19

"What was that about? Evelyn didn't even stand up to her." Yates was outraged on Eshail's behalf. It would have been endearing if it hadn't been so pointless.

"Evelyn can't. This is Tarwa's territory now. She's the only hope we've got of staving off disaster, so her word goes. I mean, she normally gets her way anyway."

They clomped back toward Eshail's house, this time at a more defeated pace than the trip to the tavern.

"But the whole village was in there. They all saw it, and this is your town."

Eshail had nothing to say to the obvious statement. Tarwa was one of the most powerful witches in the Evermoss—if not *the* most powerful—but her tact was always lacking. She didn't see people as individuals who had feelings and expectations; they were just the next person in a long line of people who needed her expertise. And even her daughter fell under the same curse.

"What do we do now? I can't just sit and do nothing." Yates's voice lowered as she whispered, "I did this. Maybe not intentionally, but I have to help. And this negative feeling . . . ? Or energy . . . ? Or whatever it is that follows Tarwa around doesn't help."

Eshail felt it too—the tingle of the guardian's magic.

It was infectious. It was the promise of a warm spring day, growth, and expectation. It'd always been ironic to her that Tarwa, of the four guardians, had attuned to spring. Almost any other season would have made more sense—the blasting heat of summer, the decay of fall, or the closed-off silence of winter. Instead she got the young cat waiting to pounce.

"We have much to do; you heard her. My stores are empty, and that is unacceptable. We're going to go forage. Normally I do my spring gathering with Hedwarg, but I imagine he will be at the council's beck and call, so you're it. I need your help gathering as much as possible, processing it, and storing it. I'm hoping you've got some experience . . . ? Your wagon was exceedingly well stocked." Eshail glanced at her companion, hoping fervently for approval.

"I have a bit of experience from childhood. I'd help my nanny gather for the family."

Her nanny. Of course.

"And the wagon full of the rarest ingredients west of the desert?"

"Bought mostly. I did study books a bit so I knew what was what and the benefits of them all. I knew you could make love potions when you were interested in heart thorn. That's a dead giveaway."

Eshail rolled her eyes. Nannies. Books. This woman was of noble stock. No wonder they'd arranged a marriage that she couldn't refuse. The village had a dozen books outside her residence, mostly owned by Evelyn, and none of them would have been given over to something as mundane as herbology. Thayatesh was nothing less than a runaway princess. Eshail attempted to hide her judgment and disappointment on her face. She wasn't Tarwa.

"Okay, well, that's a start. Are you ready to get a first-class education in harvesting and processing?"

"Very much." The words were emphasized and

genuine. Eshail didn't have to turn on her Witch's Sight to see it. For all, the princess was enthusiastic.

"I'm surprised, given your experience in the Evermoss. I would say it seems to target you, but honestly, it's just how the swamp is. It eats the unwary alive."

They'd reached the shop door, and Eshail pushed it in. She'd have to get someone to fix what was left of her doorframe. The witch went to her workroom and looked up into the rafters. Her baskets and drying racks hung from the ceiling.

She'd had Evelyn help her assemble a system to store the mess. It had all been lying about her bedroom and stillroom, taking up every surface, which didn't seem like a good use of the space. The witch went over to the corner of the room and began unwinding twine that was wound around a wooden peg. As the tension was released, various implements lowered from the ceiling. A large wicker basket given to her by Melody, the matron of the wash, was best for thrushes and reeds. Her secondary carrying basket was lowered with a clang. It was full of jars and cloth bags for general collection. It was bigger, heftier, than the one she used in the winter. Her four drying racks came down. One was on its last leg. It creaked and threatened to fall over when she unfolded it.

"I've got to get the other half of these down." Eshail pointed to the opposite peg on the other side of the room. "Can you hang this sign up in the window in place of my normal one?"

Eshail handed over one of her favorite possessions. The first year she'd come to town, the only person who'd befriended her, who wasn't afraid of her, had been the town herald, Evelyn. At that point, Evelyn had been newly appointed. Many said she was too young to hold the office. Many thought Eshail was too young to be the village witch. They'd bonded, and one of the first acts of real friendship had been Evelyn hand painting a sign that said "Closed for

Harvesting," which had green reeds and swamp ivy. She kept the sign hanging in her workroom, a keepsake of a young friendship.

"Sure, but then you'll have to tell me what all of this"—Yates waved at the tools and baskets and implements of a witch's harvesting production—"is for."

Eshail nodded, waving her off as she untwined the second peg. This side of the room had to be let down much more carefully. Several crates of jars were tied up. One of the things Tarwa had drilled into her over the years was the careful washing and storage of her jars. A good alchemist didn't run out of glassware, nor did she use dirty ones. Each jar would be sealed tight. During the year, Eshail thoroughly washed the jars, and each crate had a simple sanitation charm on it that would continue the magical cleansing until this moment, when she would break the seals on the crates and test them for magic neutrality.

They lowered slowly. Her arm muscles might not be substantial, but she had the wiry strength most swamp goblins did. Sheer bulk didn't help one survive day in and day out—it was about agility and endurance.

Three stacks of crates stood full of jars. The final thing to be dropped from the eaves was another basket full of her good harvesting tools. She had a set she'd use daily when she needed to quickly gather something or go out into the garden.

These tools, however, were enhanced. One of the gifts—typically given to a young witch by her family when she crosses the threshold into adolescence—is a nice set of harvesting implements: a brush cutter, a bog scoop, two sharp snips of different sizes, a hand trowel, a bog net, and a mud rake. Her gathering vest snaked down from the rafters. She had a waterproof wax tally sheet on which she'd list her priorities after she'd chalked it all out and a grease marker for taking tallies in the field. Eshail checked to make sure her most prized practical possession was still in its triple-buttoned pocket residence (she didn't want to ever drop it accidentally into a murky pool, or some other unfortunate mishap). The reassuring weight of her finding stone sat in its pocket, lined with stitching to charge it.

The finding stone had limited charges for the year, but when she got down to her last few objectives, normally, it would steer her into the right area of the swamp where the rarer herbs had propagated that year. Some things stayed the same, like the aspen on the Firedrake Island; other herbs like the heart thorn moved around to the most ideal location for their seeds from the previous year.

Eshail knew where things generally grew year after year—like reeds; she couldn't sneeze in the swamp without hitting a patch of them. Others, though, were the perennials that poked up because a bird gifted the swamp with its dropping or a squirrel just happened to forget its buried treasure. Those were harder to track and spot. Some years, depending on her luck, she did not use the stone at all. Other years, it was the only thing that saved her from absolute disaster.

"So what now?" the Easterner broke her from the reverie of remembering past hunts.

"I'm going to get you suited up—wool socks, your shoes, and I've got a shoe sheath for you. I'll admit, I should have given these to you when we went out yesterday." She handed what looked like a pair of giant socks over to Yates. "Put them on over your shoes, and it'll mostly keep you dry. What's better, though, it'll keep the leeches off your skin. They can't climb the fiber, so you'll be fine if you don't go into deeper water."

Thayatesh's face was a study of self-control. Burning leeches off wasn't a fun experience.

"So you had a solution to leeches that I could have used?"

"No one said witches weren't vindictive." She paused for effect. "But normally we don't wear these until spring. Winter swamps, there's just not enough leeches to bother." Yates paled at the assertion, thinking of the pools having *more* leeches in them now.

"I mean, that's probably one of the top traits my people associate with you all. Vindictive, evil, eaters of babies."

"Well, one out of three isn't bad."

They shared a smile. It took two hours to get all the equipment ready, distributed, and dressed. The reed hats Eshail insisted on were the last bit. They had longer floppy brims meant to kick any snakes falling from above away from the wearer. Although having a snake land on the brim wasn't fun, it was better than having a blue marble wriggling in one's hair.

Eshail took a moment to look at her chalked-out list, adding bits to her wax paper to remember. On this first trip into the bush, she had a routine established, grabbing some of the most common items. If Tarwa had sprung spring as she'd promised, this first day would be about finding the first blush of life. If things progressed as she suspected they would, by the end of the week, every mid-season herb would be up and blooming. Tawra had that effect on an area.

"I look like a witch." The Easterner couldn't hide her distaste.

"A witch? No, you don't have the glint of magic around you. You've got the look of an Evermoss native. Most of the village has some version of this outfit. Many make a living harvesting from the swamp and sending it north to the mountains or to the coast through trade. Your wagon, while odd for this time of year, is normally a common site in the northern villages. We have many of the continent's delicacies wriggling in our waters."

"Yes, my mother used to talk about the legends of some of the food that came across into the East. I must say, I've been pretty unimpressed with the fare here so far."

"Do your peasants in the East eat as the king?"

Thayatesh turned red at the commentary. Of course, the answer was no.

"Let's do this. The first trip is going to be a quick turnaround. We're going to get some young cattail shoots; they'll enhance the diet. Another reason you haven't been feasting while here is that we don't have much in our stores from the long winter. We're going to look for gorum plants. They have bladed leaves that are found near your feet and grow near cattails."

"What do you use them for?"

"They're good for digestion but, more importantly, can help with aches. I often prescribe them to the elderly in the village. I've used my last stores on you."

"You didn't pack any jars in my bag."

"I have a few in case we run into a rarer varietal, but these first couple trips are going to be about quality."

They left out the back door, avoiding the men undoubtedly still watching the front. Eshail hadn't had time to turn her barren garden at the end of the season, so dried vines and dead bushes adorned its beds. If she'd been honest, it hadn't been about time—it had been about desire. She hated digging into the ground in the last part of the year. It gave a finality to a season she always hoped to avoid. Being low all winter hadn't helped either.

The two fell into a companionable silence as they left the village. The hard pack of the streets gave way to the springy nature of a ground made mostly of detritus and water. The coming of Tarwa and the magical spring she brought had turned the chirps from the previous day into a cacophony. The migratory birds hadn't returned yet, but the bugs, frogs, and anything that'd been hibernating had come out. This meant Tarwa would *have* to stay until the winter fully turned, or she risked killing off a vast collection of the swamp's native wildlife.

Cattails were typically found at boundaries. They

were used in some otherwordly arts that Eshail had never dabbled in. They helped establish boundaries in magic between the living and the dead. Chalk lines that wouldn't hold up against powerful spirits or creatures when woven in reeds did just fine.

Eshail took them north of town, toward the deeper waters. The edge of the swamp into the patchwork of mini-lakes that made up most of the northern expanse of the Evermoss was a prime location for cattails; the shallow lakes in the summer were choked with lilies, and the unwary fisher could get capsized by a jumping carp.

Eshail repeated the words her mother had told her as a child: "You'll need to put on those gloves when we get to the area. Cattails are hearty, and the edges of their leaves can be sharp. We will reach down and pull from the base, bringing the roots with us. We're going to process a bunch onsite. Most of it I'll personally use, but the blades of the leaves we'll bring back for the weaver's collective."

"What do they give you for the leaves?"

"Nothing. Cattails are too numerous to be particularly valuable, but I don't like leaving waste when I harvest when I don't have to. We're going to collect the core of the shoot, the roots, and the cattail slime."

"Slime?"

"You'll see."

They walked under cedars, the air spicy with their scent. The cedar stand was one of Eshail's favorite places to go in the summer, baking in the warm aroma. She'd frequently prescribe young mothers to take themselves into the cedarwood and allow themselves a moment of calm. They'd started calling the grove the Motherwood. Eshail approved.

It didn't take long before they broke through the forest. To the uninitiated, one might naturally assume they'd broken into a clearing, but five steps into the muck and six inches of water would cause those illusions to be dashed.

"My people have stories of this place, too."

Eshail raised her eyebrows, demonstrating how to pull a cattail. "Yeah?"

"Yes, they consider it cursed. This is where the western expansion stopped cold. An army's logistical needs could not cope with these lakes."

Eshail hadn't ever thought of her home in those terms. She pulled another clump and watched as Thayatesh joined in. "Was it bad?"

"The worst. They bogged down immediately, and then the fever came."

Sweat fever was common near the lakes; the mosquitoes that bred it liked deeper pools of water than the standard variety. The sweat fever could be deadly if, like the Easterners, one wasn't aware of the crush of sweatbane root, a fibrous chew that most in the Evermoss gnawed on habitually.

"I'm going to start you processing while I pull some more roots." At this point, they had a pile several feet tall. "What you're going to do is cut the roots off and throw them in their own pile. Then cut between the white of the stalk and the green of the leaves." This left about a handspan of the stalk and the rest of the leaves. "Do ten to twenty and let me know."

Eshail watched the first few, but the woman was inept and slow, though good enough for now.

Eshail went on the hunt for gorum. It grew in the matted grass groundscape closer to the firmament. Finding some, she reached down and pulled at the base. The ground was moist with the spring thaw. It'd been a while since she'd been able to draw anything with any success out of the soil.

"We have a tradition in the Eastern Empire among the women."

"Yeah? What's that?" Eshail's voice was muffled as

she bent down to pull another gorum out of the cattails.

"Storytelling, legend weaving when doing work like this." Eshail looked at Yates in mild astonishment. She didn't expect it from the Easterner. The woman was crouched over a pile of cattails dutifully slicing them in the prescribed manner. Her floppy hat folded around her face, framing it with her hair pulled up. She looked like an Evermoss native.

"Did *you* do much work like this?" Eshail asked, but thought it didn't matter. Yates was suited to the work.

There was silence for a moment, then Yates raised her head, brown eyes meeting Eshail's. "No, but I listened sometimes." More proof that the princess theory was correct. Yates gave her a smile that lit up her face. For a moment, Eshail found herself entranced in the glow up. "I'll give you a story of my people if you give one of yours."

Eshail, intrigued, agreed, "Alright, you first."

She was used to doing this work alone or with Hedwarg or Druff. Neither were talkers, but that didn't mean the work *had* to be done in silence. And for a moment, she wanted to just listen to Yates's voice.

Chapter 20

My story comes from a time before the Blight, when the desert was full of life and magic.

Thayatesh waved off the question that immediately came to Eshail's mouth: *Magic? In the desert?*

A prince of the sand existed, and his power was that of the sand people. Every twenty years, with the flooding rains, the sand people would emerge from the wilderness muddy and full of life from their hibernation. They came into our cities seeking food and companionship for a season, only to return to their homes in the end. It was a time of festival and celebration. One prince, Hedestrol, was more handsome than most. They were all handsome people, though, not an ugly one among them.

Hedestrol went into a village and fell madly in love with a summer companion: a maiden who stole his heart, Teona. She had long blonde locks and skin as smooth as milk and honey. What impressed him most, however, was her old soul. The sand people could sense these things. She spoke with grace, and they shared their knowledge of life and the cycle.

Eshail had so many questions, but she kept them to herself. This was a moment of listening. She bent down, pulling at another gorum plant, her ears fully attentive.

The tragedy of Hedestrol's people was that they were doomed to leave. The call of hibernation was too strong for anyone to resist. Every time they emerged, the elders would warn the people not to commit the sin of loving a dry-lander, for ultimately, that was a love on barren soil. In every cycle, someone would forgo their lessons and enter their hibernation with a shattered heart. Many times, this resulted in death, for who can survive twenty years on nothing but sorrow?

Both peoples knew the risk of their liaisons and kept their trysts light. The sand people, you see, lived the same length of life as us mere mortals, but it was broken out along the line of centuries. Each emergence lasts less than a year of a normal life. Teona had also fallen for her prince, however she was wiser than he. When the cycle came to an end and the rains stopped, she knew he was destined to return to his own people. To the sleep of two decades.

She loved Hedestrol such that she didn't want him to die of a broken heart, even if it meant she'd have to deal with the separation. So, on the last night, before the people were to make their trek home, she stayed with him, listening to his plans to stay. He concluded with what he thought was his masterful avoidance of fate: giving up his magic to join the mortal realm. Teona held his hands, looked into his eyes, and told him the truth.

"I love you with all of my heart, but you can't stay here with me, my love. I will be here when you return, and my heart will be yours, even if I share it with another."

The prince's mouth was full of objections. He was willing to sacrifice everything, you see. Even for the slimmest possibility of success.

The maiden waved him away. She promised her love and the twining of their lives.

The next time his people emerged, she was no

longer a maiden. She had a husband and a set of children and ran the cactus processing for the village. Hedestrol was still young, still beautiful, and still deeply in love with her. Teona came to him, as promised, and her beauty was enhanced with the passage of age, not diminished.

"My love, you remembered me?" Hedestrol asked, tears in his eyes as she greeted him at the emergence. Although she had a husband, they'd married with an understanding that this moment would come and that they'd be separated for a season.

The two lovers spent every waking hour together, gathering in the fields, bouncing babies on their knees, and hunting kinsnap among the sage. They lived and loved harder than the first emergence. This time, the prince was even more determined to stay, knowing that twenty more years would be harder on his matron's body. Many didn't live beyond fifty, the temperamental nature of time.

Again, wise beyond her years, Teona resisted his insistence. "My love, you will die here in the dry sun of my life. You need to return to your people. I will be here when you emerge again, as will my children."

Distraught, Hedestrol offered the prize all mortals wished for. It was something given once every ten generations and something he dearly wished he'd done when they'd met. "My love, what if you were to come with me? Join me in the undying cycle?"

Teona gave him a smile, which they both knew was a rejection of the gift. "You will have my heart until the end of time, but my life I must keep, my children, you see." She didn't mention her husband, for while she loved him, she hadn't given him her heart.

"When I emerge next time, will you join me? Your children will be older," Hedestrol pressed, needing something to tide him over until the next cycle in the sun.

"We'll see, love of my heart, now go," Teona said, pushing him, like a young lover, toward his home as the

sun rose high in the sky. His skin had already started to dry out, and she worried that he'd turn into stone if he didn't hurry.

Years passed, and the matron became a grandmother. She now had smile lines and crow's feet encircling her face. Her hair was no longer blonde but a glistening silver. She had handed off the day-to-day cactus processing to her eldest son and had shifted to a simple life of weaving.

The emergence happened earlier in that cycle. Some whispered as they emerged that the prince had brought them early into the mortal realm. The prince came at a run to the village at the edge of the immortal resting. He was greeted with a smile and a hug as he ran unerringly to his love.

"You've grown even more beautiful with age!" Hedestrol was still young and spry. He hadn't aged more than a year since they'd first met. "I feel as though I've grown old dreaming of this moment with you."

Teona gave him a smile, and they spent every waking moment together. She told him of her life, her children's pursuits, and the sorrows she'd endured. As she told him of her plans, her new craft of weaving, and the mastery she was pursuing, the prince knew the truth. She was not going to return with him this cycle either.

Hedestrol didn't let his sadness impact their time together. They had a love that transcended mortality and time. They walked through the wet desert and watched cacti bloom for the first time in twenty years. In his world, this was the desert, full of life and abundance. He never experienced the struggle of life on the edge and the constant fight for a living that Teona had. She rejoiced in the beauty, the water that gave her village life. She knew what he didn't: that if he stayed with her, the cycle would stop. It was the prince and his people that brought life to the desert.

When it came time to return to the great hibernation, the prince was determined to stay. He knew that she wouldn't return with him, not with her life as it was, and he was going to make the most of the rest of her life and spend it with her.

Teona would have none of it. Their love wasn't worth putting the well-being of the entire village at risk. She told him no. She even lied that her heart didn't belong to him anymore, that time had stripped them away from each other—but he saw through it.

The way of true love is always the way of forgiveness, and despite their fight and differences, Hedestrol forgave her as he returned to his undying meadow. He looked back as he entered the realm of his people to catch one last sun-soaked vision of his love, knowing that it would likely be the last image he had of her.

The next emergence was late. Hedestrol came with a heavy heart, knowing that Teona would not be there to greet him. To his utter amazement, the glorious vestige of his love stood leaning against the fence. She was hunched and wrinkled but as beautiful as the day they'd met—more so because her presence was such a joyous surprise.

"You're late!" Teona greeted him with a smile comprised of tea-stained teeth.

"Not possible," Hedestrol stated, grinning as he hugged her gently. They spent a season together, slower this time. She showed him the work of her family and the master weaving that she'd done in his honor. The weave showed the four seasons pinwheeled from a handsome replica of himself.

"You see," Teona said in a voice leathered with age, "this was how it was meant to be. The weave wills it. It is sad but also right."

"I think there's a mistake," the prince said softly, realizing from the very beginning of the visit that this time there would certainly not be another. "The weaving depicts

a circle. When you depart this realm, it will be finished. I wish you'd come with me, or I stayed with you."

"Ah, my dear, you live so shallowly that you don't understand the way of things yet. Love is eternal. Just because my mortal body fails doesn't mean we won't find each other again."

They spent the season together. As the way of all seasons, it came to a close. Despite Hedestrol's pleading, Teona declined to join him in the immortal realm.

Twenty years had passed—a blink to the immortal, a lifetime to the mortal.

Eshail had stopped harvesting. She was completely invested. Marveling in Yates's way of words, in the story of immortal love.

The prince of sand walked slowly to the village of his love, knowing what he would not find leaning against a fence post waiting for him. Hedestrol followed the obligation of his people; he knew his duty. He walked forward, ready for disappointment. Now that he knew what true love was, his heart wasn't in the dance.

He squinted into the sunlight. The fence line was empty, but to his amazement, Teona leaned against the lone tree on the horizon, as young as the day they'd met.

"My love, it is so good to see you." The immortal rushed to the woman, never so happy.

Her smile was like coming home. "You sound familiar, but I don't believe we've met."

The lesson hit the circle, the beginning after the end.

"I think we've met in another life," the prince said, "but let me introduce myself."

"Well, what'd you think?"

Eshail wiped a tear from her eye. A couple. It took her a moment to remove the frog lodged in her throat. "It was good." The words weren't eloquent, but the emotion behind them was genuine. "I, ah, I didn't take you for a romantic."

"I always loved that story as a child. I'd ask my nanny to tell it as a bedtime story. To know that my love, whoever she was, was out there. I'd just have to find her."

Eshail bent and pulled more gorem up. Her basket was filling quicker now that she wasn't listening to a love story. If this story was the heart of Thayatesh, then what was she doing looking for a love potion for a loveless marriage? The question was too obvious to ask.

"Alright, I'm ready for whatever's next."

"Ah, time to harvest the slime."

"Ah, right. Lovely. I've been so looking forward to this part." Yates laid the sarcasm on thick.

"Here, let me show you." Eshail grinned, pulling out a jar and sat down on the grassy bed Thayatesh was crouched in. She nestled the jar in the grasses and grabbed one of the cattail hearts. "You've got to peel off a layer and then scrape both sides against the curve of the jar." Thayatesh leaned close, trying to see. Eshail used a fingernail to peel the top layer off, and a gooey slime separated the layers. She moved the freed leaf quickly to the jar and used her hand to apply pressure to the edge. "If you do this right, most of the slime will pool to the bottom of the jar. If you do this wrong, you'll be covered in it." Eshail said this, knowing very well it was impossible for a novice harvester not to end up covered in the antiseptic slime.

Thayatesh tried it, the layer of reed slipping through her fingers immediately and sticking to the grass. Yates giggled, a sound Eshail hadn't heard from the serious woman.

Eshail leaned in, whispering, "You've got to hold it tighter." The light scent of Yates alluringly filled her senses with sandalwood and patchouli.

The world froze for a heartbeat; the swamp silenced in Eshail's mind. The words between them hung in the air.

Time resumed. It was only an instant and a breath caught in the chest. Eshail knew, though, that she was in for trouble.

Chapter 21

Eshail and Yates processed five loads of cattails that afternoon, including two jars of slime that could be used as a soother and for keeping wounds clean. They also brought back bundles of reeds to the weavers, who always looked kindly on materials they didn't have to harvest themselves.

They'd washed the roots and set them out to dry overnight so they wouldn't rot stored wet.

Which left the hearts. Eshail had put each of them into jars, several of which now adorned shelves in the main room of her shop. They'd returned to find the door restored. Eshail suspected Evelyn had a hand in the repair. Yates began stripping out of her swamp harvesting gear, and the two fell into a comfortable rhythm, taking care of the packs and supplies. There was an ease to their interactions Eshail hadn't experienced before.

Eshail began heating the stove to work on dinner.

"You owe me a story." Yates was lounging in the front room chair, the dark curls of her hair had been released from the confines of her hat. She was now outfitted in one of Evelyn's more masculine green and blue button-ups with baggy pajama pants. The woman looked completely comfortable and at home. Sore but healed. The day's labor had been good and productive. It'd taken both of their minds off of the trouble brewing. It was exactly what they both had needed.

"I'm not one much for fairy tales. Can you imagine Tarwa telling a bedtime story like that?"

"No, although are witches not the thing of bedtime stories?" Yates shifted to see better where Eshail was cooking. "If you can't tell me a fairytale, tell me something real. Something of you."

A thrill of pleasure and fear, *something of you.* Eshail mentally pictured the chalkboard of the memories of her life. She didn't want to be too personal, but also not too distant.

"Tell me about Evelyn. The two of you."

Eshail winced. Not the type of story she really wanted to share. "Nothing to tell. We're just friends. Evelyn is special—you've seen that surely yourself. She's admirable, loveable even." There was a wistfulness she couldn't hide.

"She is an interesting woman."

"I told you before, she's built differently. Her energy is almost irresistible to a witch, that safe confidence. It is something we don't have enough of in our lives."

"Okay, then, something else. Tarwa?"

"You know how to hit the sensitive parts, don't you?"

Yates just smiled. "You know all my secrets. It's only fair. Wasn't she supposed to join us for dinner tonight?"

"I sent her a message to swing by for breakfast instead." She'd sent it in the way of her childhood: with a firefly illusion blinking in their family code. "It's been a long day. A good day." She gave Yates a soft smile. "I wanted to avoid having her spoil the mood." The lie was waiting to be discovered.

"Okay, so tell me of you and Tarwa. She's your mother?"

"She's *a* mother. She's my third mother. The one who bore me—my birth mother—died during my arrival to the world." Eshail didn't know it, but the lit candles dimmed a moment. "The second who took me in as a squalling child unnamed died of a fever after we fled a village, almost burned by an ignorant people." This time, she noted that one of the candles flickered and died. A portent, perhaps. "Tarwa is my third mother, given to me from the generosity of the All Mother. She's the one who took me in as a true orphan and taught me much of the craft."

"Yet you're at odds; I can see it. Anyone in the same room as the two of you can see it."

"That's a story I suppose I can tell," Eshail said, going into the back room and bringing forward a stashed bottle of wine. She'd changed into a light multicolored skirt she'd gotten from the wandering folk. Its bright colors were those of spring. She wore a sleeveless blouse since she'd be cooking. The material was cream colored, soft and breathable. A nice change after the winter's wools. "You want some? I'm going to need a little to get through this tale."

"Sure, I'll take a glass. But if it's that bad, we can talk about something else."

Druff sat on the counter, ever watchful. Eshail considered taking the out offered by Yates, but the cat stood in judgment. It was time to lance the wound. With a swirl, she danced two wine glasses off of a shelf. Looking at the mostly unused second, she took a moment to dip it in wash water, removing the dust.

The cork gave a satisfying pop and smelled of fruit and spice—a perfect pair for her story.

"I'm going to tell you not of the beginning, but of the end." The end spoke more of who she was today, not her childhood hopes and dreams.

Tarwa never really took to being called mother. She

wanted an apprentice much more than she wanted a daughter. I'd been living as a young barmaid in my hometown for six months after my mother was killed. I think the reason she came for me was because she'd hoped for an heir to her power.

I disappointed her in all of the ways that counted. My expertise turned out to be love potions, something neither of us valued. My harvesting skills were average, as was my mastery of every other skill a powerful witch needed. I wasn't the powerful witch apprentice she needed, but an average, fairly unambitious child. When I called Druff from the ether, I thought I'd finally stumbled upon something Tarwa would be proud of. Familiar casting is a sought-after skill, and few, as young as I'd been, were successful. You see, a familiar is one of the things that make our lonely lives a touch more bearable.

I'd been contemplating leaving for a bit, but I wasn't sure I'd make it on my own. My mother hadn't, and she'd been a witch for decades by the time I entered her life. Our southern villages are close to the Blighted Lands, and its taint reaches out occasionally. Poisons the flocks. In the South they rely on livestock more than the North. A disease got into the herd, and they blamed the only person within reach that they could.

It's challenging to balance people's misfortune with the finicky nature of fortune and mortality. Witches are like cattails. We exist on the border of society. We are the willing gatekeepers between life and death. Villagers are not always so discerning between cause and effect, between those who can sometimes tip the scales, and the true power of the Nest Mother.

Eshail walked over to Druff and petted his silky fur.

The day I summoned Druff was the best day of my life. Hands down. Consequences be damned.

Tarwa had not taught me the summoning spell. I snuck into her casting room and read it by candlelight.

When I read it, it blazed in my head. I repeated the incantation from my memory every night before bed. I think all of my frantic energy wrote the enchantment on my soul. It took me a month to gather all the ingredients and prepare, and I kept it all in my head and soul. The night I performed the magic was a full moon. It's not a requirement, but I knew it'd be the time that worked best.

I snuck out of the house to the meadow I found most peaceful. I'd pulled away the weeds, herbs, and brush to create a patch of bare firmament. With the Witch's Sand, I drew out the figure as told in the book, and I wove the magic. It was like nothing I'd ever experienced. I saw the web, the weave, the circle, and I tugged on a thread.

Eshail looked lovingly at Druff, who headbutted her arm.

Druff was the thread. He didn't come to me that night. At first, I was distraught. I'd stayed up all night, waiting for my familiar, sure they would come trotting out of the mist that'd developed. When nothing came, I thought I'd failed, which was silly because I knew what I'd done. I'd seen the threads of my life, all of them. I didn't know where they all led, but I knew they were out there.

It took Druff a week, but when he sauntered out of the woods and into our house, I knew.

And so did Tarwa.

See, what I hadn't understood when I wove my great magic was that Tarwa once had a familiar. She lost it. I don't know how, but losing a connection to one's soul as deep as a familiar's . . . There isn't a pain much worse.

I'd ripped open a wound so deep, so festered. I'm fairly certain she has never forgiven me for the sin. I could feel the tether, the weave between us, stretch, break.

She did not kick me out—that's not the way of witches. I was no longer her heir. Not that I made a good one, but there wasn't an ounce of warmth in the house after that. I made plans to leave, to start my life as a village witch—a caretaker. She did what one expects of a mother once I let her know. She found this village, set up the wards on my home, and introduced me to the locals. Then she left.

In the six years I've lived here, she's never visited, outside of now. There'd been a winter where the flu was particularly harsh, and I'd caught it. She brought supplies to the village to get us all back to health before there were deaths. A friend of hers, another witch, came by and took care of us all.

Being a witch is lonely. One reason why I put so much of my heart into Evelyn is that, while she might not be my love, she's given me the kindness of friendship over the years. Between her and Hedwarg and Druff, they've kept me whole in a world where I don't have much in the way of friends or family.

Her story wasn't as happy as Thayatesh's, but it was the story of her life. It was a piece of her that she hadn't uttered to a soul in the world. In some ways, the fact that the Easterner would be leaving made it easier. That someone out in the world would know a fragment of her story, would know her heartache.

Two arms wrapped around her in a hug. "I'm sorry you've had to bear this all alone." Eshail didn't know what to do at first. Her body tensed at the unexpected touch. The warmth of Thayatesh's words and the squeeze of kindness melted something in her. For a moment, she indulged and leaned into the woman, pretending she was someone who cared about her. That cared *for* her.

She closed her eyes and imagined Yates as a thread, *the thread* she'd seen stretch out into the world—her mud prince, even if fleeting.

The moment didn't last. The fire popped, and Eshail instinctively opened her eyes and made for the stove. Her iron pan was hot, ready for the cattail hearts. Yates followed her to the waiting stove. Eshail put a bit of butter in the pan, watching it melt. When the moment was right, she upturned an entire jar of hearts into the mess of butter, stirring the sizzling pan.

"This smells good."

"You're in for a treat if you haven't had these before." Eshail added a few spices she'd saved for a special occasion—a bit of salt, a grind of pepper, a touch of sweetness, and a dash of heat. The hearts grew limp like the noodles Talin sometimes worked into his specials. Eshail slowed her stirring, letting a few edges get a touch brown, then she scooped them off into a bowl. Grabbing two forks, she walked back into the main room. She didn't have a kitchen table like those in family homes. Instead they dragged her two chairs close, putting the plate of food on the footstool between them.

Yates reached out and petted Druff's head. "I think it was worth it."

"Tarwa would disagree."

"It was time for you to venture out on your own. If it hadn't been Druff, it'd have been something else. You were meant to stand on your own two feet. You're not a Tarwa replica, and at least this way, you got to do it with Druff. Can you imagine starting this life without him? Doing it alone?"

The woman had a point. Eshail gave Yates a fork and stabbed one of the hearts, bringing it to her mouth. It was fibrous but tender, holding the spices well. The morsel was sweet at first, and as it sat in her mouth, the heat of it grew. Yates followed her lead, stabbing one and blowing on it gently before stuffing it into her mouth. She watched as the woman chewed, contemplating the seasonings. Eshail drank another sip of wine.

Yates closed her eyes, a smile tugging at the sides of her mouth. She was savoring the new taste.

"This is good. Why don't you eat it all the time?"

"Well, it's a lot of work. It's a treat for those who work hard."

They ate in silence for a while. The fire was still popping, and Druff curled up to watch the two dine.

Eshail wasn't sure if it was her curiosity or the wine that made her brave. She may have just been drunk on sharing a part of her own truth. "Is that why you're going back? Because you can't imagine starting a new life alone?"

Yates had been savoring each bite as though it were a rare delicacy brought before a king. It probably was to the East, beyond the desert.

"It's more than that," she said in a way that told Eshail that it probably wasn't. "My family, as I imagine you've gathered, is one of importance. My marriage would be one of the keys to my father's strategy in playing in the sands of time. It will secure an alliance between us and a house we'd been at odds with for years."

"That sounds like a cold way to treat a daughter."

"Perhaps to you, but it is the way of those who seek power within the Empire. My father is better than most. He let me grow up as I willed it. I learned the necessary things, such as reading, weaving, riding a horse, and arranging a household."

"I have a hard time picturing you arranging a household."

"Believe it or not, I could probably sweep through your system of storage, even the village's system of management, and make significant changes for the positive."

Eshail raised her eyebrows; she didn't believe anyone, but maybe Evelyn could make good on that claim. It was hard to imagine the princess in front of her accomplishing such a feat. Her cheeks felt warm from the wine.

"The problem is, I got to be my own. I read books on adventure; I learned how to swordfight; I climbed trees and dreamed of a life that was never meant to be mine."

"You ran away in the end." Eshail was trying to be

kind.

"Only to find a solution I could live with, a way to turn off my brain from wanting to be me. The man I am betrothed to—I've met him. He's not an unkind soul. He's my age, well-spoken, and . . . not an idiot. My father could have done much, much worse. It's just . . ."

"It's just he's not *your* mud prince—or rather princess."

Thayatesh gave her a pained smile. "It's crazy, insane to me how casually you make that connection. Something I've fought my whole life, you never questioned."

"It's not a question; you know it. But witches have always known the truth. The arc of humanity is wide, and the variations are infinite. There are worse attributes to be stuck with."

"Cursed with, you mean. In the East, it's a curse."

This time, Eshail reached out, squeezing Thayatesh's arm, "It's not a curse here."

The two women looked down at the last cattail heart. Eshail did the only acceptable thing and waved Yates to take it. She watched the eager woman chew, and she studied her face—the arch of her nose, the brown eyes, the line of her jaw. Her hair was extra curly from the humidity of the day. She had a distant look on her face, enjoying the cattail heart and contemplating her fate. Either way, there was something irresistible about the look. Eshail had to pick at it.

"What are you thinking now?"

Yate's dark brown eyes snapped to her face, and Eshail found the new heat in her face had nothing to do with the wine. The woman swallowed the last of their meal. "I was thinking that in a different time, in a different place, I could see the appeal of this little town you've made home." The words weren't quite right, but the smile on her face was perfect—a sunbeam at the right temperature on her favorite chair—just right.

Eshail gave in to the feeling and leaned forward, bringing her lips against Yates's. At first, she was frozen, firm, in shock. Eshail's heart dropped, realizing she'd made a mistake. Before she could pull away, however, Yates returned the kiss, leaning into it. They floated in time, and the witch's heart sang. The kiss made the world anew. Her future changed in front of her. She closed her eyes, savoring the feeling, a kiss to remake a life.

It ended abruptly, Yates pulling away. "I'm sorry. I shouldn't have—I can't—this isn't—" The words came tumbling out of the Easterner's mouth, crashing through the illusion Eshail'd conjured.

"It's okay. I'm the one at fault. I shouldn't have pushed your boundaries." Eshail said it calmly, hiding the wave of disappointment and dashed hope.

"I'm going to go to bed if that's okay."

Eshail nodded numbly, the blossom in her heart wilting on the spot. "No problem. You should probably still sleep downstairs in case we have another uninvited guest."

Chapter 22

The next morning started early. When Eshail woke, the Easterner was already up, filled with nervous energy. Tarwa's ambiance may have healed her body, but Eshail's presence fractured her mind. Eshail felt guilty. She'd known that the kiss and those feelings were anathema. She had no right to push the woman's boundaries. The moment had just *felt* right.

Eshail was bad at reading those moments, at reading people. As evidenced by last year and the Evelyn debacle.

She tried to make it right. "About last night, I'm sorry. I didn't mean to offend you."

"Just a misunderstanding, I'm good." The words belied the room's mood, but Eshail wasn't going to push it.

Eshail nodded. "Yeah, everything's fine with me. It seems as though you've been busy . . . ?"

The Easterner had gotten several buckets of water from the well and had been washing various jars. She rearranged the ones they'd collected the day before and seemingly scrubbed every surface in the front room.

"Yes, your shop, it needed some help. It had been bothering me since I arrived. I wanted to do something for you to thank you for everything you've done for me."

"I see." A small part of Eshail wondered if there

was more to it, but she decided she'd take the statement at face value for the woman's sanity. "Well, thank you, I think. I know you told me you were good at household organization, but I'll have to trust you for now. I did have a system."

"Oh yes, I know. You had your ingredients separated by purpose. I know enough to know that, but I think it's more helpful to have them alphabetically. If magic is like cooking, and from what I've seen you do of it, it is. Then, your different herbs have multiple applications, so you can quickly find whatever you need. Plus, as a bonus, those who *don't* practice the dark arts can find what they need too." She'd grinned at her joke.

"Well, I guess that works, although it ruins the mysterious ambiance my spell webs created when the ingredients overlapped."

"You know it's better this way."

Eshail wasn't going to give in yet, although she could see the appeal. "Are you ready for another day of collecting? Today's going to be a bit different. We're going to visit several sites for a variety of plants to restore some of my main stocks."

"I'm here to serve. I'm feeling much better, but I probably shouldn't leave your or Tarwa's care until this leg rash heals." She pulled up a pant leg to expose a circular rash along a couple of spots where they'd removed leeches. They were infected.

"That doesn't hurt?"

"Not really. It just itches."

"Itching is good. It means it's healing. Let's get a bit of the slime we collected yesterday on it, and I'll prioritize a couple of collections today that will help. Today we're going to have to be more careful. We're going into the true Evermoss."

"We weren't yesterday?"

"Not quite. We were still at the edge of the village

knoll. Those lakes are beaver-made, but you tend to get safer species of snakes and other inhabitants in the deeper water. We will go back to a place like where the firedrakes live. There will be swamp puppies, multiple varieties of poisonous snakes, frogs, and leaves. Also, I'm sure you won't forget the leeches."

"I don't think I'll ever forget the leeches."

Eshail crooked her head. "It'll be better this time."

"If you say so."

"I do. Now suit up. I will run to the tavern and check on the progress the village has been making on the Blight. I will be back quickly, and we'll head out."

Yates acknowledged, and Eshail skipped out the door before either of them could make it more awkward. She walked slowly to the tavern, trying to give her head a moment to clear. The shop talk had helped smooth things over, but it was still awkward. She cursed herself for making it such. She knew better. She'd just thought. Well, in a moment of weakness, she'd thought they'd made *that sort* of connection.

Even now, her heart fluttered a bit, which she cursed. First Evelyn, and now the first stranger that walked into the village with the same bend of her nature. Eshail shook herself. Was she really that desperate? The answer, in short, was yes. The part of the story she didn't reveal to Yates was she'd been able to see the threads of her life extend out before her.

Eshail had called Druff, her familiar, at that moment, but she'd seen more. She'd seen lines of friendship and one of a more profound love. The type they write stories about. She'd seen those lines in others as she called their familiars and made their own families. Hers had always been dormant, distant, but she had the knowledge that it was there. That she had the capacity for that sort of connection. It made her want it.

Another reason her love potions were such a curse

was that she could brew up that sort of love and keep it. She could force Evelyn to settle down with her and have a passion for her. That ugly truth wasn't even tempting, and it didn't make her heart ache less.

She found herself at the tavern's door, and with a breath, she pushed inside. The room was packed and quiet, doused in the unsettling impact of Tarwa's aura. Magic floated in the air, angry, anxious magic.

Eshail walked over to the command table. If her birthright had no other privileges, her position in the village granted her the privilege of knowledge. Before she could open her mouth, Evelyn shot her a look that said *keep your mouth shut*. She wisely followed the herald's order, waiting patiently as the small group talked.

"It's spread to three more pools along this route." Hedwarg pointed at the map as Evelyn marked it furiously with a red grease pen.

"Why is it spreading so fast? It's spread more in the last day than the previous two weeks," Talin asked, worry lines creasing his face.

"I don't know, but I must set new quarantine lines. We will have to block off a huge section at this point. Choke it off here and here," Evelyn said. She was ever the practical, focusing on the actions required.

Hedwarg spoke again, "That's one of the main veins of water down to Altlaris. They'll be upset if we cut off their primary source of fresh water." He knew the water ways of the Evermoss better than anyone, spending weeks in the push with his companions.

Tarwa's harsh voice cut through the opposition. "They'll be angrier if they get cups full of Blight instead of water. We need to cut it off before it travels further south."

The group looked at the red angry marks snaking through the map, and none argued. Tarwa was right.

Evelyn picked that moment to give Eshail an opening. "Eshail, how's the gathering going?"

"Good, I've processed a fair amount of painkillers. Now I'm moving onto a variety of plants, giving us a bit larger range of options should we need to treat a variety of wounds, or if Tarwa needs to cast something more significant."

"I don't need any of your stores for anything I'm going to do. I brought my own supplies." Tarwa's harsh voice matched her disposition. She looked older than Eshail remembered, the stress of the Blight and the winter etching deeper wrinkles into her face.

Evelyn cut in, trying to save Eshail a bit of pride, "That's great, Eshail. The village will need your services when this is all done." Evelyn gave her an apologetic smile. She was dressed formally, in her white work shirt with her ridiculous purple cloak of office about her shoulders.

"They might. If you'd worked on your aura, you wouldn't have as much need for your skills as an alchemist." The table sat silently, not surprised by Tarwa's rudeness. They'd grown accustomed to her ways in the last day. What was shocking was the way she was treating a witch. No one treated a witch like that for fear they'd be cursed. Little did they know that Eshail's ability to curse someone was as limited as her other greater magics. It was almost nonexistent.

Understanding her mother's dismissal, Eshail gave a curt nod. "Alright, well, I'll be going. We've got a bit to do. Mother, I'm assuming you'll have breakfast here?"

"Oh, I forgot. Yes, I've already had breakfast. We'll catch another meal, once things are less dire." Tarwa waved her off. Eshail grabbed a couple of available travel ration bars for breakfast and left. Evelyn followed her out.

"Eshail, please be careful. We're going to need you eventually," the herald whispered as though Tarwa's ears could reach past the doors and into the street. She was wise to be careful. Eshail'd seen the witch hear a lone cricket across a meadow in the cacophony of summer.

"I'm doing what I can. Yates is decent at the work, so we're moving faster than I expected. What's really going on with the fight against the Blight?"

"It's gotten much, much worse in the last day. We're not sure why, but the growth has spiked significantly. Tarwa's devising a plan, but we'll have to move quickly, or the whole village and surrounding area might be lost." Evelyn dropped her voice further. "If it keeps growing at this rate, the entire Evermoss herself may be in grave danger."

Eshail stared at the herald. The woman wasn't one given to exaggeration. If she was worried that it might not be able to be tamed, they were in dire straits. Eshail found herself contemplating the horror of a world without the swamp.

"We can't let that happen. If it's getting to that point, please bring me in. I would never be able to forgive myself if we lost the village and the Evermoss, and I wasn't in the fight at all. Tarwa's never going to bring me in on her own."

Evelyn nodded. "I will. Right now, do what you can to gather everything you can. I have a feeling we're going to need it."

Eshail returned home, thoughts mired in the war that she wasn't allowed to fight. The awkwardness between her and Yates evaporated as she explained what was happening with the Blight. She handed over the breakfast biscuits as they suited up. She moved much quicker than Yates, taking a quarter of the time it took the Easterner. This time, Eshail took them west, deeper into the Evermoss. The growth was wilder, more prolific, and far less tame.

Fifteen minutes into the journey, a snake fell on top of Thayatesh's head. The impact was loud as it hit dead on. Thankfully the woman had attached her hat correctly, and the snake rebounded several feet away from their heads.

Eshail put herself between Yates and the snake, her snake stick extended. She hummed a small cantrip, calming the blue-marbled snake. She convinced it that they were too big to digest easily. It slithered away unhappily to seek another tree to climb and get into place.

Another five minutes brought the two to their first harvest, the sassafras tree. The tree sat by itself in a small pocket of dryness, the mulch around its trunk built up.

"We need the roots, but we'll want to harvest away from the trunk so we don't damage the tree too much. This is the only sassafras tree close to the village."

"How do you know it's sassafras?"

Eshail leaned into the question, trying to return them to normality: "If you look at the bark, there's an orange interior. That has many uses, but you've got to harvest it sparingly, for it damages the tree. If you look at the leaves, this is a magical tree. Some leaves have one point, while others have two or three. Trees don't do that; most produce only one leaf shape. But because of the magic, sassafras don't follow that pattern."

Yates examined the leaves and stuck her face close to the trunk to see between some cracks. Eshail thought it was both hilarious and adorable.

"I see what you're saying," the woman said, face scrunched against the trunk.

Eshail and Hedwarg had marked a spot where they'd harvested previously, and the stake pointed to an area where they began picking at the soil with her trowels. The soil was moist and loose, easy to remove. Before long, Eshail and Yates were prying at the roots, breaking off chunks and throwing them into bags.

"What do you use this for?"

"A little of everything, but you can't use it too much. As with most things, there's always that thread of something else you don't want."

They continued in silence.

"We're going to visit another tree next, a willow. It's not too far away."

They slogged toward their next goal, their packs a little heavier. As always, Eshail was on the watch for lurking trouble in the swamp. For every "Don't touch that!" and "Stop!" there was a subtler problem Eshail just handled without Yates even being aware. It was irritating. Thayatesh wasn't a native and walked through the swamp like a newborn. She knew this from their trip to the firedrakes, but it hadn't mattered as much. Back then she hadn't truly *cared* for the woman. Now she walked with the anxiety of trying to anticipate every dumb mistake Yates could make.

The emotional flip from simply helping a stranger to caring about the stranger annoyed her. Eshail was tired of her emotions, her attachments. She almost gave into resentment of Yates's presence. Then the woman would flash her a smile or crack a joke and she'd forget her frustration a moment, only to have it returned in a rush.

They went from willow to willow, collecting bark. Then Eshail needed some fire-ash honeybee comb for the folks who had allergies. Finding a nest was always challenging, and while they'd been looking, she'd walked right into a bunch of nettles. She had, in fact needed nettles, which was serendipitous, but it hurt like hell.

Her frustration levels grew until each step in the swamp became a stomp. The bees they couldn't find buzzed in her head like angry wasps. When her boot caught on a vine covered in leaves and she tripped forward, landing face first in the mud. She'd surpassed the boiling point.

"For all the snake-eaten eggs in the nest, be damned swamp!" Eshail let loose in a torrent of curses as she sat up, her entire front covered in a layer of thick muck. The Easterner stood impassively, waiting for the storm to pass.

"Are you alright?" Yates offered a hand up, which Eshail rejected. She just sat in the mud boiling in her irritation.

"Why in the wormwood would I be alright?" Eshail huffed. "I've got to babysit you while I harvest to fill my stores in an off-season harvest because my village is about to be overtaken by the Blight in which I've been deemed useless in the fight against." The hurt bubbled up. "I'm just as useless as I was five years ago and just as alone. The Evermoss is the most challenging and rewarding environment a witch can belong to, but I've only encountered the challenges. You come waltzing into our village with enough supplies to save us from the winter, and the only thing you ask for in return is my integrity. Now we don't have your supplies, you've managed to steal my pride, and we're all doomed, so why am I even trying?"

Thayatesh plopped down in the mud next to her. Eshail had treated both their pants in repellant and increased the salinity of the exterior to keep the leeches away for the moment. The thought was idle and ridiculous; why Eshail cared that there were leeches at this point was beyond her.

"I'm sorry. I've caused more than my share of trouble."

Eshail turned to Yates. "And you!" She pointed, mud flying off her finger as she emphasized her words. "You're *nothing but* trouble. I can't decide if you're just an absolute moron or actually just this naive about how the world works. Why are you still here? You've been magically cured by the powers that repulse you; why are you not yet miles away from my shitty little village?"

Eshail looked at the woman she'd berated, belatedly realizing that when she'd pointed, a plume of mud had flown between them, landing right on Thayatesh's nose. The Easterner, her curls done up and brown eyes wide, just stared at the witch for a moment. She calmly looked down at the muck they sat in, reached into it, and lifted a handful.

"Oh, don't you dare—" Before Eshail could fully

finish the sentence, mud flew between them. It landed right on her forehead. She returned fire, and the two engaged in an old-fashioned mud fight like two of the bairns from the village.

The anger broke when Eshail accidentally landed a glob of mud partially in Thayatesh's mouth. The woman sputtered, spitting it out while dishing one firmly over Eshail's eyes. They stopped, thoroughly covered in grayish brown mud. It caked their clothes, oozed in their hair, and smelled atrocious.

"Oh, Nest Mother, we look ridiculous." Eshail said, wiping the goo from her eyes and cracking a smile as she held back a laugh.

"If my family saw me now, rolling around in the mud with a witch, can you imagine?" They eyed each other, trying to imagine. Then Yates started to laugh. "Retfait's family wouldn't agree to the marriage. That'd be one problem down." She chortled. "My family would disown me. Two problems down. By the seventh dune, I don't recognize myself anymore." Yates found a sturdy tree to lean back on. She looked up at the sky.

Eshail stood, walked over, and sat beside her, back against the same tree. She tipped her head upward.

Yates continued, "Is it crazy? It's the same sky as mine—the same clouds, the same blue hues. The air smells different here. The weight of it is different. I can breathe."

Eshail kept quiet. She wished she could breathe.

"I am sorry I came here and ruined everything for you. I don't think I could have imagined this place, or you, or caring that I'd ruined things for a witch before I came here."

"I guess I should be happy you do now." Eshail wiped some of the mud off of Yates's nose. It would have been an intimate gesture, if successful. Instead she just accidently smeared more mud on the woman's face.

"I don't think it makes anything easier for you. I feel

like the chafe of sand. You get it between things, and each movement makes it worse. I make things worse. Once we conquer this Blight, I need to leave. I can't until I know the outcome of the mess I've made. Until I repay at least some of this debt."

Eshail knew the truth: Yates had to leave. She stood up and offered out a hand. "Well then, let's get to work and finish what we started today."

Chapter 23

Eshail and Yates walked into town like the ancient bush people of the swamp. They were camouflaged entirely in mud. They smelled like Hedwarg on his worst day. It'd been a successful journey though; both of their packs were bursting with their harvest. Eshail had also learned something that she suspected Hedwarg had known for a long time: the creatures of the swamp hadn't bothered them hardly at all, as they'd looked and smelled like they belonged.

The two had repaired what had been broken, at least superficially. They came into the village smiling, clomps of dried mud falling off, leaving a trail. Many who worked in the swamp came in less than good shape; a public wash had been set, and the two dropped their packs off at Eshail's house and walked down to the shower. The water that dripped out of the shower tower was cold, icy even, but they were able to get most of the dirt off. One of the adolescents in the town was tasked with hauling the muck back out to the city's edge every week. They'd left a considerable amount. The two weren't clean by any means, but they were at least not going to flake off mud chunks walking around town. The two borrowed ratty clothes from the communal pile and hauled two buckets of water back to

Eshail's. She promised she'd heat up enough for both of them to get respectably clean.

Evelyn found them both as they rounded the corner of their block with their water haul. They both looked like destitute beggars, still several shades darker than their natural skin tones in oversized moth-eaten rags.

"I heard you two were back," Evelyn said, without a single look at their attire. Instead she looked nervously around the street. "We've got to talk."

The two's jovial moods evaporated instantly. Eshail unlocked the front door of her shop, and the three shuffled in.

"What's going on?" Evelyn eyed the open door and quietly shut it before responding to Eshail's inquiry.

"Things have gotten much worse," Evelyn said in a hushed tone, as if saying it out loud made it real. "I think we've made a fundamental mistake in our strategy against the Blight." As Evelyn started talking, her animated nature took over, each word falling out more rapidly than the last. "It's Tarwa. We know she's the Guardian of the Spring, of growth. The woman walked into our town, buds began forming, flowers blooming, and the world came alive. We didn't account for what that effect would have on the Blight."

Eshail gasped, putting it together.

Thayatesh was still in the dark. "What do you mean?"

"We haven't had to fight the Blight in three hundred years—not here, not really. We don't have the same tools our ancestors did. Tarwa's abilities make things grow. She has made the Blight *grow*." As realization dawned, the horror of the situation became reflected in Yates's face.

"She needs to leave immediately," Eshail said, cutting to the marrow of it. "We need to call in one of the other Guardians. The Guardian of Winter?"

Evelyn shook her head. "The other Guardians are

dealing with other emergencies. Tarwa's all we've got, but I agree, she's got to leave."

"We've been out in the bush. She's more powerful than she was when I was a child. " Eshail waved a hand at the wilderness. "Everything out there is exploding with the pent-up growth of a late spring."

Evelyn was pale. Eshail sensed that she knew it was true, but confronting Tarwa wasn't easy, and they were seemingly doomed either way.

"I'm going to talk to her. Someone has to talk some sense into the pig-headed woman." Eshail watched the tension lines fade in Evelyn's face. She'd learned long ago not to use Witch's Sight on Evelyn for fear of what she thought. But that hadn't prevented their friendship from letting her pick up on the herald's unspoken cues.

Evelyn and Thayatesh flanked Eshail as she marched into the Toadsprigen Inn. Eshail still looked like she belonged to the swamp—she hadn't waited the minutes it'd take to change. Talin and half the village looked up as they entered. Tarwa sat at her table, evaluating the new maps. At a quick glance, Eshail could tell the swamp infection was *much* worse than it'd been a few days back. Tarwa didn't look ruffled. She just sat, her lined face examining the evidence as though she was dissecting a bug. The murmuring of the village stopped as they realized Eshail was there on business. She looked like a wraith come alive to extract the swamp's vengeance.

"Everyone needs to clear the tavern," Eshail stated, using her most commanding voice. Admittedly, she wasn't used to such command or authority. No one reacted, so she tried again, "This is *witches' business*. I want you all out!" The mention of witches' business got folks shuffling to the door.

Evelyn helped, lending her power as village herald. "You too, Talin. We'll let you all back in, but we need an hour. Out, all of you!"

The grumbling increased, but so did the migration to the door. It took a minute, but soon, it was just the four of them.

Tarwa's dry voice broke the silence between the group. "I suppose you have something you want to say to me? Did we really need the theatrics with the townsfolk? They're under stress enough." Evelyn positioned herself halfway between Tarwa and Eshail, indicating she would try to play arbitrator.

"Mother—" Eshail knew instantly the appellation was a mistake. "Tarwa, I'm the village witch. I am owed an update on the progress with the Blight." She knew if she told her mother what was happening, it wouldn't go anywhere. Tarwa was a woman who had to come to her own conclusions or be led to them.

The woman's face soured. "I'm sure Evelyn's told you it's not going well. If you look at the map, you can see the expansion in the last day." They all stepped closer to the table. Yates couldn't hold back a small gasp. The map was covered in red grease. Each pocket of the outbreak had grown almost tenfold, many merging together.

"What's your plan?" Eshail had to push hard. She had to be cold and relentless. She swallowed the fear Tarwa always elicited; this was her village, her people, and her nest.

"I've been executing my plan: monitor the infestation and try different cleansing methods until we identify one that works."

"And what have you tried?" Eshail's voice was unwavering. It was working. She had Tarwa answering *her* and not vice versa.

"We've tried drowning it, which made it spread faster. Pulling up the infected plants just made those touching them sick. I've used some frost magic, which slowed it down temporarily, but spring is finally here, so keeping it frozen isn't a viable option. Right now I've got several of the villagers mixing two different concoctions, one acidic and one poisonous. We'll root out this evil; we just have to find the right method."

Her methodology was sound. The problem was that Tarwa wasn't considering *why* the growth had increased. Spring hadn't come to Lushwood. Tarwa had. Eshail was sure that if they took a journey three to four days around the city, the world would be as frozen as it'd been the previous week. They weren't already enveloped in the Blight when the gully rush had originally capsized Yates's wagon because the swamp was still frozen.

Eshail saw it clearly, so she urged, "And why do you think the infection has grown?"

"I don't know what you're getting at, child." The witch only used "child" to belittle her audience.

Eshail was relentless. She refused to be belittled, to be silenced. "What changed? There's only one logical conclusion as to why the Blight has proliferated."

"*Me?* You're suggesting *I* brought on this?" Tarwa waved at the map in outrage.

"That's exactly what I'm suggesting. It makes sense, doesn't it? I've been in the field for the last two days, and everything is *growing*. Even if it's not your growth magic, the magic of spring, just that you've thawed the Evermoss in this location has sped everything up."

Eshail waited. Her eyes flicked to Evelyn, but the woman's face was impassive. Ever the arbitrator, she didn't want to appear swayed, even if it was her argument being posited. Tarwa's eyebrows were knitted together in thought. Theoretically, it was a good sign; the witch only thought when she wasn't immediately dismissing someone as an idiot.

"Suppose you're right—and I'm not saying you are—what is your proposal?" Tarwa's voice held an almost undetectable quiver. Eshail's eyes flickered to Evelyn's for confirmation.

She went for the kill. "You've got to leave. The quicker, the better. Every moment you're here, you feed the Blight, making it stronger and harder to kill."

"And what will *you* do when I'm gone? It will be a month before we can bring a different Guardian. The moon isn't in the right phase. In a month, we could lose the whole of the northern Evermoss." Tarwa made the statement with the disdain she had always had for Eshail's skill. Every failed attempt at her craft sat between the two of them—every disappointment.

Heat burned Eshail's face at the jab. Her mind fled back to childhood, and the sense of failure began to creep in. She began crumbling in on herself. She didn't have an answer for what was next.

"She'll save the village. That's what she'll do. Continue the work to identify a treatment and then execute it. And she'll do it without your fertilizing influence on the operation." Eshail and Evelyn looked at Yates in astonishment. She continued, "This witch, this daughter of yours, has nursed me back from the brink of death. She will do the same for the swamp."

Everyone held their breath, waiting for Tarwa's response. Eshail'd seen Tarwa destroy someone for much less of a trespass on her ego.

"And you, daughter, what do you have to say?" Two green eyes turned from Yates to Eshail, awaiting her pronouncement.

This was the moment where fate would twist for better or worse. Everything in Eshail, every lesson and indoctrination by Tarwa, told her to turn heel and leave—to run away from her mother, the problem she hadn't a hope of solving, and all of the consequences. Something in her flipped from fear to anger and then to ownership.

"This is my village. These are my people. I revoke my request for assistance." In the old laws, it was always a village's right to request or deny assistance from the

Guardians. It was one of the pacts of a time long ago when non-witches were terrified of their power. The Guardians' power rested on the trust of the people. It was what separated the East from the West: trust. That trust meant that those without magic, without the power to influence events supernaturally, had to have the power to command those who did.

"Witnessed," Evelyn intoned, formalizing the ask.

"I hope you're right." Tarwa stood. Her tone wasn't bitter. In fact, it didn't hold any emotion. She spoke not as a mother but as the Guardian. "If you can't stop this, at the rate it's growing, I won't need your permission to be involved; every village in the North will be sending me messages for assistance."

Yates, in all of her princess imperialness, answered that which Eshail couldn't: "That won't be necessary. Eshail will stop this." Eshail lifted her head, as though the naive Easterner's words held truth.

Tarwa stared at the Easterner, at the imperial raise of her nose, and snorted. "I will leave it to your fate." With a curt nod, the Guardian left. Eshail could feel her take her power with her. The air grew cooler, and the ambient magical energy in the tavern decreased. The doors swung on their hinges, and the three women left in the room released the explosive breath they'd all been holding.

Eshail felt faint and leaned against a table. "I can't believe we just did that."

"Where will she go?"

"She'll retreat back to Firedrake Island. The old-growth tree can be used to cocoon her power. She can't moongate out of here any more than we can moongate the Summer or Winter Guardians here. But this way, her power will be removed from the vicinity, and we can actually work on the problem ourselves. Evelyn, I hope you've got a plan. I can take over as our magical assistance, but I don't have a hundredth of the power of my mother."

"Well, we've got the forward course for the moment planned, poison and acid. I've got an idea of the next experiments; I can walk you through them. Now that we'll have the time to perform them, we've got hope."

When the villagers gained the courage to enter the tavern after one of the Guardians of the Evermoss stormed out, they found three young women, two covered in smudges of mud and tattered clothes, poring over a map and talking animatedly about the next attempt to stem the infection in the swamp.

Chapter 24

"Why was she batching it up into such large quantities? Wouldn't it be better to try a hundred different things and then batch up the one that worked?" The more Eshail learned about Tarwa's strategy in dealing with the Blight, the more irritated she grew. She almost wished the Guardian was still present so that she could scold the woman herself.

Evelyn sighed. "I agree. She was convinced that she knew how to handle it and that at the rate it was growing, the only chance we had of stemming the flow was to go all out using one of these methods."

"Falcon feathers, she's so stubborn."

The night had grown cold. The three women moved their operation back to Eshail's house, not wanting to troubleshoot their approach in front of half the village. They'd kept everyone calm, reassuring them that they had a plan. Eshail thought that Evelyn had even lied a bit, telling them that Tarwa'd just gone to get help. It was a lie, but if they didn't solve this quickly, it would be true. All four Guardians would have to descend on Lushwood. The whole northern half of the Evermoss would be lost.

Temperatures had dropped, just as they'd hoped. Eshail threw another log into the hearth. Druff sat curled on her lap, attentive to the discussion. He'd been absent lately, understanding Tarwa's distaste of his presence. He would toe the line of politeness with her but mostly tried to avoid her altogether. Eshail was reassured that he was back. She wasn't sure how much he understood any conversation, but he seemed to be tracking everything.

"I should be thankful that it's getting colder, but I was ready for winter to be over," Evelyn said, pulling a rough woolen blanket tighter around her shoulders.

"What this means is that we probably only have a few days to harvest the things that we need." Eshail stood and began making a list. "If we take Yates's advice and try out every possible potion that I can concoct, we're going to need a few things. I'll need Hedwarg's help on more collections."

The list was extensive, but she only had half of the ingredients. Most were simply cures and treatments for ailments common to the swamp. She had non-magical balms, antivenoms, antiseptics, and a variety of itch reducers. They all agreed that these likely weren't worth trying. They'd try them if nothing else worked. The magical potions she could create were a bit longer list, although they were mainly the standard variety: potions of lust, forgetting, remembering, finding, communicating with nature, fertility, removal, hair growth, healing, poison, acid, fire, winter's breath, and growth. She had magical charms that she could create; these she was a bit less practiced at, depending on the type, but she could do charms of containment, abatement, attraction, and finding.

"Surely she tried a charm of containment?" Eshail asked.

"I don't think so. She'd been so sure that her initial try would work," Evelyn said, shaking her head at Tarwa's ego.

"What *did* she try initially?" Yates asked. She'd clearly gotten over her resistance regarding magic and was fully participating in solutioning.

"She tried some sort of spell work she called Oblivion."

Eshail's eyebrows shot up. Oblivion was one of the most potent spells a witch could cast. It erased the subject entirely. It was never used and rarely taught. Only the Guardians knew how to cast it, and it was said that they only did so at a severe cost.

"What happened?" Eshail whispered, though she didn't really want to know. "Were you there?"

Evelyn shook her head. "No, she didn't let anyone go with her, wary of a backlash."

"That spell." Eshail couldn't believe Tarwa would try it. It was anathema, only used in desperation. "She was right to be wary. It had no effect on the Blight?"

"None that I could see. The vegetation might have been a bit charred, but the infected area still had the miasmic churn to the soil."

They returned their attention to her list. Eshail's hope was withering. If a greater magic like Oblivion had no effect, what hope were her workings?

"Are these the only potions you can make?" Evelyn asked, wanting to be thorough.

"Yes—"

"No, that's not true." The Easterner stood, walking over to the chalkboard. She took a piece of chalk and wrote *love* on the board.

"Not sure what a love potion will do to a Blight infection," Eshail said, red-faced.

"If we're trying your hair growth potion on it, we might as well try a love potion. " Evelyn eyed her with curiosity.

"Just because I can do a thing doesn't mean I should. Love potions are evil things. I might as well list out all the curses I can perform." This created an argument within the group that Eshail lost. She ended up writing down a concise list of curses. They'd been one of the forms of witchcraft she'd been so against that she barely knew the basics.

"I guess I don't have to worry about you granting the wish of a scorned lover?" Evelyn's offhand comment was meant in jest, but it hurt. Eshail sat for a moment with the two women she'd held any interest in in the last five years, and her heart sank.

"Nope, guess you don't have to worry about that." She kept the words light when she felt about as tall as a blade of grass. Loneliness encroached, and Druff drove it back with an increased purr. She petted his back. He was right. She was never genuinely lonely with his company. The irony of her two primary skills being love potions and the ability to build a connection with a familiar was not lost on her.

Evelyn plowed ahead, a problem predator. "Which of these could you do tomorrow?"

Eshail looked at the list and started writing down ingredients, circling the ones she didn't have. "Give me a moment."

"You should add your familiar skill. Spell? I'm not sure what you called it the other day." Yates was right. She wrote it down, too, not that it'd do much in fighting the Blight.

Eshail sat and began writing out the long list of her skills. It wouldn't be too long. Tarwa could fill up several tomes with her knowledge. Eshail kept her demons at bay and focused on the task at hand. She had multiple varieties of love potions available. She used a bit of green chalk to give that one a checkmark. Little good it'd do. They'd already been mixing the acid and a poison to try. Green checks. She could brew a fire potion, but no one asked her for that one, even though the ingredients were readily available. She also had enough for a small batch of healing and, stupidly, hair growth.

The list of items that Hedwarg would need to collect had grown large. She was tempted to go out with him instead of performing the experiments on the Blight. The potions she could try just seemed like a waste of time.

"If we're being thorough, nothing is a waste of time. We must try every possibility available to us, and if we exhaust that, well we'll have to try some new possibilities. How hard is it to learn more potions?" Evelyn was in her element. She had a mission and parameters, and she could boss Eshail around in a way that'd been impossible when working with Tarwa.

"Let's just say if it comes to that, we're doomed," Eshail said with a smile, but it was true. Learning a new potion without the tutelage of a more senior witch was painfully slow unless the Nest Mother blessed one with a knack for invention. She already knew this wasn't a skill she possessed.

Yates yawned, a sentiment that they all could get behind.

"I'm going to go back to the tavern, calm folks down, and get them focused." Evelyn stood and then hesitated. "I'll come by early to copy down what you need and get Hedwarg started. There's no point in sending him out at night. It's too dangerous with the environment changing so drastically."

Eshail agreed. Nature tended to not take too kindly to dramatic shifts in temperature. There were going to be many angry creatures in the swamp tonight.

Evelyn left, and the energy she brought to the room left with her. Druff stood, stretched, and went to his food bowl for a snack. Yates stood, looking forlornly at the hatch to the basement.

"It's going to be so cold down there tonight."

Eshail disagreed. The glory of a cellar was that it was the same temperature, summer or winter, although that temperature was a steady cold, so perhaps the point was moot. She shrugged. "We could bring the bed upstairs." It was hard to muster much enthusiasm for the suggestion. Even with the two of them, it would be a struggle. Getting the spare bed downstairs was a much easier task.

"What do you think of your bed? Is it big enough for two?"

The witch froze at the suggestion. Did Yates really suggest they share a bed? She cautiously looked at the woman and instantly realized it was an innocent suggestion. There was no innuendo, no ulterior motive. Yates looked exhausted.

"It's small and not super suitable, but we could probably make it work," Eshail answered before really thinking too hard about what she was saying. "Go take a look and tell me what you think."

She returned to the chalkboard, trying to tamper the pounding of her heart. She'd made a short list of herbs, bark, roots, and other bits of nature needed to finish some of the other concoctions she thought would work.

"It looks big enough. My soldiers would share smaller pallets than that on the road. Plus, it'll be good to be warmer. I run cold, unfortunately. It's the desert in me; I don't do well with your northern winter weather."

The hammering in Eshail's heart grew. She just nodded, not trusting her voice to answer. They gathered the blankets and pillows needed. Both took turns changing out of their swamp garb into something more suitable. They both disparately needed full baths, but neither was enthusiastic about the prospect. The temperature had plummeted. It was as though winter was trying to make up for the mistake Tarwa's presence had caused.

Bundled under four layers of blankets, the two lay side by side.

Eshail kept her mind occupied by inventorying the wooden beams that comprised her ceiling. She counted them twelve boards across. Her mind strayed to their touching arms, and counted the boards again just to be sure. Twelve again. A good, witchy number. At least she could count under duress.

It was almost comfortable, except for the bite of freezing on her nose. Druff had joined them, lying between Eshail's feet. Conveniently it pushed her leg closer to Yates's, making them touch. The snap and flicker of the small iron stove was their only witness.

Yates shifted, turning her body on its side, facing Eshail. The witch barely breathed. "Do you ever wonder what it'd be like?" Yates's voice was quiet, sleepy.

"What'd what be like?"

"You know, living your life for yourself? No one to disappoint or make proud?" The words were spoken right into Eshail's left ear, making her shiver involuntarily. "What would life have been like if Tarwa'd never come and got you from that tavern? If you'd just lived out your life as a barmaid?" Yates's voice was broken by another yawn. She'd asked a question she wasn't incredibly invested in.

"Does it matter?" Eshail wanted to dismiss the query. It wasn't real. Real was where she was at, the village witch about to lose her village to the worst ecological disaster since the creation of the Eastern desert. Part of her heart couldn't hide the answer it came up with. "I think I'd be happier."

"Me too," came a sleepy answer as Yates shifted back on her back and succumbed to the warmth and closeness. The day's worth of tromping and standing up to one of the Guardians of the Evermoss had taken its toll, and soft snores filled the room.

It took Eshail considerably longer. She couldn't help imagining a future where they were both free to make their own lives what they wanted.

Chapter 25

Eshail awoke abruptly. It wasn't a leisurely moment-by-moment movement into consciousness; all of her consciousness was alive at once. Although the two had fallen asleep side by side, shoulder to shoulder, she'd awoken to Yates's body, snuggled up onto her shoulder, and her own arm resting under the woman's head.

Yates was utterly unaware, still snoring softly. Eshail felt guilty, rejoicing in the length of the woman's body against hers. It was a cheat to a life she didn't have—and may never have. But for that same reason, she lay in bed, completely awake, savoring the moment.

If doom were to fall upon them by the Blight, then at least she'd have this. A perfect moment, where her imagination could pretend she wasn't alone in the world. That she had a partner to wake up with. A perfect glimpse of a hummingbird's glory, before it flitted away out of sight.

The world stopped for no one, and as long as the moment drew out and Eshail's heart threatened to beat out of her chest, it was destined to end. It was fitting that Evelyn's knock at the front door startled Yates awake. The woman quickly withdrew. Eshail pretended not to notice, to save them both embarrassment.

Eshail gave her best fake yawn and bleary blink. "Did you sleep well?"

Yates nodded, at least partially sleepy herself, even if the speed at which she withdrew was suspicious. Eshail didn't bother pressing. They didn't have a future, so it wasn't worth investigating.

"I'm coming!" Eshail stretched, savoring the feeling of a warm bed before taking the plunge into the crisp morning air. Druff eyed her from the dresser, judging her silently. She waved him away.

Evelyn's knock was insistent and precise, just like the woman herself. There wasn't another soul in the village with that knock. Eshail didn't bother changing but just unlatched the front door in her dressing gown. Evelyn burst into the room in proper morning person fashion, ready to complete the day's tasks.

"I'm glad to see you're up," she said, ignoring Eshail's state of dress and the sleepy-eyed Yates behind her.

"You need anything for breakfast?" Eshail asked for politeness's sake. She already knew the answer.

"No, thank you. I ate at the tavern before coming here. I brought you some sausage rolls." Much could be forgiven for sausage rolls from Talin's oven. Eshail greedily took the basket, unwrapping the cloth napkin they were wrapped in. The smells of cooked spiced sausage and flakey dough immediately overtook her senses. She let Yates take one, a true act of love, before grabbing one herself. The pastries were still hot.

Evelyn ignored them both; she had a notebook open and was copying down the chalk list from the night before. For a moment, the world was simply the burst of savory sausage flavor, the sound of a scratching quill against paper, and the touch of cold air on their skin. After the first roll, Eshail stoked the fire in the main room, trying to generate some heat. Her efforts were met with mild success as Yates pushed her aside to soak up what little heat the fireplace was giving off.

"I decided this morning that we should try anything you've got pre-brewed—or can make on the fly—first. Later today, we can try what you can make this afternoon. Tomorrow, we'll use what Hedwarg's able to dig up."

"I have nothing of worth pre-brewed. We're going to have to wait until this afternoon."

Evelyn stopped her scratching and looked at her friend with hard eyes. If there was something the woman hated more than anything, it was inefficiency and laxness. It astonished Eshail that it'd taken her this long to realize the witch was suspect on both accounts.

"If it needs to be this afternoon, then so be it." She returned to her paper. Yates looked at Eshail with upturned eyebrows. Eshail shrugged. Evelyn was universal in condemning folks who didn't have their act together.

"It's been a long winter. I haven't had much to pre-make anything. Once you use an ingredient, it's done. You can't unmake something to make something better suited to a situation." The words were valid, and if she'd had a stockpile from the fall, she probably would have kept most of it in ingredient form for that reason. Evelyn didn't have to know the main reason she didn't have anything was because her stocks were empty. She didn't have to understand that the only reason she could make anything now was because she and Yates had gone harvesting the last two days.

Eshail was floating high, and Evelyn's judgment wasn't going to affect her—which was a first. The woman's judgment would have normally sent her spiraling into self-doubt. Instead she found herself giving Yates a mischievous look.

"It will take me all morning to prepare the potions I can fix. Could you send one of the boys over with more food? A water boy wouldn't hurt either; we must scrub the cauldron between brews. You know how things can get contaminated?" In truth, she had a shortcut that made this statement not precisely honest. She had a rope lattice stretching over the cauldron and could float six or seven jars in the bubbling water bath. This would allow her, if careful, to brew seven different potions at once. Admittedly, they'd be in smaller quantities, but rarely did one need a whole vat of any one potion at a time unless there was an outbreak of crotch rot or something else as contagious. They wanted to try a multitude of potions, too, not a giant vat of one potion.

"Alright, I'll be here this afternoon, and I'll send the Chaplyn boy." Evelyn left with a final flourish of her quill.

"That way, we can have enough water to wash up," she explained only to Yates, who was chewing on another roll.

The morning improved as they'd fallen into a rhythm. Although Yates wasn't trained by a witch, she knew her way around plants and herbs. She attributed this to her nanny. A woman that Eshail was suspicious of, but every move that Yates made in the workroom was the right one. She may not have gone out harvesting much, but she did know how to process ingredients.

They'd set up two wash bins. One to dunk the cooled, dirty glasswares in to wash away any significant bits of ingredients, the other to scrub more thoroughly with soap. The woman had a good sense of how much scrubbing was enough and had even set up the dry racks for glass near the fire so they'd dry faster.

She'd also take cues from Eshail when she needed help corking, stacking, and labeling the finished brews. Their production went fast, and Eshail made twice as many potions as she thought possible that morning.

"Are you sure you don't want to be my apprentice? I mean, I'm not sure I'm a high enough quality witch to take on a pupil, but you're a natural. If Tarwa had taken on your training, I'm positive you'd disappoint her only half as much as I did."

"Th-Thanks, I think? And no way would I want to work with that old bag. I'm happy right here."

Eshail was pretty happy too. It'd been a near-perfect morning, even with Evelyn's interruption. They'd worked as a team almost seamlessly.

Eshail packed the wicker basket full of their prizes. She'd transferred many sample potions into smaller, lighter glass jars. She'd guessed that most of these they'd want to simply throw at the Blight, not get close enough to pour them in. No one needed to be any closer to the Blight than necessary.

"Alright, I think we're ready to go," Eshail said.

"I'd agree, but you're missing something," Yates said with determination.

Eshail frowned. She couldn't think of what they'd missed. She looked across the room at their drying dishes. She had some stacks of potions, but they were leftovers from vials she'd already packed. It hit her then what the Easterner meant. "You're talking about the love potions?"

"Yes, the ones in the basement. I don't think I saw you make any of those this morning. We need to try *everything*."

She didn't make any and wouldn't have. Those potions formulas were secret. Without magic, Yates couldn't replicate their effect, but she could take the base recipe and find someone else with a touch of magic to do it. Eshail'd been watching the woman work all morning. She wasn't wholly convinced Yates didn't have a touch of a bit of magic herself.

"Right. I guess we should take a couple of those." Eshail was uneasy. Yates was right, but she didn't have to like it. "You stay here, and I'll get them."

She climbed down the stairs step by step. She hated going into this part of the cellar. She walked over to her storage area, which was still unsealed. At this point, she'd trusted Yates not to break her trust again. Druff had also been keeping an eye on everything.

The secret compartment slid open. Five shelves sat before her, each with little divots in which rounded potion bottles sat. They all glowed with magic, some more brilliantly than others, but they were all magic. She'd discovered that not all love potions were the same. Some potions would make a slave, willing to sacrifice themselves. Others would create maniacal stalkers. Or you could potentially land anywhere in between. A gentle pink one promised what Eshail considered the perfect amount of love, that of true love. Of the main web of a person's weave. She hated every single one. To her, it was an abhorrence to break the weave of a person's life so completely that they wouldn't know their destined love if it hit them in the face.

It was the opposite of familiar weaving. Finding a familiar was about sending a ripple out through a destined weave so that the being would appear. It was reinforcing something that already existed. It was not using molten metal to fabricate a bond that was never meant to be.

She grabbed one of each. There were worse ways to dispose of the potions than throwing them into the Blight.

"You alright down there?" Yates called.

"Yeah, I'll be up in a moment." She grabbed one of the lust potions too. Evelyn would not be able to accuse her of not being thorough.

Evelyn guided them to the Blight. The journey took a lot less time than Eshail expected. It was only an hour away from the village and getting closer every moment. The invasive seeds had dug in, and the growth Tarwa's energy had encouraged had caused them to take root and multiply. Eshail had never been close to an infestation, and the sight of it made her sick.

The once green, verdant countryside was drooping

in death, in brown, red, orange. It wasn't the turn of fall. It was the splotch of disease, infection, and rot. She'd always questioned her attunement with the Evermoss. Hedwarg didn't have a magical bone in his body, but the man knew the swamp. He could dance along the bog waters unhindered. She'd be cursing and charming and dodging the entire route, all the while being eaten alive by mosquitoes.

The Blight, however, was wrong. It didn't just look and smell bad. It *felt* like a funeral, a sunless summer solstice, a failed spring.

"The air's off. Do you see the boiling spark of fire in the air? It's like the Cabastain in the heart of the caldera. The heart of the temple and a place people do not go." Thayatesh's voice held awe and terror—the Blight was awe-inspiring in its terribleness. Eshail could envision this disease eating its way through the heart of the Evermoss, leaving nothing untouched in its wake.

"This must stop. We've got to stop it." Eshail's words trembled, but her resolve did not. Eshail began unpacking her backpack slowly so she didn't break a bottle. She'd lived in Lushwood for six years, but until then, she'd not fully realized what the village and the swamp meant to her. She would give her life to stop this madness.

Evelyn was the only one in the trio who was calm. She'd been at the cusp of the infection the entire time. This wasn't a new horror; it was the battle she'd been fighting and intimately knew the stakes. She calmly took out her notebook, quill in hand, ready to write down the effect of the different concoctions.

Eshail looked into the boiling infection. This was only one pocket, and the map in the tavern was covered in red splotches. Talin had sent out villagers to check on the various infection points and get updates on them. The hopelessness of the task before them grew, chipping away at her confidence.

Snap! Snap! Evelyn snapped her fingers before

Eshail's face. "Stop looking at it. It's magical, remember? It will warp your mind and your thinking. You must be stronger than that." She moved down the line, nudging Yates a bit to snap her out of the trance she'd also been put in, "I swear the two of you would be hopeless without me."

"I had no idea. I just . . . no idea." Eshail concentrated on unbuckling the back of her bag and focused on the rough edge of the first potion jar. The glass wasn't completely smooth—it'd been a reject from the glass blowers—but it held liquid fine. That's why she'd taken it.

"This first one is a potion of growth." Eshail held it out, working the stopper off the top.

Evelyn scratched out *growth* on her notebook. "We'll probably want to back up. If it has the effect I think it will. The Blight might expand like it did with Tarwa here. She couldn't see the truth with her own eyes." Evelyn's tone was biting.

Eshail was surprised. She'd never heard the herald criticize her mother so. It was nice to finally get validation against the Guardian's ego. "If it makes you feel better, she never could." Tarwa's stubbornness would be the end of them all. The three moved back, and Eshail held the growth potion out and threw it underhand with the cork just minutely wedged in place. The goal was that as it hit, the cork would fly out, or the bottle would break, giving them the desired saturation. In no world did she expect to get any of the bottles back.

They watched as the bottle hit the ground, bounced off the spongey soil, and rolled a few feet away, cork still intact.

"Well, that was unexpected," Yates said, making light of the mistake.

Evelyn looked at the witch, clearly disappointed with the result. She scratched a note in her notebook. "Which one is next?"

Yates got the next one to explode. She threw it

harder, hitting a stump, causing the hair growth elixir to coat a tree. Eshail'd never tried the hair growth potion on anyone but humans—and Druff once, when he got stuck in a honey trap and lost a chunk of hair. The moss on the moss-coated stump grew three inches before their eyes. It was a healthy green for a moment until it, too, succumbed to the unnaturally heated landscape.

"Next, what do we have?" Evelyn was all business.

They threw a potion of lust to no effect. Evelyn said the trees looked hungrier, but Eshail was positive she was teasing. The potions of forgetting, remembering, and finding had no visible effect. Those she was most hopeful for, the potions of removal, healing, poison, and acid, had no effect. They'd tried several variations, strong and weak versions. Ones that burbled a bit more. The healing came in specific varieties for cuts, bruises, internal damage, healing of the mind, nail regrowth, and the typical six varieties of crotch rot. The Blight ate them all as though nothing was wrong with the swamp. As though there was nothing to heal.

Eshail was disheartened, but Evelyn was motivated. "Well, we've made more progress in one morning than Tarwa did in days. We just need to try more. The answer is here. We just haven't found it yet."

Eshail wasn't so sure the answer was lurking. If the ancients hadn't had another way besides scouring the infection enough to create the Great Waste, she was positive that a hedge witch, a herald, and a princess wouldn't do any better.

"Yates, I've been thinking about your comment. What did you call it, the Cabastain?" Her face grew red as she butchered the word. "The infected regions of the desert—how big were those areas? How much of the desert boils like this?"

Yates paused, as though contemplating her words. "My family is one of the privileged few that has this information. The Cabastain is considered holy by some; the monks watch and pray to it. We've always guessed the truth, but the stories of the Blight are old. This isn't something you worship without being warped in the mind. What was the map's scale on the table in the inn?"

Evelyn thought for a moment. At one point, the herald disclosed that she had a memory that could take a painting of what she saw. She could close her eyes and see it. Eshail had been a little jealous. Something like that would have undoubtedly made her studies as a witch easier. Evelyn disagreed with that assessment. She'd said it made things too physical to believe in the metaphysical. "The whole map is for the second quadrant of the fourth most northern section of the swamp."

This meant nothing to Eshail. She'd never had to walk the length of the swamp. When she was younger, Tarwa would moongate them when they needed to change locations. Thayatesh, the merchant, however, whistled. "By that reckoning, this infection is already bigger than the ancient one that created the desert. Assuming the Blight in the desert is the original size of the infection still. It may be shrunk, but I think the Monks of Cabas would have indicated if such was true."

The enormity of the problem in front of them was disheartening. They'd lost before they even had a chance to fight.

"We're going to need all the Guardians." Eshail stopped before she said her next thought. *And even then, the best they'll be able to do is turn Lushwood into a barren waste.*

"No, I mean yes, but no. Stop, it's the Blight again, trying to make you feel hopeless. Every problem has a solution." Evelyn's stern hopefulness was the only thing that kept Eshail going.

Yates shook her head. "And what if it doesn't?"

"Who cares? I want to live in a world with

solutions. With hope," Evelyn said, taking their hands and pulling them together. "Look at me, even if there isn't hope, wouldn't you rather go down swinging? Trying everything we could? We'll call the Guardians, but it's going to take them time to get here. In the meantime, we've got a handful of potions left today and a bunch we can brew for tomorrow, right?"

Eshail looked at the last bottles in the bottom of her bag. Three pink potions. Three love potions. They were screwed at this point, so who cared? At least if she threw these into the Blight, she wouldn't have to worry about them getting into the wrong hands. Typically, potion disposal was a big deal. One had to pull the magic out of them slowly. Throwing them into an environment like this produced various magically enhanced locations. Mostly the Guardian's job was to investigate such areas and decontaminate them. No one wanted a wood of lust or a fog of memory loss. Even the potions she approved of brewing could be disastrous if misused.

She picked up one, handing it to her years-long crush. She kept one herself and handed Thayatesh the potion the woman started all this mess trying to achieve. Yates held it gingerly like she was holding the most fragile delicacy. It'd taken Eshail a long time, but it finally clicked what saving her life from the firedrake had cost the woman. She turned to the Blight, at once overcome by its oily wrongness.

"Ready? Three, two, one." Yates threw hers. "Throw!" The other two sent theirs sailing. Eshail watched as the pink bottles flew end over end to their fate and decided that if they survived the next couple of weeks, the least she could do was give Thayatesh a potion to take back. If she were the friend she'd hoped to have, she'd want Yates to be happy. Even if that happiness was artificial, it'd be a thousand times better than the torture her life would be without the potion. She didn't want Yates to stay because the alternative was horrible; she wanted her to stay because she couldn't imagine any other choice. It'd become obvious to Eshail that that would never happen.

The three potions shattered as they hit the ground.

Something unexpected happened.

Chapter 26

The Blight itself was damaged growth and, worse, damaged attachment. It was an illness put into the world by a mage who'd been broken by life. It ate at the natural world, distorting, destroying, ever hungry in its conquest. It broke apart the bonds of trees, worms, and birds. It fed on what was sent to it, the despair, the loneliness of the world. The reaction was always destroy and contain, but the Blight was unquenchable, unrelenting.

Until it wasn't.

Eshail watched as the potions hit the infection. A dense and malignant fog erupted from the point of impact. The fog bubbled up from the grass, trees, and water and then swirled into a ball, disappearing in a violent pop. She held her ears.

"Wh-what just happened?" Yates was confused.

"I thought you said that wouldn't do anything?" Evelyn stood, notebook in hand, writing implement poised. She didn't know what to write.

Eshail stumbled a few times before finding her voice. "It shouldn't have . . . ? I have no idea why that happened. But it did work . . . didn't it?"

She took a tentative step forward, reaching out with her senses, trying to find the filament of hate, of rot and wrongness. Each step became more hesitant. She paused at the border between what'd been right and blighted. There was a difference. The ground was less lush in the blighted area, but it was recovering before her eyes. Druff, who'd been very standoffish since they'd come near the Blight, rubbed up against Eshail's legs.

He stepped forward, brave where the women weren't, and put a small paw pad on the infected soil. Tentatively, he took another step forward. The cat closed his eyes, sniffing the air. He opened up his mouth and breathed the air in, tasting it. He looked back as if beckoning them forward.

Eshail followed suit, closing her eyes, trying to sense how it felt different. She reached into the swamp and didn't ask for reconnection. Instead she watched as lines of connection snaked into the blighted area and rebuilt it, lovingly reconnecting the area to the great web of life.

"It's like calling a familiar, except the swamp is healing itself. It's knitting everything back together!" Eshail's voice rose in joy, and she stepped forward confidently, no longer doubting the miracle that was taking place. Finally something *good* came from her primary skill.

Evelyn turned to her as though she was the Nest Mother herself. Tears coursed down her cheeks.

Yates grinned beside Eshail. "I told you love potions weren't all that bad."

They watched the patch clear up and the plant life return. Evelyn insisted they stay to make sure it wasn't a temporary effect. She'd brought lunch, ever prepared. Sandwiches wrapped in cloth and little apple turnovers. They were far enough north in Lushwood to have a small apple orchard on the city's knoll.

After their meal, Evelyn wandered off for one last check across the whole of the infection. Thayatesh and Eshail lay stretched on a blanket. Yates leaned in, close enough that Eshail could feel the heat of her body.

"I think you've done it. Things will change here very quickly," Yates whispered. The words sent a shiver through Eshail's body. She was about to become the witch of Lushwood in more than just name. She'd go down in the history of the Evermoss. It was unimaginable.

"I'm not sure I want things to change." A fear struck her. The solitude of her existence would fundamentally change. She could even see, so briefly, a change in how Evelyn looked at her—not the eccentric friend, but someone worthwhile. Yates leaned in further, wrapping an arm around her in a hug. Eshail gave into the hug, closing her eyes, and believing the illusion for a moment.

"Once this is taken care of, I imagine you'll be leaving?" Eshail broke the illusion herself, preferring a clean snap.

Yates moved away, sensing the change in mood. "Yes, I need to get back to my obligations. I'll stay, though, and help clean everything up. This is my fault, even if Tarwa deemed me innocent."

"That's good." Eshail tried to put more distance between them with her words. "I'm going to need to be brewing almost every moment to meet the need, to stamp out the Blight. It will take some long hours to rebuild the connection to the swamp, the forest, and the creatures." She hated that her voice quivered a bit. She was about to be in a ray of sun, spotlighted for the entire village, to the entire Evermoss. There wouldn't be any more growth for their connection, and there would be no more illusion.

"It's okay. It'll be okay." Yates's word were kind, but she didn't come closer. She didn't close the gap between them. This was the breaking.

Evelyn came back, skipping, humming to herself. Eshail couldn't help but smile at the sight. Her oldest, dearest friend looked happier than she'd ever seen her.

"I take it we've got success?"

"It's gone. It's—it's like magic." She looked at the witch with something akin to adoration. Eshail didn't like it. Not one bit.

"Let's head back. I have the feeling our work has only begun," Eshail said, wanting the moment to end.

It took three weeks. The Blight had indeed gained a foothold in the Evermoss. Eshail's skill and discovery had turned the village into a machine. She started each day with Hedwarg and his brigade of harvesters, giving them a list of ingredients she'd need later in the week. By the third week, they had to go far afield to find the wild herbs she needed. After her morning meeting, she'd go to her expanded workroom. It had a much larger cauldron procured from the laundresses. Yates had usually, by that point, brought breakfast from the Inn where she'd been sleeping. She'd be poking at the fire to get it going and had sausage rolls or pastries ready to be consumed.

The two would spend hours tweaking the potion, stirring, and heating. Eshail weaved her magic, instilling in each drop the emotion that she was furthest from in her life. She'd had some breakthroughs in her magic, recognizing the effect the love potions had on the connections to the Nest Mother. She'd realized that her familiar skill was very similar. She tweaked the recipe not to be one of love but one of connection. It would probably produce love if drank by a human, but it was more nature-based. The color had turned from a pink to an awful pink-green combo. Thankfully, the look of it didn't take away from its effect.

It'd been hit or miss the first few days, but once they got into a rhythm, the Blight shrank more than it expanded. Tarwa was still ensconced in the old growth. The full moon had yet to pass, so the moongate was still closed. Eshail didn't care.

Her stores grew full of various collected herbs, bark, moss, fungi, and other assorted bits she'd needed. The harvesters always returned with what was required. After

Hedwarg's constant coaching, most knew what foraged resources would be helpful to a witch. They were bringing extra ingredients in as thanks, and for the first time, she felt that the village understood that keeping her well-stocked in turn served them.

Evelyn was running the place. Talin may have been mayor, but the herald took control of the village in a crisis. She had work and inventory lists. She had a scouting contingent that gave her thrice daily updates on the Blight.

By the fourth week, they could map out the end of the Blight infection. Production was starting to slow, and the foragers drew back to their normal tasks. Evelyn and Eshail contemplated pulling Tarwa out of her self-imposed quarantine.

Eshail found herself alone one morning. One of the village boys had dropped off a pastry with a nutty center and honey glaze for breakfast. She thought about going to check on Yates, but she figured the Easterner would arrive as soon as she could.

The brews were getting easier—nothing like a swamp-wide emergency to grind at the heart of her skills. Eshail had been thinking about the changes in her magic, and Druff's thoughts were coming through clearer. This was a detriment sometimes, as the cat was temperamental, like all cats. She imagined with this new application of her primary skill, her progress as a witch would be uncorked. The future looked surprisingly bright for the Guardian's castoff.

The nature-love potions were becoming some of her most effortless magic. In her heart, she could admit that most of the change came from a change in her. She wasn't afraid of her magic; she could see the good in it. She could see the connection. Turned out, intention mattered when you were a witch. The joke was on her.

She knew it. But now she believed it.

A dull knock came at the front door. Eshail looked

up to find Thayatesh looking guilty. The entire time the woman had been in the village, she'd never knocked to come into the store.

"You're late. Is something going on?" Eshail studied her friend. She was dressed differently, not as a wetlander, but in the linen garb of the desert. She had a hefty backpack strapped to her shoulders.

Yates gave her a sad smile. She opened her mouth, but the words were stuck. Suddenly it was all too clear to Eshail what was going on.

"You're leaving—but you can't. We've still so much to do." It was true, but also a lie. There was a lot to do, but she, Hedwarg, and Evelyn had it handled. She didn't really need Yates anymore, not for the physical labor.

Yates nodded, and the nod sent a blossom of anger. Why hadn't she warned Eshail? The thought bounced around for a moment. She managed to stop herself from snapping. If this was the last bit of time together, she didn't want to end it in a fight.

"Can you stay a day or two longer for a proper goodbye?" Bartering was a more acceptable mode of communication than yelling. She knew this, even if she still wanted to yell. Even she could admit it'd been better that Yates had stayed at the inn. There really wasn't a reason for their enforced closeness once the Easterner had healed.

"I've tried to tell you that I was going to leave a few times in the last couple of days, but I just couldn't. I think a quick break is probably the best."

She hated herself for wanting to say the words, but she knew she'd hate herself more if she didn't. "You could just stay." *You could just run away and stay with me. We could build a life together, an authentic life. We could explore the swamps and heal the hurt in the world. You just have to stay.*

A genuine tear traced down Yates's face as she shook her head. The woman choked out what she had to say, "You know I can't."

What spark of hope Eshail had kindled died. For a moment, she felt like quitting. She'd work to heal the world, to connect it, yet she was hopelessly incompetent at connecting herself.

"I'll be okay, Thayatesh. You've got your duty, and I've found a purpose."

The woman looked as forlorn as she felt. Eshail knew that this day was coming. She didn't think it'd be this soon, but she knew that Yates itched to move on. That whatever power Eshail had to hold the woman in place was waning. They turned from almost something back to friends and now, at the last, strangers.

"I'm going to go. Evelyn's given me an old wagon and a horse. Was going to ask you for a return charm in case I need to move forward on foot."

"Done. Is there anything else I can help you with . . . my friend?"

Yates looked at Eshail in the eyes. Two Eastern brown to two witch's green. "I will figure things out. Very grateful for all your healing and cleaning up my mess."

They both smiled awkwardly again. Eshail contemplated the decision she'd made weeks ago—to give Yates the potion she desired. The decision still felt right.

"Let me go get that charm. One moment." Eshail went to her back room and rifled through her charms, picking out the two best return charms. "First, here's a return charm for the horse. And a second for you. They're both keyed to Lushwood if you ever need to find us again."

Yates grabbed the charms and added them to the red-winged blackbird whistle Eshail had insisted she keep after the firedrakes. The three keepsakes sat around her neck, strung on a hemp string. Yates was touched, but before she could offer thanks, Eshail interrupted her, "I have something else for you. Before you leave, hold a moment more," she said, going to her room and unlatching her private storebox. She'd stayed up late one night to brew a small batch—an old potion that she'd always hated to the very core of her being. Holding the glowing pink bottle in her hand, she looked back across the stillroom to the figure in the door. One last moment of thought before she made a decision she couldn't take back.

Eshail realized immediately it wasn't a decision. She turned back to Yates. "I've got one last gift for you for the road." She held out the love potion. It pulsed in strength. It would be enough to hold a bond with anyone forever. The potion was terribly dangerous in the wrong hands. It could destroy a person, change an empire, or even save a friend from a horrid fate. Eshail knew she could trust Yates with it.

Yates took the potion with trembling fingers, her face in awe of the salvation she had given up. "Th-thank you," her voice trembled. If Eshail had been another witch, one less ethically inclined, she might have used the power the potion represented on Yates herself. She wasn't that witch though. This wasn't that kind of story.

"Will I see you again?"

"Probably not. There isn't much reason for someone of my station to cross into the Evermoss. We're normally not welcome." They smiled at each other, for it was true. "But now I have the means if the opportunity presents itself." She held up the charm of return.

Rowl. Druff trotted up with something caught in his mouth. Eshail felt he was determined to give his own goodbye. The cat sat and spit out a patch of moss on the floor in front of Yates. Both the witch and the outsider stared at the cat for a moment, unsure what to do.

Yates moved first, bending down. "Thank you, sir, for your gift. A bit of Evermoss to take with me, eh?" Druff preened in pleasure, his intent understood. Yates reached out and stroked the cat along his back. She finally gave him a rub under his chin before standing back up with her prized patch of moss in hand.

"You'll always be welcome here." Eshail gave a sad smile.

The two friends hugged. A long, lingering hug of farewell and good luck.

Yates turned and left. She walked out of Eshail's shop, out of the village, and was gone in an instant. She left her life like she entered it: in a blink.

Epilogue

A season passed, then two. The way of the circle of the Nest Mother. This time, however, as the seasons turned, things were less the same. Eshail's life had changed entirely. She wasn't a simple hedge witch anymore. She was the Savior of the Evermoss. Emphasis on *savior*. True to her heraldic office, Evelyn had sent runner after runner telling villages across the swamp what to do in the case of an outbreak. There had been a few, many of which Eshail had to contend with. Someone in the Eastern Empire was more than willing to wage biological warfare, and Yates had been one of many delivery agents.

It was hard to imagine that their desperation had managed to accidentally stop a war between the two countries. Biological warfare only worked when it was effective. The onslaught continued, but now they had a solution that worked.

Tarwa had stayed in hibernation. Except for a quick message in the wind congratulating Eshail on her success in combating the Blight, the Guardian was suspiciously quiet. Eshail was beginning to worry at Tarwa's continued absence.

Druff grew to prominence in the town as the familiar to the Savior. Everyone had a treat or a pet for the cat. He was lapping up every bit of attention. The witch and her cat's connection grew more every day. He couldn't quite talk in words; he didn't fully grasp the human language, but she could receive pictures and feelings from him in complete form. As their bond grew, Eshail had grown more at peace with her skills and connections.

She also knew she no longer had to fear being alone. With her new celebrity status, she'd been pursued by men and women alike. She hadn't indulged; the celebrity status was too close to the effect of a love potion for her comfort. But it gave her confidence. There were options where there used to be a desert. No one pulled at her heartstrings yet though.

Evelyn had made it known that she was going to throw a party on the year anniversary of their triumph. A spring festival, she hoped to make it an annual holiday. Eshail didn't mind. After a long winter, they all needed something to celebrate. The heroes sent to deal with the culprit causing the last long winter cycle had been successful, but winters would continue to be extended for a few years as the cycle rebalanced. It turned out the cause had been a newborn frost dragon who didn't understand the cycle of the world. They'd solved the problem without killing it, a relief to all those who held the Nest Mother in esteem.

Eshail's part in the festivities was to give a toast of sorts. It wasn't something she was particularly looking forward to. Being a celebrity hadn't replaced her tendencies toward wanting peace and quiet. Evelyn wouldn't hear of it. She'd badgered her about her responsibilities and had shamelessly used the leverage of their friendship.

Eventually Eshail relented, but now she was stuck with the reality that she had to prepare a speech. Evelyn had become a political powerhouse in the Evermoss, and Eshail, the savior that she was, did not have the appetite to stand in the woman's way. Besides, as heralds go, she still thought Evelyn was one of the best.

She practiced in front of Druff. Hedwarg didn't want to hear it, and Evelyn kept trying to change it. Druff, however, listened.

"I want to thank everyone for celebrating with me today. I have often gotten credit for the magic that saved us from the Blight, but that's not a fair assessment of what happened. We saved ourselves. You all worked tirelessly to find the right supplies and track the infection's course. Tarwa came and provided us with early leadership when running the operation. And Evelyn's constant drive toward a solution she knew we just had to discover was, in my opinion, the one actual pivot point on which our success relied. I'm just the tool that helped you get us there.

"I've learned that intention is as important as action. When we act without a purpose, without a lens, our lives are empty. I'm so grateful to serve as this village's witch. With the Nest Mother's blessing on all of us in the coming year, we will prosper together."

"What do you think Druff? Will it pass muster with Evelyn?"

"I think she'll like it. Although you left out that pesky Easterner." Druff looked behind Eshail. "She had *something* to do with it if I remember correctly."

Eshail turned around to find a princess in her doorway. The woman's hair was pulled back, her face tan, and her eyes merry. She wore a masculine silken ceremonial garb of deep blue with a patchwork of green vines and red flowers—the garb of royalty.

"How—"

Eshail's question was interrupted as Yates swept forward and kissed her lips. The two stood, locked together in a kiss for the ages.

"You came back," was all Eshail could say when they breathlessly broke apart.

"I did. I think a witch put a spell on me. We should

look into that," Yates said with a roguish grin, daring Eshail to disagree.

"You were going to march off with my potion to your fate. What happened to your family? Your fiancé?"

"It was that witch, I tell you." A twinkle glinted in her eye at the tease. "I am, alas, an outcast. Rumor of my corruption is undoubtedly making its way through the Empire."

"You did that for me?" Eshail should have been happy, but she frowned. That was a lot of pressure to put on a new relationship.

"Well, not exactly just for you. Would you believe it if I told you I tossed your potion into the *Cabastain?* They can't wage a war with the Blight because it no longer exists in the East. Suffice it to say, that was an unpopular choice, especially with the Cabas."

Eshail kissed Yates lightly on the nose. "The choice is popular with me."

"Me too." Yates grinned. The smile spread from ear to ear. If Eshail could bottle that smile up, it'd be her most popular potion—one she'd treasure always.

"I think we're the only ones who matter in this opinion."

The air between them was thick. "Why'd you come back here?" Eshail knew the answer, but she wanted to hear it out loud.

"Isn't it obvious? In the end, you were right. Once I knew what love was, I couldn't force myself to live a lie. It was an unkindness I didn't deserve."

They stood in the workroom, arms wrapped around one another, hearts thumping in unison. Thayatesh had changed, but she knew her heart. She knew this was a connection worth taking a chance on.

"Should we go to the banquet, my love?"

Eshail's heart soared with the appellation. She could feel their connection exploding in the warm spring soil.

"I think they'll be fine without us for a while. I'm sure Evelyn's got a backup toast planned that's way better than mine," Eshail said, walking over to her window and flipping the shop sign to closed. Eshail turned back to Yates and her doubt slipped out, "Are you sure this isn't a dream?"

Yates grinned. "No love potion required. I'm here. We're here, together." The connection vibrated between them, a magic of their own.

* * *

Thank you for reading "Potions and Perils: An Evermoss Cozy Fantasy." If you enjoyed this book, please consider leaving a review. Every review helps boost the book in algorithms and makes it accessible to more readers!

Coming Winter 2024

Sand and Sorcery An Evermoss Cozy Fantasy

The second book in the series

Thank You

I'm very grateful to the team of folks behind Potions and Perils that have helped give this book the extra glitter it deserves. Kat Hamrell with DTP has constantly lifted the art, marketing, and content. She's been the belief and the push behind the book. A notable thanks goes to Jen Kirmer who patiently endured mad late-night typing, and early draft feedback sessions to make this a reality. Hope Houtwed, my editor- words are not enough. Thank the Nest Mother for your diligence – the mud people might not be your biggest fan, but I am. Finally, to B Pranger (future intern), I can't wait to see what you do next.

A special thanks to the artists that have brought Potions and Perils to life. Sienna Arts has done an amazing job on the cover and font art. Additionally a big thanks goes to Amy Cerasi for the witchy art for all of the chapters. You created the visual magic for Potions and Perils, and I could not be more grateful for your help. And a big thank you to our beta-reader, Roman Haen, for those last-minute corrections.

Reck (they/them) is a romantic at heart who writes cozy fantasy and litrpg stories. When not out in their garden, they're found biking the trails around Topeka. They can best be described as an author, avid fencer, cat daddy (4 cats), and full-time nerd.

Follow Reck Well on social media!

@wellrecked

@dtp.reckwell

@wellrecked

Follow Dragon Tomes Publishing on social media!

@dragontomespublishing

@dragontomespublishing

@dragontomespub

@dragontomespub